Beth !

# Woman to Reckon With

## MEGAN'S JUSTICE

Please Enjoy !
Barbara Frain

## By Barbara Frain

Our parents had taught us that we should not harbor hatred for anyone, but a black speck of hate started deep in my soul as I stood by Megan's grave. I felt it grow and swell until I nearly burst with its fullness. Slowly it drained down and settled itself firmly in my hurting heart.

A hard cold, vengeful feeling burst from my pain; demanding to be heard, and I gave it voice. Silently I told Meg, *One way or another; I will give you Justice Sis. I promise by The Graces I will!*

ISBN-10: 098869820X
ISBN-13: 978-0-9886982-0-8

Chapter 1

I am leading my family on this long journey to start a new home in the western land of Montana Territory, but you need to understand who we are; who I am, and why women are making this journey.

My seven roguish sisters call me Katherine the Great. I am Sarah Kathleen O'Reilly and, just to straighten out the record, I am capable, but not great. Not to say I haven't toyed with that notion; I have that right as matriarch. Besides, I always evened the score, and then some, for that nickname whenever the opportunity presents itself.

Our Mother and I were in charge of the day-to-day running of our family's sawmill. It was one of the larger operations in our part of Tennessee, and our family worked diligently to make it a respectable, and profitable, venture.

Father put the base operation in our care as he went oft times into the vast wooded mountains to inspect, and purchase standing timber. Many times I went with him, but Mother and I split the tasks of paying bills, hiring and firing workers, maintenance, and selling the finished product.

With five of my sisters working at the mill under my direction, there were O'Reilly women in every corner of the operation, working the mill from 'stem to stern.'

Father always said, "If ye not be knowin' a thing, then ye've not be having the right to be tellin' someone how to be a doin' it." He had imparted that wisdom to us time and again about knowing what we were learning, and why.

Mother imparted another kind of wisdom to me. The matriarchs of our lineage held a secret for all those to follow. There are many beliefs in mankind.

We have our own.

Women working at a saw mill may sound a little out of sorts to most folks. Lord knows we were a source of gossip, but we brushed it aside for the prospects it brought to the business, AND to the men it paraded in front of we girls. We forgave most of the gossipers; they should have known better, for they knew we were the O'Reilly women.

Businessmen came to buy the best product available, and the young men came to get a glimpse of us trouser-wearing women. We were roguish, and a bottomless source of scandal for the gossip bearers. Of course that just inspired more shenanigans from us to keep their tongues wagging. Our mother said the wee folk in the faraway, didn't have a tinker's wit on the O'Reilly girls: Mary, Ellen, Say'ard, Matilda, Jane, Meagan, Shannon and I. Mother said it best; we were 'rogues.' Lovely, green-eyed, auburn-red-haired ladies one and all, but still rogues!

That's not to say we didn't have to abide by the Rules handed down from that long ago grandmother, and my namesake. These were ironclad rules. Anything outside of those rules we could indulge in, but the Rules held sway over all. We never really broke man's rules either, but we did leave a few badly 'keeled over' as Father would say.

Mother would smile; Father would shake his head, and take a draw on his old hand-carved pipe that had an overly long stem, and Red Oak bowl. Father was Irish as decreed by Rule One. A good man; dark of hair and eyes, and who stood a big four inches over six feet. His name was Patrick Martin O'Cassidy.

Mother was a match for him in all respects, even height, as she herself was an even six foot tall.

So am I.

A lady of bearing; proud, full of fire, capable, and a dead shot; she could ride or drive horses as well as any man, and better than some.

She had an intenseness about her for our hidden knowledge and the mysteries of nature, honor and fair play that I have been schooled in.

Many were the times she'd tear into the lumber yards or along the pasture lane leading to our home; her horse at a high speed, flat out, run. Riding bareback on her favorite stallion, Striker, her long, red hair streaming out behind her, and a flush on her face. She represented everything that I wanted to be.

I'm still trying to be worthy of carrying her blood, her name, and keeping close in my heart our secret beliefs.

When Mother sang the auld Irish or Scottish ballads, everyone stopped what they were doing, and listened. Her voice had a sweet, rising lilt that I still can hear. The memory even now, miles from where we left them; lying in their one grave; brings a tightness to my heart and throat.

I don't have her gift of singing, but my sister Say'ard does.

My grandmother Kate was only five foot eight, smallish of stature, but blessed with a true Irish temper to make up for the lack of height. Grandmother was a fighter, and we must naturally take after her.

From schoolyard skirmishes; hassling each other over boys, and outbidding the other timber buyers; we would have made all my namesakes proud!

Being the eldest daughter of this generation, I had been entrusted with their name; a hand forged, silver wedding ring adorned with an old line writing that I alone can read, and a small wooden box.

The box and ring went beyond old; handcrafted, and darkly stained from the oil of many hands. The contents were precious to my family, but especially to me.

It holds a small pinch of Scottish soil that comes from a time when our ancient tribe lived there in prehistory. The box also holds a strand or two of hair from each woman who have held the matriarchal position of her generation. Mine is there also.

I hold these treasures, values, and Rules, deep in my soul; for they are what guide me, and it is my job to care for this generation. Care for it, guide it, and protect it.

A curious thing happened in 1850; some twenty-eight years ago, and before I was birthed. A tremendous storm erupted; blew a horrendous, gale force wind over the north of Scotland, and uncovered the stone foundations of a village of an unknown people.

Grandma Kate; with a sly smile, simply said about the news article, "Ah. They've found Skara Brae. Tis our true home soil."

THAT'S how old we are!

Our Rules were simple enough and added to the Ten Commandments. One...marry pure Irish, or Scottish (which ever shows up), and only for the love of heart. Two...USE YOUR MIND, that's why you have it. Three...keep your pride up, and your skirts down.

I am named after a six times great grandmother, Sarah Kathleen O'Reilly, as of course are the women before me. Our name is much older, and it was spelled different long before the family immigrated into Ireland.

She was a hot-tempered child of Ireland. Head strong, sharp of tongue, and wise in our pagan wisdom.

My two times great grandmother fled to America after settling her score with a gentleman of some social standing who; it later turned out, wasn't much of a gentleman at all.

Her adventurous tales, along with many stories of the other grandmothers, have been re-told, and passed down through the years. When the far flung O'Reilly women gather at family celebrations, such as weddings, funerals and birthings; the Rules, our beliefs, and tales are reviewed. They are told time, and time again, with all the truth, wit, and deviltry we are noted for.

O'Reilly women have been known to get our way about most things, and compromise on the rest, and after five generations in America; we still carry her family name. Our husbands use their own names. A few men voiced objection to this, and they were still objecting as they were being rejected.

I can explain the origin of my capable stance.

Back in Ireland, my namesake's knowledge of the plight of women living a second or third class existence did not sit easy on her mind. So she marched off to do something about the inequality of the situation by using the Church's own words to her advantage, but with the sweet wit she was noted for; she accomplished her self-appointed task.

I don't have quite that sweet wit, but I do get my jobs done.

Oft times the bloodline of the horses, and other farm animals were of greater importance and value than that of the womenfolk. Since she had mastered many an unruly horse or sheep, her 'value'; she reasoned, should stand above those beasts.

Her story comes down to me like this:

Being a headstrong lass, and a member of the church in good standing; she borrowed her idea from the Good Book, and the often-mentioned matriarchal lineages of those long ago times. She figured that with a little diligence on her part; such as pointing out in that fine Book the many women that had held high positions as Judges, Priestesses and Chieftains, and had helped build their nation, to the clergy, they, the clergy, would have to come around to her way of thinking.

The church had long ago recognized the role of women in the days of Exodus; therefore, she reasoned, they would have to recognize the women of her family, who had contributed to the success of their husband's estates, and allow them to take back control of their own lives, and be accepted as equals of their men.

The true story of how that grandmother shamed many a vestryman into accepting the truth written in the Bible, was a highly public challenging of an injustice that had stood for generations. "If a thing were allowed in the Bible, as with the brave Queen Esther and Rebecca, then it will be allowed now." She had proceeded to tell the clergymen that they had a double standard: one for men and another for women, which was wrong according to the Bible, and she would have no more of it!

She wasn't allowed in church.

When the same church sent the law after her for blasphemy, she simply faded into the heathers, and shires of the forests; hiding with the help of the wee folk. Although no one really believed that except her mother; the women of her lineage, and me.

The church finally gave up on her, and she obtained what she wanted. Independence.

The next grandmother made the final change for all O'Reilly women, and their daughters. Eight generations back from me; the then Sarah Kathleen O'Reilly took a steely eyed, jaw-clamped offense to the idea of her father marrying her off to a man who offered a decent, but common grade horse as dowry.

That Grandma Sarah truly loved her suitor, but she wanted his best horse.

Furthermore, the first girl child she birthed would carry her name because she herself would retain her name, figuring that it was equal to her husbands, and the horse would be hers; not her father's.

The bridegroom-to-be, it was related, was supposed to have been a high stakes betting man. Being that he was completely enamored with Sarah; he struck the bargain. Maybe it was because he thought if he'd get the strong-willed, green-eyed, hellion into his bed, he could change her mind, and keep the stallion.

Handed down to the present, the story tells of a turbulent start to the marriage, with the bridegroom spending many a lonely night in his bed while his bride bedded in the haymow.

As he was a thick-headed man, his training had taken a bit of time, but he finally figured out that his fiery wife had meant every word she had said. After that rough and rocky start, a long solid marriage gave life to four tall, self-assured O'Reilly girls, and four tall, handsome Darrin McTavish sons.

All of the children were equals; as their parents had come to be. Each child was fully educated; which was unheard of for women. This caused the rest of the O'Reilly women near them, to want the same for themselves, and their daughters, and that elicited an uproar from their men.

So, being the woman on the path she had chosen, she converted her whole family to Protestant. Many other families; led by wives and mothers, followed their lead, and used that religion to screen their true belief.

The O'Reilly women, one and all were; for all appearances, Protestant, but on the inside: Pagan. Staunchly Pagan. Especially the matriarch. We refer to our pagan guides as our Graces. We shape our lives in the times we lived in, but carried the wisdom of the old ways as our true belief.

As Gram Ma Kate would say, "To each her own, but OURS is best!"

Even back then, over 150 years ago, and on a different continent, we O'Reilly's were stirring the pot and leading the way. It's not any stretch of the mind to know that some fifty women have carried the matriarchal name of Sarah O'Reilly and all descended from the first born girl child in each generation. The name could only be passed down through that mother's line, and not those of her sisters; unless the first girl didn't reproduce. Then the first girl born to any sister could claim the right of heritage.

In my line, in America, I am the fifth honored to be a Sarah Kathleen, and the tenth in line. As I indicated, we are a large family of old, and there is that whispered truth, that the name goes much, much farther back.

As it should.

I know it's an old heritage I carry, for when a picture of the 'lost village' was printed when I was eight, along with the article of discovery; it looked very familiar to me. I had been there.

When I hesitantly voiced that curiosity to Grandmother Kate, she quietly whispered, "Yes me darling girl. All we matriarchs have been there," and she had smiled whimsically as if remembering her long ago visit. "Tis very special to us 'Sarah's.'

Some of the Sarah's have taken a double last name by adding their husband's surname. It makes for a lot of writing, but it does help keep the family lines more understandable.

Mary and Ellen, the first set of twins, and next to me, are the best of us for enticing men, and getting what they wanted. We've never broken a law, mans or Grandmother's, but the Rules seemed to sag a little to one side when things settled down.

Our life was good back in Tennessee, but times have a way of changing.

An unusually wet spring brought more rain than we had ever seen to our mountains. In the space of three days, the runoff overflowed the creeks, and flooded our huge millpond. The decade's old, immense earth-and-log dam could hold the pressure of the acres of water for only so long before giving way.

We had fought hard against the rising waters. By adding more pilings, brace poles and logs below the dam, and opening up a second and third spillway, we had hoped to save our business, but the Forces of Nature, for whatever THEIR reason; were not to be stopped.

Late one afternoon, twenty-six of our workers, and family, were fighting desperately to lay more bracing. We were driving more bracings into the leaking dam when it gave way; bursting over my parents and sixteen workers.

Only yards away from me I heard Father scream the warning. I saw him reach for Mother, and gather her to him. Wrapped tightly in each other's arms, I watched in horror as they disappeared beneath a thunderous mountain of earth, logs and water.

It is a sight that I still see whenever I close my eyes, or think of them.

I remember screaming for them even as I felt strong hands holding me back, and carrying me to safety, but I also heard a voice in my emotion filled mind, whispering above the roar of the tragedy. *We have them. They are home with us,* and my horror ease a bit, for with those whispered words, I knew my parents were beyond pain.

It took a long time for me to accept their deaths, and even longer for the thought of how close I came to dying, to subside in my trembling body. Only the lost looks in my sisters' eyes, and my mother's constant whispers of; *Now child, 'tis your turn to take the lead,* and *we'll be with you always,* pulled me back to reality, and I joined in the task of recovering those who were swept away. I realized we needed; I needed, to put our lives back together, and start over, for I was now the matriarch, and therefore…this was my job.

It was a long grueling seven days later that their broken bodies were found miles downstream. It was another night before they were brought home. The next day we bid them farewell.

We lay Sarah Kathleen O'Reilly the 9th and Patrick Martin O'Cassidy to rest in the same grave, arms entwined as I had last seen them; protecting each other forever. Face to face we lay them. With our eyes full of tears, we bid them God's speed to a gentler life, and I didn't ask my Pagan Gods to accept them home to the green woodlands, shires and hills of ancient Scotland.

They were already there.

We girls had stood alone at the gravesite with only our reverend attending. Not that we needed him, at least me, for my beliefs ran contrary to his. It was an intensely private time for us girls, and I could feel the presence of all those ancient ones surround us.

I was not alone.


Back at the main house dozens of neighbors, friends, hired hands, and business associates waited for us to join them. I knew speculation was running rampant with what we would do with what was left of the mill.

The truth be known; at that very moment, I didn't know what was to be done either, and it was up to me to lead the family.

Among the mourners were good people like Hendrik Steinbury and his family, who were as devoted to us as our own family. Carl Tillison was quiet and reserved, his emotions overpowering his usually cheerful nature. He was father's close friend and financial advisor for all these years. We all had a high degree of respect and honor for him, but, as I was about to find out, these qualities did not get passed on to his son Morris.

Morris had approached me at the funeral luncheon to remind me the debt on our timber loan would still have to be paid at the month's end, which was just sixteen short days away.

The bastard's timing was exceeded only by his haughty arrogance. No man or woman of decency would broach such a subject at such a time! The little, weasel-nosed rodent! His lack of manners, and guile, riled me straight out of my mourning as my O'Reilly blood boiled!

The loss of the logs in the mill pond, and the water wheel that provided the power to the large saws to cut the logs into lumber, could not to be replaced in time to meet Morris's request of payment. So I met his smug challenge as I knew my parents would have.

As a true O'Reilly woman would.

Rising to my feet, lifting the skirt of my brown taffeta dress slightly off the floor, my chin held high, and auburn tresses crowning my head; I stepped up three treads on the grand staircase that led to the upper floor of our expansive home to address the people gathered in our living room and adjoining parlor.

"May I have your attention please?" I had asked in a clear, ringing voice, which sounded so much like mother's that it startled me for a moment. "Thank you all, each and every one, for coming today to share our loss, and to honor our parents. Your kindness will always be held dear in our hearts, and I thank you all for showing your respect for the men lost along with our parents. Your honor shall not be forgotten.

Mr. Morris Tillison has reminded me that our family's loan will still be expected to be paid on time; sixteen days hence. To accommodate his request, and to fulfill our family's financial obligations, I shall have timber contracts for sale immediately. Any and all who are interested, please meet us in our late parents' office in a few minutes, so we may ease Mr. Tillison's fears. Thank you again for your presence and friendship."

With my actions and words, I laid misfortune squarely on the head of Morris Tillison, and the low mutterings from many people in the room rained disapproval towards the young man.

As I descended the steps, my sisters made their way to me, and together we walked into the large room that served as our office.

The room was imposing with bookcases floor to ceiling. It also served as our private schoolroom. Beautifully drawn maps, depicting our holdings, covered one half of one wall.

Father's large brass-tacked, red leathered, wing back chair, held a commanding position at the equally large desk of solid, golden brown, Butternut Walnut wood.

I motioned Jane to that chair, and wide eyed, and swallowing noticeably, she walked up; stood beside it a moment; then gracefully lifted her skirts, and sat down with all the dignity of a queen.

"Take paper and pen; write down the names, and purchases for each acreage Jane." I had spoken precisely and in a commanding voice. The other girls had filed in to stand behind the desk and chair. I nodded silently to them; asking for their support; which they gave without hesitation, but I didn't need their support.

THIS was my duty.

A large contingent of gentlemen had quietly entered the room while their wives waited solemnly in the foyer and parlor, which only emphasized their positions to me; of their not being equal to their husbands.

What can I say except; they were not O'Reilly women.

Most of the men were well dressed, and we'd had years of business dealings with them. However, I noticed there were some men missing. I excused myself and went out the door. I approached the remaining men who stood off to one side in a tight group with their families.

They were the hard-working, poorer men of the gathering, but I had my reasons for asking them to the auction. These men were our lifelong friends, we attended church with their families, and school with their children. Some held their hats in rough, calloused hands. Some ducked their heads in greeting and mumbled "Miss."

I invited these men into our office to offer their bids on parcels that I would make affordable to them.

It was a measure of my respect for these men, and their loyalty to my parents; which bore them into our office.

I held the arm of a huge German man, well over my six-foot height, and the bicep I held was as hard as any piece of forged steel. His name was Hendrik Steinbury, and it was he who had saved my life the day my parents died. He and his large family were the ones in charge of our home, gardens, fields, pastures, and stock, as estate managers.

His wife held his other arm and came with us.

I then took the distinct pleasure of dismissing Morris Tillison from the room. His father started to apologize for his son, but Matilda interrupted saying he needn't apologize for something he didn't do.

Whereupon he cited the fact that he did do something: "I gave the bastard life, and for that I'm truly sorry."

I wondered what would transpire at their home that evening as I silently waited for his departure to finish. I somehow knew I would never see the young man again. I found out later that the son was put on an outbound stage the same evening; along with his mother.

With Father's school stick in hand, I pointed out each parcel on the maps. I knew each one, as I had looked them over with Father through the years.

One by one, and in some cases, acre by acre, tracts were sold. Timber contracts were offered back to the contract holders, or to a new party. The less affluent purchased one acre or ten, and I controlled every bid. As I said, I knew the tracts, and what species of timber stood on each. I sold the top quality timber for much less than the market value so those less affluent could reap a larger profit, and thus care for their families.

I had to dismiss only one prospective buyer when he objected to how I conducted the sale. For instance, in the middle of a tract of White Oak, ready for selected harvest, and of top dollar prime, I sold acreage of small amounts to the poorer men. I had offered a price to them first, accepted their answer, and entertained no others.

At the end of the day, at 80 cents or less on the dollar, everything was sold. Everything except the 1640 acres the home, pastures, and ruined mill sat on.

That parcel, I gave to Hendrik and his large family, for as I said; it was his arms that held me, and carried me to safety the day Mother and Father died.

Among the six men who died with our parents; was one of his sons, and this man had helped dig all their graves.

This was my gratitude to him.

It was small payment for his families' years of service, and devotion to our family. I hadn't any doubts that Mother and Father approved. My sisters did, but they didn't have to, for I now had the authority to make decisions for the family.

Hendrik would keep our stock, and arrange to have it trailed to us along with some of the household items next year; after we found land to build on in Montana, but I'm getting ahead of our story.

Hendrik didn't think the gift was very small. In fact, it took the wind out of him, and we sat him down in our Father's chair. He sat a long time, and gulped at a glass of our best sipping whiskey as many a man came forward to shake his hand and mine, for the return of timber or new purchases, and Hendrik's ownership of the mill. His wife was speechless also, but her emotions were full as tears streaked her face.

The monies wouldn't be called in until after the harvest, and the lumber sold. No one had out of pocket expense. With the mill destroyed, the buyers would have to haul their logs a far distance to another mill, or here to Hendricks, after he had it rebuilt, and I gave them a year to complete their contract with us.

Every man opted to wait and do business with the Hendricks mill.

Memories of that day, in that room, are as clear as the air of this wild, open, land we are now travelling through. Somewhere in this land my sisters and I would carve out our new home.

Mr. Carl Tillison accepted the promissory notes of the buyers, due dates and wrote a receipt for me; signifying our note paid in full at that new time. The remainder was to go to our account; which was a goodly amount by anyone's standards, but far less than the sale of the high quality lumber would have given us.

We were homeless, but not broken in monies, and the O'Reilly spirit sat strong and well on our shoulders.

I spent many an evening sitting by their graves; talking in my head to my departed parents. I revealed my hopes, fears, and the doubts in myself, but in the end I knew that I was going to take my family west.

I can't put into words the growing confidence I had deep in my soul for the position I now occupied in the family. The position of leadership.

There was a part of me that grasp fully the knowledge and a deeper, more resounding truth, than what I was told at Mother and Gram Ma Kates' knees. It was as if a flood gate, as intense as the ones we opened on the mill pond, poured into my core. I believe it was the old wisdom flooding into me. Only time will prove to me if that is so.

I do know that from that time forward, I made decisions without hesitation; acted immediately upon my instincts; not thoughts, and I was handling a dozen things at once. I dreamt dreams that should have scared me; like when I was little, but I was now in awe of what those dreams showed me, and looked forward to bedtime.

Except I was only sleeping four hours a night. But it was enough.

I surely didn't know where I was rushing to, but I was caught in a male storm, and was without doubt that I could do this…my job.

I explained my decision to my sisters, and we packed up, and in a month, we struck out for a new land; just like our long ago Grandmother had done years before, and took her first step onto this soil in 1773. Only she came by ship, and we were going by horse and wagon.

I continued to spend many an evening at their graves. I knew I had to let them go. I knew that, but it took many a conversation with them to finally accomplish the fact.

The decision to go west was mine, approved I knew, by every O'Reilly woman who had lived before me. Our many aunts and cousins, who lived in the county, and along the ocean shore, abided by, and understood my choice, and many of them spent a few days with us before our parting.

I had received an answer to my letter from a man in the Montana Territory who was a land agent, and through him I purchased a large parcel of good grazing land; sight unseen.

That's what we're doing right now. Traveling. It's raining. It's September 1878. I'm tired as hell, and the Graces are somewhere over Ireland, for they're sure as hell not here!

Chapter 2

"Kate! Can we stop early tonight? I want to dry out before these clothes take root in my skin!"

The day had broken gray and low. The air was moist; carrying its burden of hidden, heavy rain. The clouds and suspended rain hadn't broken off, but deepened as the day progressed. Then the clouds opened, and dropped rain in drops so large they stung woman, and animals as good as any wasp ever did!

Say'ard never was one who enjoyed the outdoors as I recalled. Indoor sports were more her style. She was twenty-one this year past, and had that sloe-eyed look of a real beauty. When we left Tennessee, she hadn't broken one heart: she had shattered seven! One belonged to a handsome Irish man of admiral qualities, and quiet nature. Somehow I knew he wouldn't be taking lightly to Say'ard leaving him behind.

She did get around; just like my namesakes all did, if the stories were true, and Say'ard surely was upholding her part of our heritage.

*Well, I better keep the peace if possible; besides, I'm just as wet as the rest.* "Say'ard, if you promise to sing after we set up, I'll ask Ellen to make dried peach cobbler. A warm, dry blanket, spiced peach cobbler, coffee, and some singing will make us all feel better. What do you say, Ellen?"

"I'll roast one of these damned mules for dry bloomers!" Ellen yelled back to me. Ellen had a way with the spoken English language; when she wasn't being 'proper'. She was one of the older set of twins, and I know for a fact she didn't wear bloomers.

We pulled up under a grove of large willow trees lining a spring-fed stream. The rain was still pouring hard, but everything was snug and dry under the canvas rigging of our wagons. After tying other tarps between the back to back wagons for a shelter; we hauled wood from the possum belly under the first wagon where we had stored a supply before the rain started, and lit a fire.

The fire caught eagerly in the dry grass and twigs, and felt very comforting. Within an hour, the cobbler, coffee, and music were soothing the ire in each of us. The coffee seemed to me to be the best part of the meal, but I did have a second helping of the cobbler.

The thoughts of dry clothes, and a warm blanket were what I was looking forward to, as were the girls.

I didn't get either.

While the girls slept snug in the wagons, I took the wet guard. Mary would take over at about midnight, and she would have a dry watch, for the storm was starting to break even as I threw a dry, blanket poncho over my wet coat to retain my body heat.

I ached all over, my butt was sore, and I needed to stretch my back, for the day had been a trial. I stretched as I walked the perimeter of the camp and stock line.

A wheel on one wagon had worked loose, and we spent an early morning fixing it, and replacing a thrown shoe on one of the team mules.

Shannon had whined a bit about riding the wagon, and we finally put her on one of the lead team mules, which put a dark scowl of pouting on Megan's face until she got up on the other team mule. They were fourteen; in between childhood and womanhood, and had a lot of growing pains showing.

The water barrel had rocked hard enough on a stretch of rough trail that the lid came off. At the next stream we had refilled it with fresh water, and re-tied the lid more securely.

Matilda had voiced deriding words to Ellen about missing an easy shot on a small antelope which brought Mary to Ellen's defense. Mary and Ellen were twins.

I had shaken my head; listened to the squawking of my sisters, and nudged Striker to take me WAY up front for a while.

Morning brought blessed sunshine. It came creeping up to the edge of the world; slipping from under the last lingering pink storm clouds, like a smiling, elfin child that was contemplating mischief.

"Sunrises are a gift," Father used to say.

They surely were.

Mary came in from guard duty and woke the other girls, and I handed her a hot cup of coffee. We went about doing personal things, and getting a hot breakfast of pan fried bread, and antelope steaks. We ate until we were over full; which was a considerable amount of food, but still the rigors of the trip had slimmed us all. Say'ard said her slimmer waist was a good thing; it emphasized her breasts.

I looked at her with a questioning, raised eyebrow, and she quickly finished her breakfast, and we turned our hands to breaking camp and packing up.

I stood the first teams in place; Mary helped me throw the harnesses on while Jane led the next teams to stand. The harnessing took the same amount of time that it took Ellen and Matilda to saddle the riding horses, and the other girls to put the last of the night things in the wagons.

My backsides imprint was still in my saddle, and I settled into it and led out.

The air was fresh, crisp, washed clean by the rain, hung out to dry, and smelled intoxicating! Matilda took over the lead, and I rode off hand of the lead wagon Jane and Shannon shared today.

We were a week into the journey when Shannon had questioned, "Katie? Where did you say we are going? The town is not on the map." So I had sided Striker to Shannon's wagon, climbed up beside her, took the map, and put and X where Highwater should be. "There you go Little Sis. You just get us there. All right?" I said warmly into her smiling face. "Far into the western Montana Territory."

"Why that far west?"

She had me there. *Why west, indeed? I guess a little history will help explain it to her.* "Well Imp, a long time ago an O'Reilly woman came west across the Atlantic Ocean. Then much later Great-Grandmother Kathleen came west into Virginia, and I heard the story from Grandmother Kate, that on that trip, her mother rode the finest looking Irish stallion you could ever hope to lay eyes on.

Then our mother came further west into the hills and canyons of Tennessee, and she too came riding in on a fine stallion that was sired from that herd. We seem destined to keep heading west for one reason or another," I spoke softly to my youngest sister.

"And you're riding our herd stallion on this journey."

Giving her a one-armed hug, I said softly, "Yes I am Imp."

Shannon was "Imp" to us all. She was the last born of the second set of twins, and on the sickly side. She was everyone's favorite. She was still a strawberry, blonde haired child with the exact features of what we've come to believe a fairy should look like. She was a book worm, an excellent seamstress, an artist, and covered with freckles.

As a young child, Imp had spent more time in a sick bed than the rest of us put together. For her amusement one day, Father had fetched a pencil and paper, and asked her to draw a pretty picture for him. She did, and it sparked her hand at drawing.

He proceeded to prop items up at the foot of her bed. First, her own rag tag doll, then a flower, a bouquet of flowers, various clothing items, a saddle, a basket of five tabby kittens that were so young they couldn't see to crawl out of the basket, and then we girls.

One at a time we sat as still as dead bees while Shannon labored over our portraits. She was six at the time, and by age ten she had drawn everything on the place. Windmills, ponds, trees, flowers, pastures, yard scenes, every human in sight, and our animals, of which there was a goodly number, and we could recognize each one.

To me, one of her most amazing drawings was a large catfish; underwater, moving gracefully with the current! What sort of mindful insight did a person have to have, much less a child, to envision such a thing? Or did that elfin child hold her breath and go under water?

For Mother's birthday, when Imp was eleven, she sketched a portrait of Mother. It was so realistic that it was uncanny to behold. It's packed in one of the wagons; along with the sketch of Father, and they will hang over our living room once we get settled in.

Father had made a vow to do what it took for his Imp to be a truly great artist. Now, it was up to me to follow through on his vow.

I would.

"What's there for us Kate besides land?"

"A home, but we don't have to build one. The land we bought has a house and buildings already standing on it, but we have to begin again," I replied easily as I smiled at my littlest sister. She had slid into the world three minutes after Megan, and I, as a twelve year old, had helped Father and Gram Ma Kate, deliver her.

"You wait and see Imp. We O'Reilly's are going to stand this land on end!" Say'ard added with an air of authority, and toss of her head.

"I don't know about that Say'ard," Mary said doubtfully.

"Sure we will Mary!" Matilda added in her FOUR cents worth. "Folks will know us when they see us, and remember us when we're gone! You all just wait and see!"

*I'll wait* I thought, as I crawled onto to Striker and swung out to hunt up supper.

He was our main herd stallion and Mother's favorite again. She had ridden his sire often, and he carried his sire's name of old. Each of us had our own mounts from that herd, and we were proud of their blood lines.

Mother's stallion, mine now, was fast; a twelve-year-old stud, smart as a cagy buck deer, and he was a stayer. He'd go all day, and night on a handful of grain or grass; a few drinks of water, and he never turned down a treat of sweet maple sugar.

Striker's name fit him well. People didn't stand close to him or they'd walk with a limp. That included family. But there was a trick to let him know NOT to kick you; just gently touch his left front leg below the body, and he was a patient listener.

He and I swung wide behind the trail the girls were on to hunt up meat for supper and tomorrow's breakfast.

Shannon, Meagan, Mary and Jane were in the wagons. Ellen, Say'ard, and 'Til rode as outriders today. They carried the "73" Winchester rifles, and Colt handguns. In addition to these weapons; we each carried a belt knife, and had a bull whip coiled up, and hanging from a saddle tie. Not exactly what a well, dressed lady wore, but at the moment we weren't well, dressed ladies; we were protectors of our property and each other.

We were versed in the art of shooting, and had won many a contest growing up. Father had seen to our practice sessions himself, and he was renowned for his shooting ability. The rifles we carried were .44 calibers, and they were lightweight enough for us girls to handle, but powerful enough to take on just about anything we came up against; if not alone, then by the strength in our numbers.

We may have been women, but we were women to be reckoned with Father had always said of his girls.

Father had wanted a son or sons; like any man, but all he could ever sire were girls. So he made sure we could take care of ourselves, and each other. Mother made sure of the domestic side of us, and booked no fussing or backsliding.

The balance of what we learned from our folk's stands us well as we travel. I wasn't worried about the girls, and they didn't worry about me.

Striker lit out for a line of trees along the base of a grassy hill far out to the southwest. The day had warmed, and the sun was soothing on my back as I rode away from it, and my clothes were drying on my body. I didn't bother to change to dry ones last night. I just laid me down next to the fire and went to sleep.

At our approach, a small spring doe sprang from her bed in the tall grass and bounded away. As any inexperienced youngster of any animal, her curiosity made her stop to look back from the far edge of the tree line. I had pulled Striker to a stop, and was ready for the young deer's' mistake. Striker never flinched at the shot; the Winchester did its job just fine, and we had tender eating for supper and breakfast.

## Chapter 3

"How much farther is it, Kate?" Matilda questioned, it seemed for the thousandth time

"Probably three weeks at the most," I answered.

"What will the place be like?" Matilda pressed me. She never was satisfied with just one question.

"You know as much as I do. The description in the letter is all we have to go on," I replied.

"Mary?" Ellen added to the conversation, "How much cash do we have?"

"Just over $14,000. Why?"

"I was wondering if that will be enough to set us up. Will it Kate?" she questioned me.

I never lied to anyone, I had never broken any of the Rules, and I wasn't about to start now. "It won't be enough, but the ranch will be paid off free and clear, and we'll just handle whatever comes," I summed it up. "There won't be a lot left before we sell our first cattle, or horses, and that won't be for a year or two from now. So we will have to be very thrifty with what we buy, but the money from the timber sales should start arriving before then."

The five months we'd been traveling had brought us into a different kind of land. Back in Tennessee the hills, and mountains were covered with big yellow poplars, hickory, oaks, sycamore, and maple trees. There were a goodly number of pines also. The dogwood and rhododendron flowering in spring filled the air with their heady perfumes. Gram Ma Kate showed us how easy it was to make perfumed water from almost any flower, along with bars of bathing soap, and the wood ash, lye soap, for the heavier cleaning.

Hill folk, like us, are a different breed than most. Clannish, kind and giving, soft spoken, mule tough, sometimes mean, highly musical, head-shakingly dumb, and every other kind of quality you can lay a name to pretty much describes hill people.

They're Scot-Irish by decent for the most part, but we are Irish; at least for many generations. Before that

Gramma Kate said we were Scots, and before that we were…from somewhere else.

One trait which we all have, well, most of us anyway, is our word. If, and when, we give our word, our promise, or hand, it was like giving part of ourselves. We stood by it. Added to all that; the hill folk were knowledgeable in the ways of survival, and making do.

Mother and Father made sure we knew some about most things, and a whole lot about a few things in particular that we took an interest in. In the wagons were the books and articles we each had on our chosen interests. In my trunk were the things from all of the Grandmother Kathleen's and Mother that were to be passed down to the next generation.

Like it or not, I am the current matriarch of the family, and I am not being smug when I say that I truly respect the position.

Today still saw us in the same grass-covered, rolling land, where the trees are few in number, and I miss them tremendously. The waterways were usually of good size except in the hilly areas. There the small streams, or trickles, escaping from beneath rocks were cold, clear, and sweet. The land surely was different than Tennessee.

It had taken us a while to get accustomed to the openness of this land after living in a place where your view was interrupted in a few miles, or less; except on promontories. This land gave us a feeling of defenselessness, but not much vulnerability, but I carried, a little more than I liked, an apprehension in the pit of my belly in regard to the open plains.

As the weeks have gone by, I have become more accustomed to the expanse, and I've settled into an amiable association with it, but I still envision myself as a fly on a horse's rump. That's the way a human seemed to size up to this land; not too big.

The three or four of us who rode; ranged far out from the wagons looking things over, and getting a feel for this country where I had chosen to settle us. As we were nearing the end of our journey we started to pay closer attention to everything from coal seams, timber stands, rock formations, the directional flow of water courses, and of course; the mountains. They had risen higher in front of us with each passing day.

We now looked up at the top of that barrier.

The ranch land we had obtained lay in the heart of good grazing lands. After settling in, and putting things in order; I would find a workable time line, and send back to Tennessee for our livestock. I planned on meeting the herd just about this time next year.

Father had seen to the quality of our animals, and made sure they were of a pure line.

He didn't set too much store in gambling on things in general, but he hardly ever passed up a good horse race when the occasion presented itself. Because of Mother's blooded Irish horses, we had a stable of six prized racers; mares and studs, and thirty brood mares. Thirty or more teams of two, big strong work horses; the rest of our riding stock, two hundred Herefords, and the four big, one-ton bulls; comprised what I expected to be brought to me.

It would take some time to walk them here, and keep some meat on their bones, but they were worth every mile of hardship.

Judith Basin in Montana was a long, hard journey, but taken one day at a time I never had any doubts that we would finish the excursion well.

Woman to Reckon With

## Chapter 4

This basin had been settled by a few, rich, eastern men who fancied themselves as cattle barons. Conrad Kohrs was one, and Grandville Stuart headed up a concern called DHS, for Davis-Heuser-Stuart. They didn't know much about cattle or how to get along with people.

They didn't have to worry about eight women treading on their prospects though, for we had talked things out before starting, and decided we would stay fairly small; going for high quality, and keeping a pure bloodline in our stock.

I had chosen this area because it was out of the way and obscure. One had to hunt to find it. What I looked for in this area, and hoped to find, was quiet peacefulness.

The ranch would be the main establishment of the family. We would run businesses separately, and we would pull together for whichever one of us needed help.

Separate, but together. Apart, but united. If one would fail the others would stand.

Diversity was the one thing in which I felt Father had erred. His mainstay was the mill, timber, and good stock; with the mill bringing in eighty percent of the money.

THAT was why I sold out. Eighty percent is a big loss for any business. That, and I wanted to make Morris very aware of how I dealt with the likes of him!

We would try for a more balanced income. Being women, we decided to cater mostly to a woman's frame of mind. That frame of mind was usually concerned with the comforts of a woman, their menfolk and families, and hopefully it would provide a living to each sister. The ranch would belong to all of us, and I would run it, and have the final say over it. Each sister would branch out on her own if she desired to.

Judith Basin lay smack dab in the middle of Montana just north of the Little Belt Mountains, and forty odd miles southeast of a small, but solid town named Highwater. Which was near a spectacular waterfall. The mountains to the south of this basin rose upward to over nine thousand feet, and one of them, called Big Baldy, I have read, is a sight to behold.

The Lewis and Clark Expedition passed to the north of here on their exploratory journey of two and a half years. That was over seventy years ago. It seemed this area is chock full of the historical making of the western part of this country.

It is a high country; a sight to gladden our hearts, and I know that my grandmothers would have been at home here.

Tennessee has an abundance of its own history; just a lot earlier, and in a different century.

Our journey was almost finished. It had taken us northwest from the northeastern line of Tennessee; northwest to Knoxville, in as direct a route as we could lay out, to the heart of Montana. We had given the maps to Imp, and she kept a constant, critical eye to our direction and routes, and the X marking our destination.

Traveling through Kentucky was the easier part as we followed established roads. Passing over the Ohio River was our first time on a raft, and although we had always walked the logs on the millpond; this was different.

The stock didn't care for it any better than we did.

The lineman operating the raft was an older, shabbily dressed, rank man, and he was feeling too much of the corn. When he made advances toward Jane, and actually dared to lay a hand on her, I upended him into the fast flowing river before he came to an understanding about the respectability that should be offered to women. We unloaded ourselves from the raft, and watched him climb out onto the river bank farther downstream. The girls glanced to me, as if to say they agreed with my actions.

I didn't need them to agree, but glad they did.

It was my job.


Cutting across the tip of Indiana took hardly a week, and we found friendly people who granted us camping rights on their lands, and our week stay in Springfield was a welcome respite.

A few days of travel, and we saw the Mississippi River itself. The sight of that brown-tainted water, rushing past dark green hills, brought a lump to our throats. We had inherited the appreciation for the beauty of nature from the women whose blood flowed in our veins, and THIS was beauty!

After that crossing, our travel followed the Des Moines River, toward that town. Going north with the river, we made another crossing, and continued up the trail to Fort Dodge.

The terrain was bone jarringly rough, and we rubbed the soreness out of each other's' muscles every night.

A few people we met warned us of the dangers that lay ahead, and the army tried to stop us at Fort Dodge.

Neither the terrain, nor the army was much of a hindrance. As for the army; they sent the wrong two men.

The kid faced sergeant with his detachment of six soldiers who watched us cross the stream near the fort, didn't put himself on my good side immediately, when, with too much authority in his mannerisms, informed me that we couldn't continue on alone, ordered us to the fort, and wait for an escort.

Issuing a brisk, "Follow me!" he wheeled his horse; sitting ramrod stiff in his saddle, and expected me to meekly follow.

Embarrassed, he returned in a few minutes.

Embarrassed and angry he was, for I had silently sat Striker; watched him leave, and waited for him to come back.

He needed to understand who I was, and I didn't talk to anyone's back!

Riding up very close to Striker, his horse nose to nose with my stallion, the uniformed kid began to loudly berate me.

"I SAID, FOLLOW ME! I'M IN COMMAND HERE!"

"I'm not in the army," I replied softly. "And lower your voice; you're scaring my little sisters."

Striker apparently didn't like the horse so close, and being the herd stallion that he was; snapped out; ripped the horses' nose open; drawing blood, and sent the mount into an out of control, rearing, handful of thrashing horseflesh.

Striker was just being himself, and asserting his rights.

Getting the horse halfway in hand, the sergeant shouted lividly, "YOU'RE UNDER ARREST!"

Shannon began to whimper, and Jane rode over to her, and laid a hand on Shannon's leg to comfort her.

"For what? You riding a horse you can't control?" I spoke in an astonished tone.

"I'M THE LAW HERE!" He bellowed at me.

"Keep your voice down, and go get your commander," I said through clinched teeth. "Now. Before I have to hurt you in front of your men," I continued.

He fumed hotly; glared at me, but sent a man towards the fort.

The man returned very shortly with another man who looked familiar, and as he rode up I recognized him from a family back in Tennessee.

Our families had had trouble.

I heard the girls spread out behind me, as I knew they too recognized the approaching lieutenant.

The man stopped in front of me, and about ten feet away.

"I see Striker's still the herd boss," he said softly, glancing at the still bleeding nose of his sergeants' horse.

"He is. Still knows how to handle things that get in his way," I replied gently. "Your 'boy' here," I indicated the kid with my head nod, "says I'm to be arrested because his horse got away from him. You going to try and do that Anse? Arrest me?"

Anse Campbell's thirty year old cousin had violated a twelve year old second cousin of mine, and I was the one who had stumbled upon him doing it. When he pulled his hunting knife, and advanced on me; I killed him on the spot.

A knife fight with a pistol isn't much of a fight.

I was nineteen. That was seven years ago.

The hills got real tense with verbal charges against me until the doctor's report, and the girl's recounting, was made available to their family. The family had gotten real closed mouth; except for Anse.

He did his level best to get me hung for murder, but the leaders of both families prevailed, and that only left bad blood from Anse, for me.

He was remembering all that as he studied me intently. "You going to settle here?" He was asking the question, but telling me not to live here.

"I've bought further west," I answered in a bored voice as I looked around at the bustling commotion around the fort. "Someplace a little less...crowded."

"That's good," he replied. Further indicating he didn't want me anywhere he had to lay eyes on me.

I rose to the veiled challenge in my own way. "Am I going to have trouble with you too? I wouldn't have a problem with that."

He stiffened just a bit, and his chin came up just a tad. I don't know if anyone besides me saw that, but it didn't matter. I did.

"No need for trouble. The sergeant gets overzealous at times. He's...young. You be camping close by?"

"No need," I answered, still in the same 'code' talk we were having; not meaning what our words were saying, "there's still a lot of day left to use up."

"Have an easy journey then," Anse Campbell spoke lightly, touched his hat brim; eased his horse around, and the full detachment of blue soldiers followed him towards the fort.

I never took my eyes off him as I heard my sisters gather behind me and Jane say to Megan, "Head 'em up Meg," and listened to the mules tighten the traces, and the wagon wheels creak as they passed behind me.

The girls left me alone for a few hours after that. They knew I was reliving bad memories, and had to settle my feelings.

Westward a few more days from Fort Dodge, we struck the Missouri River, got hauled across on rafts again, and swung onto the wagon trail toward Fort Randall.

The days slipped by under all manner of weather and skies; taking us with them to fledging towns like Rapid City, Sheridan, Billings, Lewiston, and finally we were almost "home."

The trip wasn't without its mind-wearing trials. Nature did her level best to ward us off. Here, in these immense open plains, the storms raged in full force with little to slow them, or break them.

One of the mules was killed by a cougar, and one of Meagan's horses died of gunshot after breaking a leg while she was climbing a rocky point, for a view of the land. Meagan was laid up with a bruised arm, and lumped skull for some time; acquired when her horse had fallen.

More men, than Mother had led us to think could have existed with less than honorable intentions, plagued our way. But these bad examples of manhood didn't stop Say'ard from her shenanigans! I do love her dearly, but she has been, and is, a worry!

## Chapter 5

I was extremely thankful, when we pulled into the town of Highwater, that our journey had been completed safely.

We must have made quite a sight to the people who were accustomed to seeing the occasional wagons of traveling families. They stood, and stared as we rolled past. We smiled and stared back

The previous night's camp had been an earlier one than usual. We washed, fussed, cleaned the guns, belts, saddles, harnesses, and beat the dirt from the wagon canvases. We even went so far as to brush down all the stock. Everything was as prime looking as we could make it.

Say'ard had decided that we were going to arrive at our new home clean, and with dignity. It must have worked, for Say'ard's words of 'standing this land on end' passed briefly across my mind. Maybe little sister wasn't too far left of being right after all.

I hate it when she does that!

We dismounted in the dry-sand street. An early winter wind drove a chill into us as we tied to the hitching racks. I reached to help the younger girls from their wagons, and we took our first walk around the town which we had come so far to settle near.

It surely wasn't a whole lot to look at on first glance, but when you looked a second time; you began to see little things; such as the people didn't appear to be dirt poor like so many back east.

Signs advertising various businesses caught our attention, and the number of people in town for this time of day was surprising.

We drew every eye as we walked, for it probably wasn't too often, if ever, eight good-looking, eligible women showed up all at once in a town of this size. Especially women dressed as we were, wearing pants with blanket ponchos over our coats for the added warmth, and no men at our elbows.

The land agency would be our first stop; then the mercantile. My letter of purchase agreement and the receipt of down payment, were all we needed to acquire the deed, and with the rest of the price paid, 6,500 acres of Judith Basin belonged to us; for $6,000.

It seemed pricey, and the land agent seemed smug about something.

At the mercantile store we stocked up on provisions, and bought grain for the animals. The personal items we purchased made up for what we had done without for a while. I purchased a local paper while the girls shopped, and then we looked over the rest of the town.

Two hours later we rolled out heading west for our land. It was eleven o'clock in the morning on a brisk, and sunny Wednesday, October 2, 1878, and we were home.

The ranch lay half a day's travel by wagon; about seven miles, but a person on a fast horse could make the same trip in just over an hour.

Pulling up on a small rise a quarter of a mile from the ranch buildings; we sat speechless, and numb as we looked at what I had purchased!

Run-down and broken buildings! Not many windows and doors, and the waist high weeds, full of a light dusting of snow, overran the entire place!

The hills, covered in brown, dormant grass, stretched far in all directions. Cottonwood trees formed a staggering line as they followed the creek towards a larger river that flowed from the mountains, and in the other direction towards the open valley and town.

"May the Graces help us? What have we done?" Mary whispered.

I was totally in shock, and getting madder by the minute! What we saw, and what was described in the letter of sale were two entirely different things! The man in the land office part of the bank had written a lie to me! Maybe he thought women were gullible about the ways of business. Was that why he seemed smug? I'd remember him! And he'd damned well end up paying dearly!

Right now I had to face some difficult facts, for it was hard onto winter, and I wouldn't go somewhere else; not even into town, for we had spent a lot of our money, and couldn't waste any more by buying more comfort than we needed.

I sat quietly on Striker as he pawed the ground, digging a small hole, as if saying: "Here, right here! I'll go no farther!" And neither would I, damn it! Neither would I!

"Girls, I guess we'll have to show a few people who we are. Let's get down there and unload. We're home."

By the Graces! I wanted to cry, but damned if I would!

Chapter 6

Christmas saw a goodly amount of change in the
place. Rotten, or broken boards on the walls, and roofs
had been replaced. A few new windows were letting the
bright, late, fall sun in, and the window openings that
didn't get glass were boarded up tight. We made a few
trips to town for materials that should NOT have been
necessary.

The smug faced land agent stayed out of sight.

Matilda and I made ladders from tree limbs, and long
poles bound together with wet rope, to get us to the high
rooflines, and upper walls. I chiseled half round notches
in the poles to lay the limbs in, for better weight bearing,
and more secure lashing. Their construction was just a
part of the knowledge that father had taught us.

As I've said; we're capable.

The areas around the buildings were wide open to the
strong winds that blew like screeching banshees! Three of

us, Say'ard, 'Til, and I, rode a few miles away towards the high country; each leading another horse; cut good, ten-foot-high, branched-out spruce trees; and dragged them, and dead trees; twelve at a time, back to the ranch. There we stashed the pines around the outside of the house to create windbreaks. They would catch more snow for warmth, and further block the house from the howling, winter winds.

It didn't look pretty, but it would make the house warmer. Come next spring; we would start digging, and transplanting a mixture of many small trees to grow into a dense, living windbreak around the north and west perimeters of the buildings.

That would be spring and fall work, and in-between the other chores.

We three continued dragging in just dead wood and piling it near the back of the house for firewood. We worked at hauling wood, many hours a day, and changing horses often, until the snow stopped us.

The other girls cut fodder during the daylight, and piled the wagons full. At night, by lantern light, we emptied the wagons, and piled the hay in the mows.

Two of us worked the wagons; throwing it up to two more; who tossed the hay to the last two; who piled it high, and towards the back walls. Shannon and Meg handled the teams; keeping them in place.

We would cut on the growing pile of tree wood later as we needed it for fires.

We boarded up the holes in the barn using lumber from another old shed we tore down, and got the horses, mules, and cow a better place for the winter. To get all twenty six head in the small barn, we took out all the stall walls but two, and removed any other unnecessary walls, and left only the strong upright supports. The stock could mingle as a herd for warmth. The two stalls were for the cow and any horse or mule that needed to be kept separate for medical reasons. The large space was easier to keep clean too.

We cut fodder, hauled firewood, and patched things up every day. To get a break from one job; we went to another. This was not the sort of work a woman is built to do, but WE were all WE had. We worked steadily, and gained steadily.

The repairs were only temporary to get us through the winter, and come warm weather, and our first year here; we'd do it all over again, and do it right.

The biggest problem was fodder for the stock. Even though the girls cut daily, and we stored what could, that many animals required a lot of feed, and we couldn't cut enough to feed them through the winter, before hard winter set in. We let them forage for themselves as long as they could, but it was an accepted fact we would have to buy.

Fighting the biting cold, I worked my way into town, and put the word out that I was in the market for feed.

The folks were willing to sell, but the price was high; I paid it, for our stock would die without it. The livery man sold me part of his, at a higher price than the ranchers, but that included delivery.

The land agent was still not to be seen on my visits.

We loaded our wagons at the rancher's barns with the dry grass, and hauled many loads to our barn. The men at those places helped with the work, and a few called on the girls later. The ranchers were taken aback when five women showed up to pitch their hay into our wagons, and did most of the work for us.

We left Meg and Imp at home with Jane to protect them; keep the fire going, and do the daily chores.

Those days of hauling hay were long. We started before daylight and got home well after dark.

We met the women and children at the ranches, and left on good terms.

I believed in buying time, but not work if I could avoid it. I couldn't avoid this work, and we put the stock on short rations the whole winter.

Winter descended on us in earnest, and we stayed indoors during the worst storms; except for tending the stock. In-between these white rages, which we weren't used to dealing with, we four oldest rode out when we could; strung trap lines, set seine nets in the good-sized river, and hunted deer in the boulder, tree choked canyons on our land.

It was a bitter cold land; the likes of which I had never dealt with, but the largeness of the land and broad sky drew me to them, and I was not afraid.

Hunting needed to be done, for that was our only meat. We didn't care to eat the animals and fish we trapped, as a main diet. In the span of a week we had the cold storeroom off the kitchen, hanging full of three elk, and five deer.

The smell of raw meat and the blood trail to our door, brought many a coyote or wolf to our place. The wild ones harassed the stock and unfortunately we had to kill a number of the predators before they left us alone for easier hunting, but by then their numbers were greatly reduced. We stood guard in the barn, two at a time, until the packs moved on.

As soon as I could find them, I'd get a couple of large guard dogs. A male and female; let them raise a litter, and train them to help us.

The hides, and furs that the trap line, and predator kills gave us, were welcomed for foot wear, and clothes. We worked the hides into what we needed as easily as the store cloth for skirts, blouses, and skirts. Father had made sure we had this ability also; working hides into clothing and leather.

As I said, Christmas found a few changes in the place, and in us. We were maturing as only self-reliance can shape a person. Imp was improving, but still we thought of her as frail, and even though we tried not to treat her as such...we did anyway.

More than anything else in our day-to-day existence was the longing for warm spring to ease our routine. We knew spring would bring long days of hard work, but with each armful of wood we carried to stoke the stove; we took solace in the knowledge we were one day closer to summer.

In the deep darkness of winter, we shed tears. Tears for the lost parents, lost home, old friends, and the old life. Then we decided we had been downcast long enough, and started to act like the real honest-to-God O'Reilly's we were! Singing and music filled the snowbound, rundown house we had endeavored to make into our home, and we honored the special day of Solstice as it should be honored.

We observed our Pagan Solstice with no prying eyes, and I gave the invocations in the auld language. I was also teaching Shannon the auld language. She was the only one that seemed drawn to it. I was pleased to know that the language would continue. The other girls knew the meanings for some words but couldn't hold a conversation in it.

Jane lit many candles, Ellen poured Irish coffee for us all; even Meg and Imp. Fried bread with venison steaks dripping with milk gravy, and dried apple pie was that holiday meal in Montana. We nibbled on molasses cookies; warm from the wood stove's oven while we waited for the evening to close down.

There would be other holidays but none better. As for Thanksgiving; we had worked the day through, and only at our supper of venison stew, biscuits, and jam did we remember what day it was. We gave our prayers over that satisfying meal as we usually did, and thanked our Graces again, for bringing us this far safe and sound.

October and All Saints Hollow, had been a happy celebration for us with food, drink, dancing, and Prayer; all done quietly in our home, for that day meant more to us than the others.

Six days after Christmas, the first day of a new year for us with 365 blank pages to fill in as we wished; the weather cleared. The sky hovered overhead, a pale clear blue. The temperature was above freezing as the porch was dripping in the heat of the sun, we saddled up, and fought the drifted snow into town.

The storms, one after another, had dumped snow by the foot, and our horses floundered, and crow hopped their way through the deep drifts that blocked our way.

"Meagan. Shannon. Stay behind me," I called to the youngest twins.

"We will, Katie!" You just keep Striker breaking trail for us," Shannon called back.

She sounded happy, and the lilt in her voice made us all glad of heart. The air was drier or fresher or something, for whatever it was, Shannon was thriving on it, and we had never seen her look better! If the journey made Imp well; that was all the rest of us would ask the Blessed Graces for!

The race horses, as I mentioned, were a prized line of our Mother's, but our riding horses were from two other lines.

Their sires and dams were English pacers, and Spanish Jennets. In early Virginia, the pacers and Jennet breeds were crossed, and produced just what this vast western land needed; an all-around work, riding, race, and pleasure horse that we rode today. Our riding stock was called the American Quarter Miler, and they were from the top line of that beginning breed.

The Irish line were our race horses.

The first true American horse breed; the Quarter Miler came to be called The Quarter Horse, because they only raced a quarter of a mile.

This breed was sired by a black stud whose name was Figure, and he was owned by Justin Morgan. When Figure finally proved what he was, his breed was called Morgan. The feisty, small-built horse could outrun, pull or carry, any horse matched against him of equal size.

Striker was a Quarter Horse, but he carried the look of a Morgan more than any horse of Mother's herd. He was jet black with a mane that hung over a deep neck to his chest, and his tail swept the ground if I didn't keep it trimmed. His small build belied the drive that was in his heart and soul.

I had been doing a lot of thinking, which wasn't unusual for me; about our horses. Most of the animals I had seen here were a haphazard mixture of various breeds, but mostly a wild horse called a Mustang that populated these western lands.

Those animals had a quality about them I liked, but I wouldn't cross them with ours. That didn't mean I wouldn't see what they could do. After all, they had survived out here; on their own, for over three hundred years, and had to have learned something! It intrigued me to find out what that might be.

There would be better horses on the bigger ranches no doubt, but the area in general needed upgrading in their general stock line.

The Quarter Horse had been pushed out of the racing world by the English Thoroughbred, but Father had always said these blocky little horses were worth hanging onto. So the O'Reilly's owned Quarter Horses very early on in their history.

We rode, drove, and worked them.

We girls had rode them daily; often racing each other over the short stretches of straight roads, and sometimes not so straight. Father sent us out on this breed to gather in the stock. There they showed what they were capable of doing with cattle.

I had a good idea rattling around in my head, but I would need to improve on it if I was going to compete with the ranchers pursuing the same thing. The spark of that idea had been lit by my parents a few years back, and I felt I would follow it up. Striker and I had to spend time together working the kinks out of that idea.

"Jane!" Say'ard's scream pulled my attention from my thoughts, and working Striker through another deep drift.

Jane's horse was down and floundering, and Jane had been thrown off; half buried in the soft snow, but still within reach of the thrashing hooves of her downed horse.

I screamed at Say'ard, as it was she who rode next in line behind Jane, "Rope her away!"

Her thoughts were mine, for Say'ard's rope was already in the air, and settling over Jane's shoulders, and Jane was jerked backwards a few precious feet.

"I got Buckjump!" Matilda, next in line, called out as her rope snared the struggling horse's head, and gave it the bracing it needed to get on its feet.

Meagan started to giggle, and we turned to stare at Jane. She was chest deep in the drift; her arms pinned to her sides by Say'ard rope; plastered with snow, and she was madder than an Irishman with an empty whiskey bottle.

"Say'ard! You get this damned rope off me! Get it off right now! This ain't funny! I ain't no horse!" she fumed.

"Am not a horse," Shannon corrected her.

"Jane, you better watch what you're eating. Buckjump can carry a good load, but it seems she had to lay down for a rest, carrying all your weight, such as it is," Say'ard said.

"All what weight," Jane sputtered; spitting the melting snow from her mouth. "I wouldn't talk if I was you!"

"Were you," Shannon corrected her again.

"Were you," Jane pared. "Say'ard, you need to ride one of the draft horses when they get here. YOU need a saddle that wide!"

"Hold it," I said, stepping Striker in-between the two of them. "Jane? You all right? Not hurt are you?" I asked.

"No, I'm not hurt! Just got snow shoved up my behind, and it's colder than hell that's all!"

"'Til? Buckjump all right?" I asked trying to hide my smile by keeping my jaws clamped tight, and holding my lips in a straight line.

"Yeah. She's fine." 'Til answered.

"Jane. You owe Say'ard you know," I said looking at her. I waited until Jane muttered, "I know Kate. Thanks Say'ard."

"Anytime. Fatty," Say'ard smirked.

"Fatty!" Jane bellowed.

Sisters! Even though their response to the incident was right on, and up to the situation; I had my doubts about them from time to time!

I adjusted the poncho blanket around me; walked Striker back up to lead position, and left the two of them discussing the less than finer points of each other.


We took the town in from stem to stern as Father would have said. At one time he'd been a sailor, and his descriptions, and phrases were a part of our language; even though we'd never set foot on a sailing ship.

After shopping; getting the mail, and in general just browsing; we bought a hot lunch and coffee. Each of us had a pack tied behind our saddles when we left town, for we didn't expect to be in town again until spring, and that was some four months off by the calendar of nature.

## Chapter 7

Winter to some folks is a dull and boring time. They didn't have the wit of eight spirited women to liven things up!

There were a hundred routine things to do from sawing wood into lengths; splitting it to fit the cook stove; breaking ice on the stream for man and animal; fleshing out and stretching the hides; cleaning the barn; caring for the stock, and milking the Guernsey cow daily.

From one of the neighboring ranches, I purchased two dozen older laying hens and a three year old rooster. We had our own eggs, but we didn't have chickens to eat; they were too old and tough, but we still had to tend the colorful, mismatched flock.

The milk was turned into cream, and that into butter, the leftover milk from the butter churn was used in baking, or drank. It made the best cornbread or sourdough bread, biscuits, or flapjacks!

During the winter my sisters talked constantly about finding work, or starting businesses. Shannon had decided to go into business with Jane. Jane, being the elder, would run the place, but it was already agreed that it would be Shannon's books, and artistry that would be a big drawing card for their shop. Shannon was fairly itching to draw portraits! Jane was the most gifted amongst us as a seamstress, and designer, while all our sewing abilities would multiply the number of garments available for sale; men's and women's.

They would be able to fill any special or custom order. With the newer fashions we knew about from back east, and the fact the mercantile didn't carry a decent line; the demand for readymade clothing should be steady.

With her gift for making a place look pleasing; as she had done in our home; Shannon would set up displays of her drawings and portraits; not forgetting the hand sketches of clothing by Jane. The place would be where a body could browse; spend time, and money.

Sitting in our snug, snowed in, warm home, with Mother and Father looking down from the wall, I listened to the ideas flow from my sisters' chatterings on the ideas for the clothing shop, and, as I laid aside the rifle I had just cleaned, and picked up a well-worn book on Scotland; I knew the town was going to get a much needed store.

Part of whatever building they could find, would be set with chairs, a few small tables, a wood stove, and shelves full of books for sale, or for a credit exchange.

Shannon had persuaded us to bring along a good portion of our library. They were an added weight that we struggled with the whole journey. It was a goodly passel of reading material; most of which we were sure the folks here had not had access to. Now, as I listened to my little sister, I understood her wisdom.

Books out here were highly prized and revered, but our personal library would not be for sale, but leased out.

Meagan, Shannon's twin, was undecided as to what she wanted to do.

"Meg, why don't you do readings in our shop for those folks who can't read, like you did at the school, and for Shannon when she was abed?" 'Jane asked.

"That's a great idea Meg!" Shannon added, "I remember how well your voice rings? Like a bell. You make a poem or story fairly come to life, and leap from the pages!"

Meagan's smile was like a sunbeam breaking through a cloud. She looked at each of her sisters, coming around to me last; as if I had to approve or the whole idea would be scrapped.

"You do have a flair for it, Meg," I said, "and you could do a good turn for the girls while watching for something you'd like to set your hand to. I don't see how it would fail. I think you would do well."

"Thanks, Katie. If you think I can; I know I can," Meg fairly bubbled, then she started to cry.

"Meg? Sis? What's the matter?" Mary asked going to her, and draping an arm around the little shoulders.

Between sniffles, Meagan whispered emotionally, "Oh Katie! You sounded just like mother."

I don't mind telling you; that made all of us a little misty eyed. I went to my baby sister, and gathered her in my arms. "Thank you, Meg. I'm glad I sound like her."

After a tender moment of holding her small body, I added, "AND if you twins think that by working in a store, you don't have to finish your education, you're very much mistaken! Mary will have at least two students in her school: you, and you," I said as sternly as I could while pointing to each twin.

My authoritive sternness was met with wide smiles, and laughter from my devilish sisters!

Mary had decided to pick up where she left off back east. Being a school teacher back home, she left that position to come west with us. Weekends she had always worked the mill with the rest of the family, but coming west was a decision on which she wouldn't, and didn't take no for an answer. The teacher for Highwater had left after Christmas, and no one had taken his place, but now there was Mary.

Mary was a Tennessee state-certified teacher, and a good one, but she needed to get certified here, and was working on that.

She tried to curtail her wiles with the menfolk, but her heritage kicked up every now and then, and she's had to work on upholding her discreet image of a school marm. I had often asked Mother which of the two gave Mary the most fits; her teaching or her heritage!

Matilda had approached the bank president, and was hired as a teller-bookkeeper for the goodly sum of eight dollars a week. She was to start with the spring break-up when business picked up.

Ellen, before the journey, was a student of the law through her own endeavor by mail correspondence. By spring she would be taking what she called her 'bar' examination to pass on to being a full-fledged, practicing lawyer. In the meantime she had, in the short time we were in town, secured a job writing for the newspaper. Her articles would be on any and all subjects, and she had a knack for putting the humorous touch to an incident of any kind.

Mary intended to use a few of Ellen's short stories in her classroom to show the students a lighter side to education. Perhaps she could nurture, and help to grow in one of her students, the same talent for writing that Ellen had.

Say'ard was more headstrong that any of us, and also a tad more on the wild side. She'd do just about anything on a dare when we were growing up, and she hadn't outgrown that fault yet. She had, without anyone's knowledge, talked the saloon keeper into a singing position in his business. When she let that piece of information slip out one evening; there was a shocked silence, and not much wit, and humor was passed around.

She was determined to go ahead and do this, and we had to give her a chance. We would not, or could not, live each other's lives.

Timothy O'Toole, the saloon keeper, was a lad from the old country itself, and Say'ard's quick wit, and beguiling tongue had apparently taken poor Timothy by storm. For the tidy sum of twelve dollars a week, and a percentage of the profits, if she proved to be a good attraction, she had a good start, as she reminded us from time to time, "of standing this land on end!"

I intended to have a talk with Timothy, and Say'ard, and I liked the land just the way it lay.

In our trunks were bolts of good cloth; heavy for work, light for shirts and dresses, and linens for kitchen and bedding. While Shannon drew and painted, the rest of us settled down to some serious sewing. I spared some time to do finger weaving; a very old craft of the family. I worked fancy hatbands and sashes in thread, and wool yarns of vivid colors on a makeshift loom.

Come spring when a shop could be opened, the array of apparel would be varied enough for anyone to find something to suit their fancy, and it would take a wagon or two to haul it all to town!

Ellen spent her time studying; along with chores and sewing, and by late April she had passed her bar. She was a full-fledged lawyer, and we were so very proud of her! Mary baked a special cake to celebrate the accomplishment, and we drank a peach brandy toast to the first 'professional' in our family.

I hadn't forgotten about Shannon and Father's dream to see her an artist, but there was time for that, and we would have three professionals in our family.

With her degree, Ellen had her first client: me. It was time to bring an accounting to one piece of low life that was masquerading as a land agent.

I gave my letter of inquiry, and his return letter of description to Ellen, and she would obtain a letter from the sheriff on the ranch's actual state of disrepair. She said that would be enough to get my case before a judge, and she seemed confident that a partial refund could be obtained. I handed it all over to her, gave her full rein on following through, and nailing the bastard's behind to the barn door!

Our horizons were getting wider as we were learning, growing, and getting along like sisters usually did; sweetly and vilely. I stayed in my corner, and out of harm's way as much as possible, coming out to referee on occasion. I wasn't a recluse. I just figured they had more growing up to do than I did, and I learned a lot by watching and not taking part in their squabbles.

False spring took us by surprise in late February, and it was a welcome break to the numbing cold. The weather warmed overnight, and in a week's time, bare ground showed through. The mountains were wrapped in a shimmering blue, and there was a smell on the wind, of a greening not too far off.

The stock were let out from the barn in a rushed group, and they descended upon the brown grass like locusts. In the barn the stock wandered about as they wished, for warmth, and companionship. It was the natural way of animals to seek the comforting closeness of their kind. Animals developed friendships with each other just like humans. I knew this, and they were gentler for it. The oldest mule took to hanging out with the milk cow.

The animals were clean, for we had continued to brush them daily; even with their thick, winter hair making the chore twice as difficult.

The horses, to our delight, had ran and frolicked like colts; sank to their knees, rolled on the warming ground, and we didn't mind brushing them clean again.

We spent these warm days gathering in more wood and airing the house. All the linens and clothes were hung outside on the clotheslines. Some were freshly washed, and some just to freshen in the scented air. Snow was shoveled up, and dumped into the meat room, and the outside of the store house was covered with more pine boughs to retain the cold inside.

It was agreed we would need an ice house built next winter, and I knew that job would fall to me.

The warmer weather was welcomed, and despised. It lifted our spirits, and threatened our food.

Some things just don't seem to balance out.


Say'ard left for her singing job with a fashionable, but lady-like wardrobe. We'd had a few words over her clothes. Rather, she had a few words. I reminded her who she was and whom she represented, and that I wasn't about to let her throw a shadow of disrespect on the O'Reilly name. Things got loud and tense for a while; on her part. In the end my ignoring her toned her temper tantrum somewhat.

She had learned from past experience, as they all had, that I didn't stop talking in an argument because I'd lost. She knew better than that. I learned the silence trick from listening and watching Mother handle Father with it.

In most arguments, before Mother and Father died, I'd won. I had to win them all now, for a while at least; until the girls got started off right in their affairs. So when Say'ard left for town; I rode with her.

"Kate?"

I let Striker canter along easy.

"Kate? I know you're still angry with me, but I just want to dress the way I have to. Besides, what's so wrong with that? I have to present myself in such a way to draw the crowds in. Don't I? I need to be a bright spot on the floor. I need..."

"YOU NEED to present yourself as a LADY! An O'Reilly, Say'ard!" I spoke sharply to my sister. "YOU WILL be a respectable looking lady! One that men will want to take their hats off to; NOT their pants! YOU WILL be the lady of their dreams, for you are not a fallen woman, and you WILL NOT EVER give them that impression!

Right now Say'ard, you are going to do something that will reflect on all our lives, and will mold you for the rest of yours. You will be either a piece of meat to be had for a price, or you will be a lady who will make the men who frequent the saloon speak of you with a degree of respect.

Men don't marry, or respect saloon girls.          You will be a singer; NOT a saloon girl. And you WILL do it with the style, and quality of a lady. You'll do it OUR way, and NOT ONE DROP of liquor will you taste there!

Do that Say'ard, and no door will ever be slammed in your face. It's up to you. I've said all I'm going to say. YOU think about the taint you may be bringing down on your little sisters' heads."

The ride on into town was filled with a silence so strong it made Striker skittish.

Say'ard tried a couple of time to make me see her side of it, which I did, but I ignored her anyway. I was mad clean through, and she knew that too. I never was one to tell the girls what they should become, BUT I sure as hell was going to tell them to do it right!

Timothy O'Toole didn't fare much better than Say'ard.

The batwing doors of the place were hooked open to the inside of the room, and the closed, windowed doors held the winter cold at bay. The place was unpainted, and dank with the smell of sour, spilt whiskey, unwashed male bodies, cigar smoke, and THIS was where my headstrong sister wanted to be!

We walked along the long bar with its brass foot rail, and the bartender looked up from his reading to stare at us. A small Chinese man with a tight skull cap, and a long braid was sweeping the floor, and he too stopped to watch our passing. The man seemed ageless, but I was thinking he was probably well into his seventh decade of life.

Say'ard stopped at an unpainted door with a white painted sign that had 'private' written on it, and knocked. A masculine voice called for us, in a distinct brogue, to come in.

Timothy O'Toole was a trim older man with graying red hair; mutton chop, side whiskers ran down the length of his jaw line, and were neatly trimmed. His brocade vest was green under a well-fitting black, tailed coat. He looked like an astute businessman who could be a banker, a lawyer, or the saloon owner that he was.

He had manners and stood when we entered the room; took in Say'ard's attire, and then mine. Say'ard was dressed in a proper dress which covered her respectfully while I was attired in my everyday work clothes; trousers, blouse, vest, overcoat, neck scarf and hat. My gun hung from its usual place on my right hip, and showed through the accommodating slit I had put in the coat. My rifle was cradled easy in my right hand.

I carried two of Say'ard's valises in my left hand, and dropped them on his office floor. She carried two larger ones.

He watched me with an eye of interest and took note that Say'ard didn't say a word, but I knew she glanced at me a couple of times.

"She's pure, and a lady Mr. O'Toole. Make sure she stays that way, and no harm comes to her, in speech, or manner." I said it softly, with a hardness in my eyes, my teeth clinched, and only a fool could not have caught my meaning. I knew Say'ard knew, that I meant every word, and O'Toole would bear my wrath, if he didn't understand what my words promised.

I nodded to my sister; turned on my heel, and walked away softly before he could respond to my statement.

I left the building not giving notice to the two men in the outer room.

I wanted to stomp hard on the stained floor as I left, but Mother had instilled in me to control myself, in manner and speech, and that would keep others off their guard, and they would not know what to expect from me.

It was difficult not to stomp.

Coming from the saloon I paused, and breathed in deeply of the fresh air, and slowly let it out as I watched the other girls just riding into town. They had trailed behind us giving us some privacy.

I watched the town's activities, and was amused at how the few folks I took note of were carefully 'uninterested' in my activities; a woman coming from a saloon!

Ellen pulled up at the newspaper office to drop off some articles for publishing, and Jane, with Imp tagging along, went to look for a building to rent. In the meantime, Mary headed for the office of the mayor to see about tying up any loose ends on that teaching position, and Matilda wanted to stop in at the bank again. Meg tagged along with Jane and Imp almost as an afterthought.

I stomped down the saloon steps to the street and out along the board walkway, the rifle hanging loosely in my left hand. With Striker ambling along behind, I wandered down to the mercantile to drop off our shopping list. We hadn't expected to be in town for another two months so we'd decided to stock up on a few items thanks to the break in the weather, and Say'ard wanting to start her "job."

From the mercantile we strolled past the jail, and a few houses to the livery, for we had decided that we would need two carriages. All we ladies had were the big wagons, and we knew there would be times when riding astride just wouldn't do.

The livery man, Ben Jenkins, always had a buggy or two around that he repaired and sold for extra income. He also had a pile of hay that was delivered last week, and since he had only one horse in the barn, he agreed to sell me half of the pile, and would see to its delivery; barring bad weather, and the buggies would be ready by spring breakup.

Seeing not a sign of the girls, Striker and I headed for the post office to gather what mail we might have gotten. It was scant, but welcome. Letters from Tennessee always brightened our day.

Heading back up the street, I saw Ellen and Matilda walking with a couple of men. Those girls did move fast!

I knew that I would get all the particulars later on.

Meeting the other four girls, we went to the small eatery in town, and Striker stopped at the hitch rail. It was a clean, simple place, much like everything else around here. We seven decided to have coffee and something sweet. Pecan pie was on the menu.

I said I'd get Say'ard since I didn't want any more of us inside that saloon than was necessary. Imp brightly offered to get her sister, but I hurried away to gather in what I thought was a wayward sister.

Imp could be a little antagonist at times!

We gathered around a large round table, and were cast many glances from the people already there, and as other patrons entered, they too looked us over. The girls were feeling devilishly grand, sitting at the table, waiting to be served.

I, on the other hand, felt a sense of dread for some reason. I couldn't catch it in my thoughts, and pin it down proper, but I had a feeling that something dark was hovering over my family, and I couldn't stop it no more than you could stop an Irishman from kicking up his heels on St. Patty's Day.

I questioned the Graces, but they were strangely quiet.

I knew there were incidents in ones' life that had to happen. Some refer to them as fate or misfortunes, and I knew that the Graces had to let a person's life play out the way it was deemed to. They, the Graces, could inform or interfere only slightly, and usually unexpectedly.

I shook off the feeling somewhat, and passed the letters out. Say'ard got the most. After all, you couldn't leave seven men, and not get ANY mail!

Mine was from Hendriks about our stock. He'd gotten my letter on the time frame of travel, and planned to start the herd out in mid-February. I should plan on the stock's arrival around mid-August. I did some quick calculating, and figured that was about right. I made a note in my head to arrange things so I could meet the herd a month's travel from the ranch, and guide them in. By then the girls should be well settled in their business, and I should have things in hand on the ranch.

The information I had been expecting from our lawyer, Mr. Morris, about the timber sales, hadn't come through. I guess it was taking more time than I had figured on for him to get the information for each sold parcel from the abstract office, and sent to me. After all there were dozens of parcels to record. I reflected on that, and wasn't too upset. Besides, the payments would come after the lumber was sold, and that would happen one parcel at a time.

In the meantime, Ellen was working on the problem of the land agent.

Say'ard and I made our peace with an unspoken toast with our eyes over our coffee cups, and the tension eased greatly at the table, and I felt better about leaving her in town.

The ride home was a spirited one as the girls talked about men.

"Did you see that awful man walking with Ellen?" Meagan shrieked.

"He wasn't awful; just a plain sort of man," Ellen shot back.

"Plain! That's not what I'd call plain!" Meagan squealed laughingly.

"That wasn't such a bad fella walking with you Matilda. Who was he?" Mary asked.

"He's a hand for a ranch north of ours," 'Til answered.

"What's he do…with his hands?" Jane goaded.

"Wouldn't you like to be old enough to know?" 'Til answered sweetly.

"I'm old enough to know!" Jane yelled.

"You better not be," I put in.

"I mean, I haven't…but I could…I'm old enough, I guess…to talk about it…" Jane sputtered.

"Talk about what?" Shannon asked, mildly bewildered.

"Men," Mary replied.

"Men or boys?" Ellen smirked

"WE'RE O'Reilly women," Meagan said smugly. "WE don't take up with boys!" The twins were as different as night and day in their makeup. Megan always was in the lead of the two of them, and the bolder.

We broke up laughing, and for the life of Shannon she couldn't understand why. *Oh Mother,* I thought, *she isn't near old enough to know the difference!*

Chapter 8

The middle of April brought much warmer days, but frosty nights. The storm clouds of winter were gone except for a few strays that every now and then would bunch up on the horizon, and roll over us, turning our world back to winter white for a few days.

The girls were all living in town, with their Sundays spent back on the ranch. Say'ard was doing well with her singing and they all stayed together in the living quarters over the store that Jane rented.

Over Say'ard's objections, I made arrangements for the sheriff, or a deputy to walk her home each night.

Ellen had subpoenaed for a hearing on the land agent; gotten copies of his records at the bank, and last week the traveling judge heard the case.

The sheriff was court ordered to keep track of the man, and escort him to court. Ellen assured me he wouldn't be leaving town, but I knew from experience that cowards usually run.

The courtroom/saloon was standing room only as I walked in with my lawyer-sister, and took our places before the judge.

I was wearing a long brown skirt, a snow white ruffled blouse, my long black coat, and no gun.

I have to say that Ellen had chosen her profession well as she laid out the facts in precise order, and admitted into evidence four notarized letters from other buyers who had similar complaints against the same land agent.

The sheriff stood behind the agent, who was sweating, and openly nervous, while a deputy stood next to the judge, and watched the room.

The judge questioned the sheriff as to the condition of the ranch at the time of sale, and found the land agent guilty of fraud for my case, and for the bank/sales agency; embezzlement. For the agent had given the bank records of a lesser selling price.

Restitution was made to me of $3,000. Forty percent over the market value of vacant land, as that assessment was what the judge ruled our land fell under; the description of vacant land.

When the verdict was handed down there were angry voices from the crowd wanting their day in court. The judge regained control by asking Ellen if she could look into the voiced concerns, and bring the matters before him on his next visit.

The judge ordered all of the agents assets held until the next court hearing.

It appeared Sis was well on her way to a solid career righting many a wrong, and I was proud of her even when she took a ten percent service fee of $300 from me!

'Cost' she told me; no profit for her from my case.

Really?

I was given two large but young, hound dogs. A male I named Jim, and a female from another ranch that I called Girl. Not too original, but the dogs picked up on the names quickly. Their previous names were Cur and Bitch.

I hired two permanent ranch hands that spring to help redo the buildings, and mend the many broken fences in the pastures, and corrals. They squeezed into a small, storage area, made into a bedroom in the house with the rest of us. They were worried about folks might say about such an arrangement, but I wasn't.

The shed we had torn down to repair other buildings was the bunkhouse.

The new roof boards, replacements windows, railings, the general cleaning out, and sprucing up that they helped with, really made the place look like someone actually lived here.

Everything was painted. The house was a brilliant white, and the out buildings all red with white trim. It took a lot of time, and paint, to accomplish that. The wood would stand the weathering for a long time with the paint's protection until I could build new.

A new corral had to be built as the old posts were rotted off at ground level. The new ones were coated with creosote before being stood in place, and should outlast my life span.

The men and I enclosed an area for a large garden, and re-enforced the wood fence with chicken wire. Before we did that, we hauled all the old hay and manure to the area. Knowing this would build good soil for the plants to sink their roots into we piled it deep. We dug holes for posts to support the peas, and heavy bean vines, and nailed chicken wire along them for the vines to climb on.

We'd never get the whole area planted this spring, but that was just fine. The remainder of the barn debris would just rot down into good rich, black dirt for the next year.

I needed a dam built upstream on the creek that flowed near the buildings. It could back up into a low area farther out in a pasture. It'd make a fine small lake for swimming, and watering the stock. One of the men, Frank, said we should make sure there were fish in it too. The other hand, Chuck, knew where I could buy a few farm implements, as I knew we had need of a plow, drag, hay rake and wagon: to start with.

I would probably spend every penny of the re-turned money Ellen got for us.

In the middle of May a spring dance, and box social was to be held as a sort of celebration for the official end of winter. If these dances were half as good as the ones we attended back in Tennessee; we were going to have a great time!

The only thing different out here is that the party started with dancing, the box social, then more dancing, and finally breakfast! The whole thing broke up near noon the following day! The men said it was because of the distances that many had to travel to attend. And if what my hired men told me was true, we were in for a roughish time. As Mother would say.

The get-together would be held at a large, prosperous ranch that lay due south of town, and since it would be an overnight affair, we planned on taking the wagons to sleep and dress in.

The food we were taking to contribute to the gathering included the makings for flapjacks, and biscuits, homemade peach jam from our supply of dried peaches, tea and coffee.

Meanwhile, I had ranch work to do, and a lot of it. My days were long. The men and I worked all day after a shared hot breakfast, ate a cold lunch, and come in for supper late in the evening. The weather fought us tooth and nail sometimes, but we gained steadily.

Then something happened that put our, especially my, abilities and trust in my men, to the test.

A bear took down our milk cow near the end of April, and the cow seemed to have been slaughtered for the pure joy of killing because the carcass hadn't been fed on. Not one bite was eaten, but the carcass was ripped and slashed repeatedly.

The horses and mules had bolted into flight from the far pasture into the barn yard, and the protection of our rifles, and the slower moving cow had become the victim.

Death for the sake of killing was a fairly grim and chilling thing to see, and comprehend. We now had a dangerous job facing us, and it wasn't anything that I looked forward to.

The bear had to be killed before it started in on people.

My men, brothers Chuck and Frank Arnold, and I, roped the downed cow, drug her out of the pasture; piled dry wood over her; poured coal oil onto the pile, and set it ablaze.

I sent Frank into town to tell the sheriff what we needed to do, and to tell the girls to stay in town until one of us came for them. Chuck rode carefully over to the nearest ranch to let them know what was going down. When they returned, the cow carcass was about burnt, and I had provisions enough ready for a long haul, and we set out tracking the bear.

The morning of the third day, we came across another fresh kill with two hired hands from another ranch looking it over. We gathered wood, doused the carcass with oil, and they told us they had gotten word of a rabid bear; which we hadn't but suspected. One stayed to watch the fire, and the other came with us. It was the same kind of kill as our cow...not fed on.

The trail wasn't hard to follow now, for the bruin had been tearing up small shrubs left and right all along its path.

You run into times in your life that can try your mind, and scare the wits clean out of your body, and just thinking about that bear up in front of us surely had me tensed up somewhat!

The other man joining up with us was Hal, and he looked capable enough.

I led out on the track, Chuck rode left point, Frank rode right, and Hal rode drag between the two men.

The area we trailed in now wasn't to my liking for it was thick with brush, washouts, and hundreds of places an animal could hide. The others were just as uneasy as I was, and we rode with rifles in hand, and the safeties off.

The brush was close and getting tighter. We rode around spots where the bear had pushed straight through; swatting at things that got in its way. None of us relished the thought of that bear coming at us in this!

I kept my eyes on a point just over Striker's ears. I could see to each side and straight ahead. I'd miss a left movement if I looked right, and miss a right movement if I looked left. Besides, I needed to watch Striker's ears; he'd hear anything long before I could.

He was on high alert, for he was as tense as a fiddle string! The horses behind me were skittish, and the men were having a hard time handling them with only one hand, but they were trailing close; covering my back.

Striker tight stepped along quietly, but I could feel him tremble underneath me.

We were close, and we both knew it. Just a gut feeling that time was running out for us, or the bear, and that was a black feeling I couldn't shake.

The time had passed agonizingly slow it seemed since Hal joined us, but in reality, four hours had sped by when I pulled Striker up sharply!

The tracks turned hard right, and showed signs of the bear lunging into a full run! Since a bear can outrun a grown horse, it could be long gone, or circling behind us! Dam!

Reining Striker around; he responded instantly to the order, and I swear that horse sat on his butt, and folded in the middle he turned so quickly. I heeled him, and he covered the first few yards so fast we passed between Chuck and Frank in a blur as they were turning also. "Come on!" I yelled at them.

A horse's scream tore through the brush scant yards ahead of me, followed by a shot, and the scene I rode into was a nightmare!

Hal's horse was down, and the bear had the horse's neck in its jaws! Blood gushed from the horse, and its screams split the air again as it thrashed its legs! Hal was on his knees behind the fighting animals; covered with dust; fumbling with the rifle to jack another shell into the chamber, and I concentrated on him as I jammed my rifle back into its scabbard.

I could hear Frank and Chuck coming in behind me as I watched Hal stagger to his feet; bringing the rifle up.

The bear saw him at the same time and lunged!

Thirty feet or so lay between Hal and the bear, and maybe fifty between me and Hal. It's funny how you think of things; calculate and reason it all out in a split second when you're in a fight for your life. And I knew right then...I wasn't going to get to Hal in time!

Hal fired another shot.

Then my Graces stepped in and lent a helping hand.

In my left field of vision, I saw the hoof of the downed horse strike the bear's rump; knocking the brute sideways, and causing Hal to miss his shot! The bear regained its feet, snapping its frothing jaws on empty air, but I had Hal across his back as he clung to my saddle horn and me, and Striker kept running flat out!

When the small war that Frank and Chuck opened up behind us started, I pulled Striker down, and Hal slid to the ground; where he promptly fell to his hands and knees.

I wheeled Striker around and started back to help, but it was over. The bear was dead and we were all alive. No one had been infected. I couldn't speak I was shaking so hard inside! We had come so very close, and had almost paid a terrible price!

We sat and looked at each other. No words were spoken for none were needed. Frank dangled his rope loose, and laid it on a dead snag. Chuck and I followed suit. It would take a lot of wood to burn the two animals.

Hal walked up and knelt to un-cinch his saddle, and Frank dropped a hand to his shoulder, and said gently, "Let it be Amigo. It has to be burned; there's blood on it."

Hal nodded, and I handed him my bag of supplies. He walked away while we pulled the bear closer to the dead horse, and drug in more brush. We figured one fire was enough to watch.

As the smoke started to rise, other riders, who had been hunting the bear, began showing up at the small fire Frank built off to the side. He offered coffee, from the provisions I carried, to those who came in. They took over the job of dragging in brush as we tossed our ropes, with the blood of the bear on them, into the blaze.

In the shade of a tree, I off saddled Striker, rubbed him down with a rag from my saddle bag, grained him from the feed I always carried for him in the other bag, and gave him water from my canteen. He'd earned all of it and more. I gave him two lumps of sugar.

Hal was talking to one of the new men, finally he came towards me, and I stood to meet him from where I had hunkered down beneath Striker's neck; after I ran a hand down his front leg so he wouldn't kick me. Hal stopped; held out his hand, and I took it.

"I owe you Ma'am, and I don't really know who you are," he said with a lot of emotion in his voice.

"I'm Kathleen O'Reilly," I answered softly, for I was still full of anxiety also.

"I'm Hal Jackson. I'm hired on at the Triple Y. A big spread off southeast of here," he said.

"Is that where the box social is to be held?"

"Sure is and I hope to see you there. You the folks who bought the old Jake Snyder place?" Hal questioned.

He was getting talkative and full of questions. "Yes, we bought it," I replied.

"I'm going to double up with Jess," he stated, throwing a thumb over his shoulder towards a man on a bay mare by the coffee fire, "and get on back. Thank you again," Hal said.

"Well Hal, I won't tell you 'anytime' because one incident like today is plenty," I said, trying my best to make light of the day's events.

I must have succeeded, for Hal let a big smile slide across his face, and in the shadow of the serious business we had just taken care of; it looked good.

"Ma'am, the boys can finish up here," he said. "You'd be welcome at the ranch, if you'd like to come with us."

"That's kind of you to offer, but it's been a tiresome three days, and I'd like to get back to my family now," I answered softly. "Thank you just the same."

I was still shaking and bone tired as were Frank and Chuck. I re-saddled Striker and eased up on him. Chuck and Frank came up alongside, and I told them, "Thanks for coming along."

They just nodded. Frank reset his hat, and led us out for home. HOME! That sounded so good!

I had to buy a milk cow.

Chapter 9

Nothing happened in May to equal the bear; nothing except the box social. Not so much the gathering and feasting, as the glaring and pushing between the single men that my flirtatious sisters inspired off and on throughout the entire event! Try as I might to get those girls to be nice, and dance with each man who asked, they just naturally went about their own way of 'putting some spark in the gathering,' as Say'ard put it. A comet couldn't have thrown more sparks!

I danced first with Hal. He was as tall as me; wore a new shirt that I remember was part of Jane's inventory; had a square chin, black hair, blue eyes, and he was awkward. He beamed with pride or embarrassment, and his wide smile went well with his red ears. More than once a whisper came to me about 'her' and 'bear'.

As we box stepped around the barn floor he watched Ellen a lot.

As the social wore on; I met people; a lot of people.

There were three or four men for each woman, but I didn't see nary a man in particular who caught my eye. I danced with single men, married men and widowers.

Hal danced with Ellen as often as he could.

On the ride over to the Triple Y, the conversation turned to the men who would be there; who was going to be first to latch onto a husband, and who would provide the first daughter to carry on our line of women.

I reminded them each and every one that I had first rights on that. My witty sisters reminded me of my age, and that I was getting past the age of child bearing. I am definitely NOT that old!

I shook my head; not believing these giggling girls were the same women I had traveled well over a thousand miles with, forded rivers, and braced nature's fury. We had held our own against pretty overwhelming odds, and I was proud of them, but I wouldn't tell them that right now.

I also reminded them about the Rules. Especially the last three: the most important ones to behave by. What the thought of a man could do to my sisters was unreal!

I did manage to talk some business in-between dances and the meals. For one thing, I needed another milk cow, and I wanted to show the stock when they got here. I drew quite a bit of interest when I mentioned the drafts and Herefords. I also drew a challenge for a horse race when the racers got here.

Things were moving right along.

After breakfast we took our leave, and since I had crept off, and caught a nap along about one in the morning; I drove one wagon and Frank drove the other; with a promise from Mary to relieve me later.

I drove all the way home, pulled the wagon into the barn, un-harnessed the team, with Frank and Chuck's help, turned the horses out, closed the barn doors, and went to the house, and to bed.

I left the girls in the wagons in the barn.

It took a full day for us to revive after that social, and the family had things to talk, dream, and goad each other about for weeks afterwards. We had made many acquaintances, and we felt that with the girl's positions in town, and the dance, we had started to fit in around Highwater.

Even Say'ard had gotten along well with most of the womenfolk. She'd been persuaded to sing during the gathering, and after some tender ballads, even the staunchest holdout among the ladies, had almost forgiven her for where she worked.

Of course, a few well-placed comments from us girls, as to how well Say'ard sang the hymns, and recited the Good Book didn't hurt either.

Ellen whispered to me that it probably wasn't the right time to bring up our Pagan beliefs, and I agreed with her.

Mary reminded us about Say'ard's statement of what we were going to do to this land, and I have to admit, when we eight climbed down from the wagons; in dresses of greens, lavenders and blues; our hair braided, and piled high with locks falling alongside our ears; we did make an impression! One thing was for sure; the folks at the social would remember us.

Sometimes I swear that Say'ard had the gift! Maybe I should ask her to see, if she could, when in the future I'd meet that certain man. On the other hand...I won't. That way she can't tell me 'I told you so' for the rest of my life!

At the dance I'd made a bargain for a few beef cattle from Ray Stockman, a small rancher that touched boundaries to the northwest of me. Little did I know that in three short years I'd buy out his grieving widow. Right now I had need of a beef food supply separate from the Herefords, and in exchange for a dozen head, I gave him grazing rights for the summer, since my herd wouldn't be here until late August or early September. His cattle would eat rent free on my 6,500 acres. The deal would save me the cost of the cattle, and afford Mr. Stockman's cattle good grazing.

I intended to keep that food herd small, by selling off anything over ten head until we could cull meat from our own herd.

The grass of my ranch was for Herefords and horse flesh.

Our lives settled into a pleasant routine; interrupted only by the many men calling on my sisters. No one called on me. Things were routine, but they surely weren't dull! Ellen saw a lot of Hal and she didn't discourage him one bit.

Chapter 10

By early June things were pretty much caught up, as I had hired four carpenters to put a rush on things, and with the ice house built, I decided to go exploring.

It was a habit I'd grown into back east, and Father always fussed about me going off alone, but Mother said it was the only way to learn what lay on the other side of the ridge, and to go ahead. After all, I wouldn't be here if my namesakes hadn't explored the distant horizons of land and ocean.

It wasn't just men who had a need to see what lay over the next hill.

Mother's perspective again.

It was born in me to look things over, and this land was at the top of my list, and I didn't fight the urge. I was also a thinker. I found out the best place to think was off alone somewhere exploring and learning.

I constantly held conversations, with me, in my head, asking and answering myself. I remember Gramma Kate teaching me to do that; ask a question or make a statement, turn it every which way; look at it, and see the many ways it could be answered, until I found the one reply that clearly suited the question.

I covered the land I owned in a short time, and turned Striker's nose toward the distant Big Belt Mountains. I'd packed a good nap sack, and told Frank I expected to be gone a couple of weeks. The look he gave me was amusing to say the least, for I could tell he didn't care for the idea of me traipsing around in the mountains alone.

"Well, Kate, this is different sort of land than maybe you're used to. It lays different, and the animals are cantankerous, so you watch yourself close," he had said.

I'd read a passel on this land, and its happenings before taking the lead to move my family out here.

There were a whole lot of folks gouging pretty deep into the lives of other people that lived here, and I intended to stay out of their way. The more I had read about the army campaigns against the Indians, the more I felt the white man was going about handling the situation all wrong.

Back in Tennessee, we had many people, of all colors, that came on our land. Father dealt fairly with them all, and he gained their trust, and friendship.

I knew about shady land deals, and outright murders that happened to our Black, Cherokee and Creek friends, and I knew the government, and army, were wrong.

With the Lewis and Clark report of the riches of this land; came the greed of white men for timber, gold, and furs.

The mountain man had had an uneasy truce with the tribes, but they had respect for them.

John Colter, back in '07, somewhere around the junction of the Madison and Jefferson Rivers, had been caught by the Blackfoot warriors for a violation of some kind, stripped naked and forced to run for his life; unarmed. Run he had; eluding the best of the Blackfoot warriors, and making it some 200 miles to a white settlement.

I don't recall reading about the way he treated the Indian, but he did have knowledge about them and their ways that few white men ever had. He was, by record, the first white man to see fairy tale places like the Big Horn River, Grand Teton Mountains, and Yellowstone Lake.

I intend to see those places for myself someday.

Maybe, as Mother said, he got 'uppity', and someone brought him back down. I don't know for sure of course, but it seems to fit.

A man of the auld sod, who fared better in these high reaches, was an Irishman by the name of Fitzpatrick. He got around some also.

Even though this area I was going to be poking around in was sort of set off by itself, I intended to ease through it with care, for just west of here, and just a year or so ago, Col. Miles fought a Sioux named Crazy Horse near the Tongue River, and the Nez Perce fought the army near Big Hole.

I felt a hurt deep down in me that would never go away, for the little children, and women of that tribe. In that bitter cold, they retreated, and ran for freedom to the Canadian border. The Grandmother Land they had called it. Over five hundred women, and children accompanied their men in that desperate run.

They didn't make it.

It seemed freedom, and the right to live as one wants in this land of the free; was extended to only a few.

My family didn't live by such shallow rules, and I firmly believe babes don't hate; until they are taught to.

Shaking off the melancholy thoughts, I shifted back to Frank, and his concerns for me. "I'll be fine Frank. You and Chuck take care of things," I said and pulled into my saddle. "Tell the girls where I've gone," I added.

By midday of the second day I was rattling around in the higher reaches of the first foothills of the mountains I'd read about. Striker and I were looking out over a vast, silent array of broken peaks and canyons.

The silence was misleading.

Out there were all kinds of animals, big and small, rushing rivers, and laughing waterfalls. There were honey bees, hawks, moaning wind, whispering grass, and man. Prospectors and ranchers. Good men and bad.

Right now Striker and I were alone.

This country we surveyed was not yet a state, but it was surely headed that way. The passage of the Bland-Allison Act was proving to be a boon to this territory. The United States Government had agreed to buy some $2 million worth of silver bullion from the western region on a regular basis, and all manner of men were descending upon these mountains.

They'd need horses and I intended to have those horses, good horses, available. That was part of why I needed to be alone for a while. Solitude to think through the plans I had for my ranch, and solitude wasn't available with all the ranch work, and my sisters underfoot. When I worked, I thought of the work I was doing or something connected to it. Now I needed unhurried, thinking space, and just to get off by myself for a while.

Off a ways from here, railroaders were building a grade, and there had been some trouble. Workers called strikes against the railroad, and the army had been called in. As soon as things calmed down, this land would open up, and move forward. I would quietly move forward with it: one horse at a time if need be.

The Civil War was past, but tragic memories die hard, and I hear the mutterings, and see the lingering hate every now and then.

Grant had just left the presidency to Mr. Hayes, and his tea-totaling wife. Some folks just weren't happy unless they were gouging someone, and so they nick-named our first lady, "Lemonade Lucy." Why? Would they have preferred a boozing madam? *Wonder if anyone had asked them that question? Besides, what was wrong with lemonade? I drink it.*

I nodded at the scene before me. It'd do; even if some of the people in it wouldn't.

Striker turned us, and we worked our way past huge pine trees, gray rocks, and flowers of many colors. I didn't know all their names, but a goodly number were familiar.

We pushed up one canyon, topped out on a crest, and followed another gorge down. From crest to crest we ambled along, making snug camps in protected places, and found places to wait out passing storms. I intended to cut a wide south to west to north circle; coming home by the east trail. Things were well in hand back home, and with nothing pressing me, I took my time.

These mountains awed me, for unlike the ones of the Appalachians, these were open to vast vistas from just about any spot that was halfway high. Try as I might I couldn't quite bring myself to believe they were real. They were too beautiful and serene to be real, but I knew what lay before me was more real than my own life.

My life was to be such a short thing in the span of the ages; not like the earth.

Man was an ant. He could move mountains; dig tunnels through them, and invent some wondrous things; like Mr. Edison with his light bulb, for replacing our coal-oil lamps. Still, with all things said and done, when man stepped too high and mighty, the earth, and the ways of nature, could surely beat the man-ant to his knees, and put him in his proper place!

Grandmother Kate used to tell us that.

Early the next day with the dew still hanging on the grass, we set out. I'd made a comfortable night camp in a rock nitch that overlooked a hidden, green meadow. We were working our way down to the bottom of a rather small canyon, and Striker's hooves were leaving a dark trail through the dew.

A grassy meadow ran each side of the small water course, and yellow, white, and dainty blue flowers dotted the spring green. Snow still lay in patches in the shade of pine trees here in the high country. I snuggled deeper into my heavy warm coat, and I was tying my long neck scarf tighter when, without warning, a high piercing scream split the air.

Striker bolted a little side hop, and I brought him down with a tight rein.

126

The scream was the kind that came from a body in pure agony, and I headed Striker for a close by stand of trees; pulled him up, pulled my rifle out, leapt down, ground hitched him, and waited.

The scream came again, far off to my left, and downstream. It sounded human, but some animals sound all too much like a human in times of stress. It seemed to be some two hundred yards off.

Keeping to tree cover, I hurried towards where I thought the sound came from. No telling what I'd find. Maybe a man set-on by a wild animal or the animal itself, but I needed to make sure of the source, and not just ride off; leaving someone, or thing, in pain.

Keeping to the cover as best I could; I went quietly, for the danger in these hills was real.

The screams broke across the small valley again, and tapered off into a groan that was followed by crying. I could hear talking now, but it wasn't any language I could understand. I looked through the tall ferns I was lying in, and saw the source of the screams.

An Indian woman was trying to give birth, and she wasn't doing too well. A man, probably her husband, knelt next to her; holding her tenderly, and rocked her back and forth.

I looked to the woman as she drew her knees up, and I could see that she needed help. Right now! A tiny foot, and part of the leg was out, and that surely wasn't right! A breech birth! The woman would probably die, along with the babe, if things weren't done quickly!

I stood up, and emerged from the ferns and trees. The man caught my movement, and spun towards me, drawing his knife. When he saw me, a woman, he relaxed some, but I had the queer feeling he'd stick me proper if I acted too sudden, and not to his liking.

Easing closer, I could see her eyes were glazed in pain. I was sure she didn't know I was there. Things were bad for her. I didn't know if I could help, but I was surely going to try; if he would let me.

Slowing, laying down all my weapons, my coat and hat, I motioned to the man I wanted to help, and he took his sweet time about deciding! Then another pain ripped through the woman, and he gave me room.

As I knelt beside her, I looked closely at the little foot and leg. The other leg wasn't to be seen; only the cheek of a tiny buttock, and the tiny genital of a boy babe.

I had two choices, I could try and move the baby back into her, and get the other leg down; letting the birth be feet first. I'd have to watch the throat area; protecting it with my hand, or I could open her belly.

I didn't want to do that, I surely didn't, for I had witnessed that gruesome scene once back home, and I don't believe he would have let me do that to her anyway.

Motioning for the man to help, I put the woman flat on her back; put his knees against her shoulders to brace her, and gave him her hands to hold across her chest; pining her to the ground. I shifted around to straddle one of her legs; to hold it away from the other one, and reached for the child's buttock.

She was between contractions, which were only seconds apart, and while she was partially relaxed I had to work fast, for to push against the babe while she contracted and pushing out; wouldn't gain anything.

The baby was tightly wedged in the pelvic bones, and I couldn't get it to move! Pushing harder, I felt a slight give, then it slid backwards into the womb, and my hand followed.

Holding the baby in the recessed position, by using the straight leg, I gently searched for, and found the other leg. I pulled the bent knee, and foot towards me from where they lay across the belly. I pulled the foot down from her body, and straightened it to the first leg.

Pulling on both tiny feet with my left hand; I slid my right hand along the small frame as it moved towards me, and up to the face. Then I lifted the small body; curving it upwards, and let the head slip out.

Legs first! What a way to be born! But there he was! Blood covered and blue, for he wasn't breathing, and no wonder!

Turning him over, I patted his back firmly, but not too hard. He was still blue and making no sound. I quickly turned him face up; opened the tiny mouth; cleaned out a wad of mucus with my finger, and blew into the babe with a short, quick puff. Flipping him sideways in my hand, I slapped him firmly with the heel of my hand.

The roughness, if he was dead, wouldn't make any difference. If he was alive, he couldn't hurt any worse than he already did!   He drew a ragged breath and wailed!

The boy had a good set of lungs, and his loud wail was an emotional moment for me. I looked to the man, and a smile split our faces at that moment.

He reached for his son, and I pulled my knife to cut the cord, but he would have none of it as he reached a hand across my forearms; stopping me.

I turned my attention back to the woman, and massaged her stomach, as I had been taught, and helped to expel the afterbirth.

The man started doing things that I didn't understand, but I knew he were praying, and did a ceremony of cutting the cord. He handed the babe back to me, and went to bury the afterbirth that he had placed on a piece of leather and folded up.

By the time he returned, I had the boy wrapped warmly in a small fur I found by her side, and I had washed up in the stream. I don't know how long she had struggled to birth her son, but she was wore out from the effort. The blood had stopped flowing pretty much and he took over her care.

He went to the skin bag, hanging by the fire, and from it he dipped a small bark cup of broth. Blowing on it to cool it, and holding her in a sitting position with one arm he put the cup to her lips, and urged her to drink deeply.

Putting the cup aside; he gently laid her back down. He glanced over to me, and I smiled. I couldn't help it, nor could I stop the tears that stood in my eyes. It was a touching sight.

Turning to the woman, he covered her thighs with cattail down, and it quickly absorbed the blood. He tenderly covered her with a beautiful soft skin, and touched her face.

I turned to go, but his voice, soft and mellow, stopped me. He beckoned me to the fire, where I sank down on the fur he laid for me. He motioned me to stay, and with a sweep of his arm, I understood he wanted me to watch her.

Picking up the babe, he went to the stream. Shortly he came back, and kneeling beside her; tucked the cleaned, wiggling baby in with her, and looked at them a long moment. He touched her face again gently; said something; rose and came towards me.

He was taller than the average Indian, and bronze-colored; not the reddish hue of the natives I have encountered in Tennessee and Georgia, with coal black hair and eyes. Some of them worked for us, but they didn't have the wildness about them that this man had, and oddly; I wasn't afraid.

He scooped the bark dish into the skin bag that still hung over the fire from a tripod of poles, and held it out to me.

I took it gently, and tasted it gingerly. It was a soup, or broth as I had thought earlier, and it was delicious! I smiled my thanks, and sitting the empty bowl down, I stood, and motioned to him that I was going to get my horse.

I left my rifle, coat and hat where they lay, that way I figured he knew that I trusted him, and that I would be coming back.

When I returned with Striker, he looked at that black stud with interest. He knew good horse flesh, for his own horse was tied a ways off, and was a robust specimen; well-groomed and cared for.

Taking the coffee pot from the pack, I scooped water from the stream, and set it on the coals to heat. I had four left-over biscuits, and a small jar of Mary's wild, grape jam wrapped in a towel. I laid the biscuits near the coals to warm, and we waited for the water to heat. He seemed to relish the coffee, and food, nodding as he ate three biscuits; leaving me one.

The babe started to fuss, and he looked to me with a question that said plain as day: "What do we feed him?"

I had birch sugar in my pack, and in no time at all we warmed some water in my metal cup, and laced it with a small amount of the sugar. I pulled a clean bandana from my clothes pack, and twisted it into a thick point of sorts.

I motioned for him to bring the babe to the fire side, and he did. I didn't know if the men of their people did this kind of duty, but I assumed they did, for 'a new father is a new father' no matter where you find them.

Wetting the cloth in the warm sugar water, I gave it to him to put in the tiny mouth. The boy sucked on it greedily, and, as I glanced to the man, I knew we had solved a problem, for the next few hours anyway. He fed his son the second time; looked up at me, and smiled.

The woman started to moan, and tried to move around. He handed me the babe. Rising, he took a pinch of something from a small pouch, put it in some of the broth, cooled it again as before, held her gently, and made her drink it all She drifted off into a deep sleep quite rapidly with the herb, a drug I'm sure, that he gave her.

I wish we could talk to each other, for I could learn much from him. There were things that I needed to know, and understand. Perhaps there would come a time when we could meet again, and that just might happen, for stranger things had.

Nightfall crept upon us as a bright pink, and gold wonder. If mornings were a gift; then sunsets were pure pleasure. Working together he and I quickly built a shelter over her, and big enough for him, and a smaller one for me. We turned her on her side and snuggled the babe to her chest.

We took turns through the night feeding the boy, and tending his mother. It had been the hardest birthing that I had ever seen much less helped with, and I wondered how in the world such a fragile, newborn child could survive such an ordeal. It always amazed me...a birthing.

I had heard stories about Indian women giving birth, hardly interrupting their day, and continuing on with their work. I now knew that such talk was just that; talk. For this was a woman as any other. She felt, I'm sure, all the emotions that I did, and today, she definitely endured more physical pain than I ever had too.

One more thing that I was sure of was: this woman wouldn't be working for a while! The physical drain on her body, to have given birth in this manner, would not allow her to be up, and around for two or three days.

When I awoke at the stirring of dawn's light, it was to the sounds of cooing. The woman was sitting; nursing the child, and rocking it gently.

When I stirred, she looked to me, and her eyes said everything, and more. Wordlessly she rose in a graceful fluid movement, holding the babe to her chest with one arm, and brought ME coffee!

So much for my three-day theory!

I took the cup she offered, and knew better than to try to switch roles with her. This was HER camp, therefore her house, and she was the hostess. Their ways were not to be taken lightly, and I had a lot of respect for the young mother.

A slight rustling of grass, and her husband stood before us. He had been busy getting breakfast, for six fresh fish, of a kind I'd never seen before, hung from a forked stick in his hand. The fish were bright yellow, almost golden, with vivid stripes, and spots along the sides.

After a wonderful tasting breakfast, she came to me; touched my head, and my chest over my heart. Touching her head and chest; I knew she meant I'd always be in her thoughts. It surely was a beautiful way of putting things.

From the red tint in her dark hair, I thought she was a mixed blood; perhaps French. I knew she wasn't full Indian, for the exposed skin at the birth showed a lighter color.

Then to my surprise she started to speak in haunting, broken English, as if she were trying to recall the words from a long buried memory. There was an unmistakable overlay of an accent to her words, and it took the better part of a few minutes before I recognized the thickness of the German tongue; just the same as the Hendriks family back in Tennessee.

Slowly, through the rest of the day, her story was told to me.

As a young child of perhaps three winters old, she had wandered away from the wagon train that her family was with, and wandered into a creek, playing with the little fish, and frogs. Time got away; it was getting dark, and she was alone, hungry and lost.

During the next days, she wandered along the creek, and after many days she fell into an exhausted sleep;

tucked in alongside a dead log. She had awakened to find herself warm and safe; wrapped in a soft fur. She was being carried in the arms of a young Indian woman.

There were about twenty in the group, and they tried to talk to her, but she couldn't understand what they were saying to her. Years later they told her all they could about the morning Blue Cloud, the woman who became her mother, remembered about that day.

She had indeed been lost, as the white peoples wagons passed far to the north of their trail, and it was days before they found her. They also knew they couldn't take her back, for THAT action, someone would have died. No white man would ever believe an Indian had found her, but rather had stolen her.

She was free to leave anytime she had told me, for she was not a slave, or property. She was Blue Cloud's daughter, and Blue Cloud was the youngest daughter of the tribe's Medicine Woman's lodge, and a very important person of standing in the tribe. They gave her the name of Little Walking Fire, for her red tinted hair.

She had freckles on her face and arms I noticed, as we spent the warm day visiting.

Little Walking Fire could have left The People when she wished, but she didn't, for she had fallen in love with the only son of a widowed mother. They were not wealthy in the manner of some of the People, but the man had a kindness, and tenderness about him that pulled her young soul to him, and so she had stayed. She accepted his one fine horse; a magnificent stallion, and the best of the six he owned when he presented it to her mother's lodge, and wed him in her sixteenth year. At least she thought she was sixteen.

That was last year, and yesterday the birth of their first child had happened. She said one day she would take her son, that they named Strong Boy, to visit her 'other' family if it could come to be.

I asked her if she remembered her white name, and she brokenly said with difficulty, 'Becca Bay-burnt,' which I took to be Rebecca Brayburn.

The day was relaxed and they were a kind and tender family. Her husband, Talks to Horses, captured, trained horses, and traded them to others of The People. He was twenty years older than she, but she didn't mind for his heart was good.

*That would make the buckskin a mustang,* I thought, and was impressed by the horses' appearance. He was a far better horse than the ones I saw around Highwater. He was apparently very skilled at his work.

Early the next day; after a breakfast of fish, biscuits, and coffee, Talks to Horses tied the bags containing their possessions together; laid them over the withers of the highly decorated buckskin, leapt up onto the horse, and waited for his wife.

I walked with her to their horse, and she handed me Strong Boy to hold as her husband reached down, lifted her effortlessly, and sat her sideways in front of him.

I kissed that sweet little bundle of life; hugged him tightly for a moment, and handed him up to her.

Talks to Horses laid a hand to my shoulder, and said something to me that Little Walking Fire translated.

"My husband say...you are welcome in our lodge Green Eyes...for you have...a good heart."

I smiled broadly, and said I would come to their lodge if it was to be. Then they turned; faded into the aspens, and in moments they were gone from the little valley as silently as if they had not been there, and we had not touched each other's lives.

I put out the fire out; rolled and tied my bedroll into a tight bundle; fastened it behind my saddle, mounted Striker, and turned him north.

I had a whole bunch of new thoughts in my head about Indians, and I knew that I would offer the Indian my hand in friendship just like any other human; until I'm given reason not to.

I had read that they were honorable, and true to their friends, red or white, but death, and hell on their enemies.

I'd prefer to be a friend. I've grown accustomed to living.

Chapter 11

While I was exploring, destruction had come to town. A tight, whirling wind that we called a Twister, and fairly rare in this area Chuck said, blew up in a hot, humid rainstorm, and flung its fury on the pitiful buildings that stood in its path. The hell that swept through the town was softened by the fact that only one person had been killed.

My sisters had been bruised, and battered somewhat when their building had been lifted from the ground, and blown apart. They, along with most everyone else, had climbed down into every available root cellar, or dug out, and huddled in fear; waiting out the destruction.

The recounting they gave me left me feeling that they had been spared by the Graces, and I was thankful that all my sisters were alive.

The rebuilding of the town, and the girls store, was well underway by the time I arrived, and I lost no time in backing up the girls in their giving of a thousand dollars to others for the needed repairs. Repairs needed by folks that couldn't pay the cost of rebuilding, but their businesses and families were needed in our town. Besides that; they were our friends.

The twister had hit our ranch; damaging our barn, and making our corrals, and garden fencing disappear, and damaging the new crops.

Chuck and Hank had gone to herd the longhorns to our place; and I was exploring when the storm hit.

I knew my Graces had protected us by arranging work that took us away from the ranch at that deadly moment, and I thanked them for that.

Hank, Chuck and I put in many hours of work to help our family, and friends put their lives back in order. When we went home each night; we took a wagon load of fresh sawn lumber to rebuild the barn and fences.

The dam had to wait to be built.


July came and went. The weather brought beautiful warm days, and frequent rains turned the hills to green. The land bloomed with life, and we bloomed with it.

Each morning and night; we gave homage to those that cared for us.

The girls' businesses and jobs were flourishing, and our ranch was shaping up along the lines I had hoped it would. Hal Jackson came over weekends and we built the dam.

Hal finally got his nerve up and asked my permission to marry Ellen. I gave it, but there were things he needed to understand about the woman he'd make his own. It would be up to Ellen to explain things to him, and then it was up to him to wed her or not.

The exercise ring for the horses had been finished while I was gone; destroyed by the twister; rebuilt, and I started working Striker in it. I knew deep down that he had the instinct to do what I wanted him to do, for, like I said, it was in the breed, and I aimed to pull it out.

I still remembered how Striker had cut that hard-headed cow out from the herd, and kept her out, back on Father's farm, and how he had turned to race back to Hal on that bear hunt.

I also remember what a few of the other breeders back east had done with this new style of horse. My Father and

I had gone to various farms, and watched as the trainers put these horses through their paces.

I read articles of other ranchers in parts of the western states starting the same thing. I figured there was room for one more horse breeder. Me. It was a beautiful thing to see the intelligence that shown in the eyes of this breed, and I wanted to help the breed build on its ability.

Now that I was working on my life, I didn't ride herd on the girls too closely anymore, and they were doing just fine on their own. Hal and Ellen were to be married and he would come live here with us. He would be family.

He came over every chance he could and we built an addition house on the property; across the garden from the main one for him and Ellen. It was a good solid, stout house that would become a home to them and their children for years to come. We built it from the very stone of the land and it looked old when we were done. They would marry when it was finished.

Chuck and Hank hounded me for a separate house for them also. We would started on that one when Ellen's was finished.

Mary had ordered a whole passel of new readers for the school with the approval of the mayor. To these she would add books from our own library, for the students to read. Each week she planned to have Meg take a book to school, from the store or ranch, and read to the students.

Mary convinced Jane to let her hold a reading class in the store for the summer, and the first book Mary chose was a new one just released over a year ago, and was a fantasy that none of us had read, for we were packing to head west when it had arrived. Now Meg would read our book, for the first time, aloud to this class. It was entitled *Black Beauty,* and such a story should capture the attention of these western children right off.

For oral reports, Mary let older students have the use of one book at a time. *Cinderella, Tom Sawyer* and *The Yearling* were a few they had to choose from. Mary wanted the students to be transported far from the life that they lived.

Nothing was wrong with where they lived, but we knew there was so much more to be experienced. She hoped their imagination could be sparked with a growth of desire that might make a difference in their humble lives. A desire to delve into what life showed them through the travels, or adventures of people; written by their own hand; in their published books, and maybe push a student or two into college, and beyond.

The summer reading class was not a regular school class, but an extra one where attendance wasn't mandatory, and was free. To Mary's delight, each class was attended by a rotation of different children of all ages whenever they could make it to town for an hour or two, and parents were warm with gratitude for the chance Mary offered their children.

Mary; by holding the book class in Jane and Shannon's business where adults gathered, talked and spent money; gave the children a chance to understand what being an adult meant, and to not be apprehensive being in the same room with them, or speaking to them first.

Our parents had always included us.

The children rapidly grew to have confidence in themselves as their minds seem to open, and expand.

The girls, with the exception of the younger twins, started keeping company with gentlemen friends.

Ellen and Hal were married on the 4th of July.

Matilda was being courted, but she didn't have the right feelings for the man, and was going to find a graceful way out of the situation. She was going to go for a quiet evening walk with him shortly, and bow out gracefully. To tie yourself to a partner your heart doesn't love, is not right, AND it's one of our Rules.

In the quiet of the evenings, when I had the time, I read of Ireland and Scotland, the old, the new, their changing times and growing pains, for there wasn't a man courting me. So I read, and tried to tie modern times to the old ways.

Sometimes they just didn't fit.

Ireland was the Kingdom of Bards, heroic poems about Cuchulain, the hero of the Cattle Raid of Cooley. The Blarney Stone of Cork. The Children of Lir, who were found by St. Patrick, and changed from swans back into humans after 900 years. Robert the Bruce, and the spider's lesson of patience. Fomors, the sea giants of ancient Ireland; who were older than the gods. The Book of Kells and Oisin, the Bard Warrior of the third century; who talked with St. Patrick. There wasn't quite as much on Scotland, but enough so I gained a solid insight into what may have shaped my family. William Wallace was indeed a hero.

Now I don't know if all the stories about the lands that held me to their bosoms were true, but I did fancied it to be about half right. Added to my lore of Pagan knowledge; recanted by the O'Reilly women for generations and eons before them; to the history of these lands, made the stories good enough for me, and they would do.

You may not believe in such a wisdom; spirits, elves, fairies, wee folk, and the like, but I do, for I have seen things that I cannot explain. I don't need to explain them. I know they are real. I know they protect me, hold me close, and guide me.

Gram Ma Kate and Mother instructed me in these beliefs as they had been instructed, and I hold no doubts of the wisdom.

ALL the beliefs I hold are shared by my sisters, but not to the extent that it dwells in me. That's what being a 'Sarah Kathleen' entitles you to, and you alone. If I should be fortunate enough to give life to a daughter; I will take her into nature, teach her the wonder of those things; where the spark of life dwells in everything, just waiting to be born, and humankind is the intruder.

The man who would share my life; would have to understand this 'other side' of me, for I would not be tied to one who opposed, or scoffed at my beliefs.

Besides reading, wondering and remembering the old wisdom; I made time to make plans for the herd of stock walking its way towards me.

When Father bought his first Herefords about 1855, I was but three years old, and the breed hadn't been in this young country very long. Henry Clay had imported some for his Kentucky farm in 1817. I was fascinated by the huge red, and white animals Mother had told me.

Father had the foresight to get Herefords that could be registered, so when the time came, as Father felt it would, that the breed would be recognized, his animals would be of the quality, and lineage to be registered, and thus could be sold as breeding stock. The value of our herd would go up considerably.

Anyway, I did some fact-gathering in my younger days about where the breed came from; a place called Hereford in England, and two things still come to mind when I think of that place. One; they had a twelve-acre outside food market, and two; Hereford Cathedral had a chained Library. That was one way to keep control of your books!

I had an idea in my head about that market.

Chapter 12

It was nearing the end of July when I packed up a bed roll, filled a hefty nap sack of food, and started Striker east to meet up with our herd.

They would be somewhere close to the area of Fort Sheridan in Wyoming Territory by the time I would get there. If they were early, they had orders to rest, and wait for me. If I was early; I would do the same, or explore a little.

I figured that riding easy, the trip would take about nine or ten days. With just me and Striker making tracks, and allowing for his spurts of running, we should make good time. Once again I had time to reflect on the events of summer, and allowing for the bear, the box social, the birthing and tornado, things seemed laid back, and mediocre lately. Even the Graces were quiet.

The feeling still nagged at me of 'something' that pushed at the edges of my mind. I was watchful for it, but for the life of me I couldn't get a handle on it, and I didn't get any help by asking the Graces. They were silent.

The mediocre part was just fine with me, for I didn't want to take on any more problems than I had to.

I'm saying we O'Reilly women wanted to be independent, and capable of handling most any problem that might come to us, but we still wanted to remain women. Ladies. Women attracted honorable men for husbands. Good solid husbands. Mannish-appearing women didn't, and we didn't want to be labeled with the likes of Charlie Parkhurst!

Charlie had died this past year, and had built a somewhat infamous reputation as one of the hardest driving stagecoach drivers around; among his other accomplishments in the territory of California. Upon his death it was discovered that he was a SHE!

Therefore we intended to remain women, and to be thought of as women. Charlie Parkhurst, and Calamity Jane woman, had done enough, all by themselves, to damage the virtues of our gender! I surely don't want to add to what they had begun!

Right now I had a job needing to be done, and done right; so I would dress the part and rolled my leather leggings into my bedroll. They would be needed when I started to help haze the herd home.

I recall the first time I came into a noon camp at my ranch; with torn pant legs. Chuck had me put on his chaps, or shotgun's as he called them. They were part of the clothing that his mother's people wore when doing ranch work. Her culture was Spanish/Mexican, and the two brothers reflected that; in appearance, and knowledge. He said chaps were called for in such places. They were a blessing, and I've worn them daily since, along with good leather gloves. I have calluses, but my hands are still soft enough to make a courting fella want to hold them. IF I ever HAD a courting fella!

As I traveled, my thoughts went back over just about everything that I had encountered in many a year, but mostly what we had accomplished this past year.

Frank had insisted that we build a dipping tank for the stock, and he'd been right. The stock I had traded for from my neighbor were the lanky Texas kind, and infested with ticks. My Herefords wouldn't be immune to the Texas fever ticks that those cattle were carriers of and immune to. So the tank was built by the three of us, with Hal helping when he was there.

We broke up; shoveled, and scraped a hole in that hard dirt some ten feet wide by twenty feet long; to a depth of eight feet; lined it with thick, wooden planks, and fenced it off for safety.

The cattle would be herded into the open chute end; forced into the water to sink, then swim to the other end, and climb up an angle ramp into a holding pen. The holding pens at each end took us more time to build.

Frank, Hal, Chuck and I, though work hardened, were bone tired, and muscle sore by the time that particular job was done, and the dirt carted away to the garden or pig pen.

We built a wooden trough that diverted water from the creek into the trench where we mixed in the insecticide. After the dipping, the cattle had to be re-checked for open sores or cuts where screw-worms could grow. Blow flies laid the worm larva, and the flies were always around. Checking for screw-worm was a constant job. At the end of the dip tank we also treated their eyes to clean out the insecticide.

I had a lot to learn about cattle because back in Tennessee I was hands-on with the horses while Father and Hendrik tended our Herefords; who didn't have to have this treatment.

The men were teaching me about being a hands-on cattle rancher. At times I think it is more than I can handle, BUT, I asked for this life. I surely did!

I had hired the men for a couple of reasons that come to mind besides their being brothers. One; they were western cowmen of a long heritage, and they knew a whole lot more about raising cattle than I did. Two; they were mustered out of the army because of the injuries they received at the hands of officers because they were mixed breeds; Indians, white, and Spanish. They had been bucked and gagged for amusement by a demented sergeant; although such treatment was strictly forbidden by regulations. They had endured hours of being tied; arms and legs bent, with poles thrust through the arm and leg angles.

Upon release, they had filed charges against the officers. They were given early, honorable discharges for 'medical' reasons in exchange for dropping the charges against those officers.

The bucking brutality had left Frank with torn ligaments in one knee, and he would always limp.

Having worked and lived alongside these brothers for months; I had come to realize that they had more honor than most, and I was proud to call them friends.

During my ride to Sheridan, I lucked out, and stayed with families who were also ranchers, or homesteaders. These were friendly folk whose hospitality was warm, and giving, as visitors were rare, and I was treated very well. The children oft times were tow-headed, barefooted, solemn-eyed tots, and they could steal your heart with a dimpled shy smile.

This was a new land to me, since we had taken a more southern route on our journey out here last year, and I took time to study the land intently.

We had followed wagon trails, but now I just rode the hills in a straight line towards Sheridan. The region was fully grassed over with an abundance of low hills, draws and fresh, clear running water was to be found nearly anywhere.

Striker was always a pleasure to ride, and he ambled along pretty much at his own pace from near sun up to sun down; except when he wanted to run. He would start asking to run by pitty patting his front hooves, and fighting the bit slightly. He usually did this about a mile into our day. Just wanting to get the kinks out I guess.

The stallion always stopped just short of a rise; looked left, and right; sometimes behind us; before moving at my command. He was cautious, and left me with humorous thought of waiting for a street to clear of wagons before crossing. There wasn't any sign of life save for the two of us, but he stopped anyway.

Striker was in his prime at thirteen years old and always drew looks where ever he appeared. Most every horse we rode is his offspring or closely related; through his sire or dam, but they had a few years to go before they gained his stature, and knowledge.

He and I traveled steady, and stopped briefly every couple three hours. We circled wide of towns, for I didn't feel like constructing meaningless conversations with people I didn't know, and fend off their probing questions of a woman traveling alone.

Mother had said I was commanding in my stance. I tried to find that particular aspect in my mirror, but all I saw was a woman with backbone, and the ability to back up what she might have to say.

She didn't come right out and tell me to change but, in her motherly way, she was alluding to the slim prospects of husband material if I stayed as I am. I surely don't know if I can change. I've been in the lead far too long, and hard set in my ways.

"Wonder what he's to look like?" I asked of Striker. I'd been running that question around in my head lately since some of my sisters were walking out with husband material of their own, with one already married.

"He'd have to stand tall in height, and bearing, you know. I won't settle for a mouse of a man, but he'd not be high-handed with me either. He'd need to see me as his equal".

Striker seemed to agree.

"Of course he'd have to be Irish. There'd be no give in that aspect at all! Well, maybe Scottish. Brown eyes. I'd be wanting him to have brown eyes, and a tad touch of curl to his hair; right in front. Black hair; wide shoulders; strong in strength, but gentle, with true feelings in his heart for me."

Striker looked off to his right as if searching for something else for us to talk about.

I shook my head at the daydream of the husband I'd conjured up. "A wish on the wind. Tis all he is". I whispered sadly.

I heeled Striker up and kept an eye peeled for an evening camp. We were closing down the sixth day, and three, more or less, would put us at our destination.

We crossed a flat, table-topped mesa; found a well-used game trail down the edge that led to a narrow green valley that spilled out onto a wider grassland in the distance. Far off on the distant eastern horizon, I saw a lake glittering in the last rays of sunlight. The water course in the valley was headed that way, and we might as well too, for I could also see the darker green line of far off trees.

The greenery would make a sheltered camp, and give Striker good grazing.

I was still comparing the land to the closeness of the mountains back east. The truth be known; there wasn't any comparison. The places were worlds apart, but I was settling into this land with every passing day.

The leaves on the trees were a hard green in color; not the new, bright green of spring. They looked dull, and worn out from a summer of feeding their tree. A few were tinted with their chosen fall color already; reminding me that the return trip would take me into cooler weather.

We ladies were well prepared for winter this time.

Striker and I weren't the first people to use the trail that followed a clear running stream, for it had the hoof prints of shod horses on it.

The trail led to a stone-ringed fire pit.

I used the pit to make my supper while Striker ate his fill of lush green grass, and we both drank deeply from the cold stream.

I had two small cans of ham; some fatback meat, flour, coffee and tea left in my kit. I had ham left because I'd shot a small marmot on the fourth day out, and finished the last of it this morning. I'd spit-cooked the whole carcass immediately; warmed some up daily, and ate it wrapped in a piece of skillet fried, flat bread with strong coffee.

It was stick to your ribs food.

Each night I killed the fires, kicked them apart; dumped water on the hot ashes, and moved far away to bed down. Striker would flop down beside me like he'd done as a foal; the same as a dog, heave a sigh of contented relief, and get real still. Otherwise; if there wasn't room for him, he'd stand hip shod, knees locked, and sleep on his feet with his head hung low.

Chapter 13

By late afternoon of the eighth day storm clouds were appearing on the western horizon as I left the east end of the lake; skirted northeast, and found a small homestead. It was a tiny place compared to what we O'Reilly's owned, but it was tidy and neat.

As we approached from the backside of the buildings, I stopped near fifty yards out, and hailed the empty area with a loud hello.

Washing hung from a clothesline near a fire on which sat a heat-blackened wash tub. Two other tubs, each with a scrub board angled down into the waters, and a couple of wooden buckets, claimed their spots on a board bench nearby. The fire crackled beneath the tub, but no one tended it.

My hail went unanswered except for a cur dog that ambled from the barn, and bayed my arrival into the silent yard. Its color of brown, and black showed the dog to be a breed of hound.

The door to the back of house opened, and an older woman walked to the edge of the porch. She stood straight; unbent, her head high. Whatever life had handed her; it hadn't worn her down at all.

She had my respect immediately.

At my knee pressure, Striker eased us forward, his ears alert, and he stopped twenty feet from the lady.

Her dark eyes glittered as she appraised me, and the slight tilt of her head told me she was surprised, and curious, to find a lone woman in her yard.

I gave her time to finish her assessment of me while I gleaned more from her. Her graying hair; gathered and pinned atop her head; gave her an air of stateliness. The kinked mass of darkness, mingled with a small amount of gray, told me the woman carried Negro blood; as did her very dark brown eyes, and the slight, brown color of her skin.

Striker must have picked up faint sounds inside the house, for his ears tipped forward attentively. The woman was not alone. But was she unprotected? Or was she the protector?

"Good day to you, Ma'am," I began easily, removing my hat, and draped it from the saddle horn.

"Good days to you," she replied briskly.

*She's defensive,* I thought.

"I've been a few days on the trail, and I surely would like a dry place to spend the night. May I use your barn? I'll pay you fair." I spoke easily as I glanced towards the clouds that were piling high atop each other towards the southwestern skyline. I indicated them with a nod.

"Yo be hungry?" She asked a little friendlier.

"Yes Ma'am, I could be persuaded to be," I answered with a bright smile.

Thrusting her chin towards the barn, she spoke again, "Go puts yous stud in the barn, and come inside. We's set to eat supper; sparse as it is, but yous be welcome to join us."

"I'm sure your food will suit me fine, Ma'am. Thank you." I again gave the woman the respect I had been taught to give any person.

The barn was tight, weatherproof, and sturdy. Someone had added upright boards to the outer walls to cover the cracks. I would be warm, and dry tonight, and I wouldn't be the first person to bed down in a stable.

A grandmother had done just that, for different reasons of course, and so did a young woman 1800 years or so before that. In a different land.

The stalls; only four, were three-sided boxes with a rope across the open end to retain an animal; except there wasn't one animal in the barn but Striker.

An old, big bagged, Guernsey milk cow was long-lined out near the garden.

A makeshift saddle rack of sawhorses stood next to the stall Striker ambled into like it was waiting just for him. I put the two sawhorses side by side, and hoisted the tack off Striker, and placed it on the makeshift saddle rack. Removing his bridle and bit; I rubbed him down with an old towel I found hanging on a peg. He sucked water from the bucket I sat for him, after I made a quick walk to the creek beyond the garden, and ate the hay I'd laid in the manager.

I checked his eyes, and hooves, and thought about the lady in the house. I was curious about a lot of things that should have been here, but weren't. It was plain to see the ranch pastures stood thigh high with good grass, but the only animal I'd noticed was the milker, and she was tied close.

Finished with Striker, I cleaned up as best as I could; washing some of the grime from my face, neck, and arms with water from Striker's bucket. I rinsed it out, and refilled it for him. Beating the dust from my clothes with my hat; I dug out my hair brush, and put my long hair in order.

Slipping father's coiled whip around my left shoulder; I picked up my rifle, and went out the door.

A boy about seven years old, and a girl maybe ten, had appeared. The girl was stoking the tub's fire as the lady shook out a laundered dress to pin on the line. The scrub board had a pair of little britches on it. I leaned the rifle, and whip against the buckets' bench, and started scrubbing the small pants.

No one stopped me nor uttered nary a word, but I felt their eyes on me.

The children had more white blood than black. Only the slight kink of their brown hair, and full lips gave away their bloodline. They were overly silent for kids. Too silent. I knew life had not been a kind, happy place for them. It showed in their mistrust of me.

As I knuckle-rubbed another piece of clothing, the lady rinsed the pants in the second tub, and pinned them alongside the dresses. As I washed; I scanned the yard again.

A wire and board chicken fence alongside the coop held half a dozen white striped, black, Barred Rock hens, and a long-tailed, high-headed rooster. He stared boldly at me; letting me know the small patch of dirt inside the fence was his.

Good. I didn't want it.

An empty pig sty, and a medium-sized garden surrounded by a post-and-twig-laced fence completed the out buildings. The proper name for the fence was woven wattle, and I hadn't seen one since leaving Tennessee.

The Guernsey was staked outside the garden, and had been re-staked all around it; keeping the grass decently short, and that kept the windblown weed seeds from planting themselves inside the wattle fence.

I finished the last piece of clothing, and dried my hands on my thighs as she hung her work shirt. How did I know it was hers? It was blue with yellow flowers on it, and too big for the girl. A man wouldn't be caught wallowing in a mud hole wearing a flowered shirt!

At least not any man I knew.

Leaving the tub on the fire, the lady dug out a hole in the red coals, and propped a small shovel full of washed, cut up potatoes on the glowing chunks of heat.

*Efficient,* I thought, but said, "My name's Kate O'Reilly," and held out my scrubbed, reddened hand.

She hesitated as she studied me again, in what I took to be disbelief. Apparently having come to some sort of an agreement in her head, she reached out, and finally shook my offered hand.

"Sophie Rose Alexander. These be my grandchillin,' Mary Rose Elders and John Jacob Elders."

"I'm very proud to meet you," I said softly, and reached out my hand again to shake hands with them. Mary Rose shyly took my hand after looking to Sophie, but John Jacob hid behind his Gramma's skirts. He was on the smallish side, and cute as all get out.

"Well, we best get on in the house, and see to gettin' supper. I'll tote the waters to the garden after supper." Sophie was all business again.

"Chillin', go fetch us greens from the garden, and 'member to latch the gate," she instructed as she gently

171

pushed the barefoot children towards the wattle fence that was at least six foot high.

I picked up my rifle, slipped the coiled whip over my shoulder, and followed her inside what turned out to be a four-room building. A fireplace held a small, glowing bed of coals that warmed the room, but didn't overheat it. The usual iron pots hung from the metal rack over the fire.

A large rope-and-pole bed was near the corner, and a split-board table with benches was hunkered down; claiming its spot near the fireplace, and served as her kitchen work table.

The doors stood open to the other rooms. I could see beds, and braided rugs on the floors. A serviceable privacy room, between the bedrooms, completed the home.

Beyond the kitchen table, a couple of shelves held a small amount of dishes, cups and basins. Another shelf held glass jars of kitchen supplies; most were empty. Two more shelves held a Bible, a few books, and a sewing basket. Beside the main door a rifle hung vertically from two pegs, but the small shelf that usually held bullets was bare.

I recalled the small neat stitches that held patches on some of the clothes I had scrubbed. Sophie was good with needle and thread. A precisely stitched, patch-worked quilt lay on each bench, and larger ones covered both beds.

"I's only gots fresh kilt greens; baked taters, and butter for eatin'. I's hope that be fine by you." She just stated how things were.

"It's very fine with me, Mrs. Alexander. If you would permit me to contribute to our meal, I have supplies in my knapsack. May I bring some?" I asked carefully being mindful of her pride.

"Yes'm. That'd be fine." Her answer wasn't asking for gratitude.

"I'll be right back," I said politely, and turned for the door after gathering up my weapons.

"You'in's always carry that rifle, and whip?" She asked a mite carefully.

I stopped; faced her square on, and replied seriously, "Yes Ma'am, I do. Everywhere I go."

The children came in as I walked out, and John Jacob scooted to his Gram Ma's skirts again. He was scared of me...or my weapons.

Walking across the yard I eyed the freight wagon hiding in the barns lean-to shed. The harness, hanes, and collars hung inside the first stall next to Striker. *Where were her horses?* I wondered, and knew things were way out of kilter here and, me being me, I couldn't leave it alone. I needed to know her situation.

Rummaging in my supply sack, I took everything; both cans of hams, the flour, coffee, and sugar; along with two long sticks of peppermint candy I usually shared with Striker.

He wouldn't mind...much.

I added the last two cans of milk, the rest of the bacon, and dried apples. I had emptied Striker's water bucket; put the food in it, and went for the house.

I would re-supply in town.

I stopped by the fire; pulled the shovel out, and finger-tested the small hunks of potatoes. They were getting soft so I took them with me. I carried my rifle under the arm carrying the bucket.

Sophie took the shovel full of potatoes, and propped it on the house fire coals. I sat the bucket on the work/dining table, set my gear by the table, and proceeded to open a can of ham by inserting its attached key into the thin strip of metal near the top of the can, and twisted my way around the can.

John Jacob watched intently, his beautiful brown eyes round with wonder.

I winked at him, and he shyly smiled.

I slid the ham onto a plate Sophie laid on the table; removed my belt knife, and thinly sliced the meat. I put it in the skillet to heat and Sophie would add the greens later. She placed the skillet on the small fire next to the shovel of potatoes.

Inside of ten minutes Sophie set the ham, greens, and potatoes on her table, and we sat down to a very delicious meal.

"I'll say grace," I said and, with open palms, reached for a hand on either side of me, bowed my head and...waited.

I felt Mary Rose timidly take one hand, and Sophie grasped the other. "Blessed Mother, thank You for this food. Thank You for these new friends who asked me into their home. Walk with us, Blessed Mother, and protect us. Amen."

Sophie whispered, "Amen" but the children were quiet. There'd be questions from at least Mary Rose later.

I could sense it. Probably Sophie too. The prayer was one of Mothers. It was from long before time, and history were written down; when the old ones worshiped Nature. It was a good prayer, and I stood by it as Mother had. I didn't explain it...or me.

We dished up, and I started talking. "Mrs. Alexander, I've a herd of stock arriving in a day or two, and be taking back west. They'll be needing a break. Your pastures are empty, and I'd like to rent them to lay the stock over for a few days. Would you be willing to do that?" I spoke my request between bites of food, turning the meal into a business meeting.

I wanted to put the lady more at ease with me, for I had the knowing in my head this woman needed help, but her pride showed clear. She was a good woman; not afraid of hard work; a beautiful seamstress, and protector of two innocent children.

"How much you be offerin'?" Sophie was also a businesswoman; letting me set the price, and she'd bargain from there...if need be.

"Three or four days...twenty dollars a day." I laid the price on her table nonchalantly, and saw her hand hesitate as she pushed the greens around on her plate. It was speckled blue metal…the plate. The spoon was carved from wood, as was mine, and the $80 was more than two month's pay, but I had a lot of stock to graze.

"That…seems…fair 'nough," she choked softly.

"How large is your place? That stream, and lake part of it?" I wondered who, or what was breaking her to the point of forcing her off the land. I was sure of that now, for the land was fertile, and with water; the homestead would hold a high value. Yet she was just scraping by. Trying to survive. I needed to know the why of that. It's just the way I am. Not usually poking my nose, but not standing by either.

"I've 1600 acres. It be good land. A body'd make a decent livin' off'n it I reckin." Hiding behind her words was a hint of anger.

I shifted the conversation.

"My family and I trailed out here from Tennessee last fall. We've a place over by Highwater, Montana Territory. A few business folks put problems in our path, but that's all behind us now." I said softly, leaving out all the hardships us girls had worked through.

"Yo family?" Sophie asked, without the underlying anger.

"Yes Ma'am. I've seven sisters, and I have to tell you; they have spirit!" I smiled brightly, and so did Sophie.

"I like yo hair color," Mary Rose's tiny, shy voice crept into the table talk.

"Thank you, Mary Rose. My sisters all have the same," I smiled down at her.

"Yo truly gots seven sisters?" The girl asked in awe.

"Surely do. But I'm the eldest," I spoke lightly, adding an air of authority to the "I'm."

"Yo's gots brothers?" John Jacob whispered low.

"Nary a one, John Jacob, just us girls. But that's all right isn't it?" I asked him smiling, and winking.

"Yo's horse is pretty." Mary Rose's voice was still soft.

"That he is. He's smart too." My reply was true, for Striker was head smart, a thinking horse that learned fast; then added his own twist to what he'd learned. Father had finally stopped trying to hold the horse in a stall with a latched half gate.

I didn't try anything like that with him. If Striker wanted to leave a stall; he'd find a way; by cunningness or brute strength. He stayed in a stall because he wanted to. It was something called trust. It worked on people the same way. Right now I was working that way with

Sophie. I'd accomplish what I wanted her to do, but it would seem to be her idea.

"You chillins finish up, and go bring ole Lilly in so's I can milk her, and get you'ens off ta bed." Sophie was soft of voice talking to her babies, and there was love in the words. She had a quality about her that I liked.

I washed the dishes; Sophie dried; stacking things in their proper places as the kids went to get the milk cow.

I put a measure of coffee in the pot, ladled in the right amount of water, and set it over the fire as Sophie took the cloth off the top of the milk pail, and waited on the porch for the cow.

"She gives 'bout two buckets a day, but I's pour most of it out since I ain't got no way ta haul it ta town ta sell, and we cain't use it all."

I had stopped beside her and her words gave me an opening.

"Why can't you get to town? You have a wagon."

"Ain't gots no horses ta pull it no more since J.B. Hutchinson took' em for a debt payment he say I's owe."

"Do you...owe the debt?"

"No Ma'am I's don't. Bought this here land free and outright five year ago. Then my daughter, and her man

179

died of the 'thera two years back. Thought I'd lose John Jacob, but the Lord spared him."

"So whose debt is it?"

"Mr. Hutchinson say it was my son-in-law who took it on. He says I's owes it now, buts Tom said he paid it off 'long time back."

"Your name on it?"

"No Ma'am it aint' but don't seems ta make no mind to that...man." The word 'white' was on her tongue, but she cast me a look and let it die there...on her tongue.

"Sophie, some people are born bastards. I've been pushed on by a few of them. Color didn't enter into it."

"What happen when dey pushed on ya?"

I smiled broadly at her, winked, and said, "I pushed back."

"What happened?" She needed to hear what a woman could do, I guess.

"They lost," my words rang with Irish deviltry as I wiggled my eyebrows, and she smiled.

She milked the cow. I poured the first pail to the chickens and hound. She filled another bucket; set it to cool, and the cream to rise while the children, and I walked the cow to the barn. I toted the rinse water to the garden while Sophie put the children down for the night.

Sophie knew how to coax a garden into full crop, and she practiced multiple plantings for a continuous crop. She was capable.

Striker and I would have company tonight with the milker sharing the barn with us.

Daylight was fading; the moon was cresting the east horizon, and the first stars were blinking on, but they wouldn't last. The rain clouds were building high, and taking over the sky.

The tots were in bed. Sophie and I were in rocking chairs on the porch drinking my coffee. The milk was in the cold creek, and safe in a wooden box anchored with stones, and we were listening to the night sounds.

Far off in the upper valley, a pack of coyotes let loose a wailing song, and I turned to look; knowing I wouldn't see them. Habit I guess.

Sophie broke our silent vigil. "So you's mean if'n I didn't sign that loan, I's don't owes it?"

"I'm pretty sure that's what the law would say. Especially if you have a paid off receipt. Have you asked the law? There seems to be something wrong here. It just needs to be sorted out."

"But Hutchinson, he say he's gots Tom's name on it!"

"Does he now?" I questioned with a brogue to my words. "Can you read Sophie?"

"Yes 'em. And write too!" She replied curtly, and her chin lifted with pride.

"Have you seen the papers at the bank? Yours should be a direct copy to the others."

The look of surprise that came immediately to her face indicated the overlooked fact that Hutchinson didn't know she could read, and I now knew one set of the papers were forged. *He wants the land. Why not? Good grass, but more important...the water.*

Time for another roundabout question.

"Your lake and stream dry up or is it year round?" I led her mind where it had to go.

She looked at me a good long while, and in the fading moonlight; I saw the realization come into her mind, and then her face: "He be a breakin' me down to gets my land ain't he, Kate?"

By using my first name, I knew she was almost there. Almost understanding there was an intentional wrong here, and I believed it was as simple as adding a number in the right place.

"But what's can I's do?" There was despair in her voice.

"First, I think you need to ask yourself, if you can, or want, to stay here. How have other folks helped you, and the children? Has anybody stopped by to check on you? Is there the possibility others know what Hutchinson may be doing to you, and they're waiting for you to give up and leave? Perhaps they'd profit also if you left?

Give me your answer then we'll figure out what can be done. I know some about the laws of property sales, and loans. One of my sisters is a lawyer."

We drank our coffee before it turned cold, and I took our cups inside; washed them, and sat them on their shelf while Sophie thought on my words.

My rear had just touched the rocker seat when she softly spoke. She had tears on her face, and slowly brushed them away. "Nobody. No body's stopped by, but the doctor. He be a good man."

"What about the sheriff? He honest?"

"Yes'em he is."

"Does the judge fit that billing too? An honest man?"

"He does seem that way, but he be friendly with Hutchinson. Their wives be all friendly like towards each other."

Sophie was getting talkative, her answers quick, and sure.

"And your son-in-law could read and write?"

"Tom Elders was a full white man. My daughter was near white. Both of 'em could read and write real fine. They's taught me, and the chillin'."

I had the question in my mind as to how this woman had birthed a 'near white' daughter, but I knew things happened to women that they didn't ask for, nor had control over. The Civil War was supposed to put an end to such things. I would not ask her, or hold her accountable.

"Do you have any paperwork, or any loan papers with Toms' signatures on them?"

"Sure I does. Kept every scrap 'bout the land, and stock, since we'ns bought here!"

"May I see them?"

We rose together and went inside. Sophie disappeared into a bedroom while I turned the wick up on the coal oil lamp on the table.

It didn't take a minute to see Tom Elders' beautiful script on a number of legal papers with a $100 loan. There was a receipt of a loan payment of the $100 with a Mrs. Cora Copeland's name on it. The loan was paid in full, and dated; a long time ago.

There was a separate, sealed letter that caught my eye. It was a Trust, and Sophie's name wasn't on any of the papers.

"Tomorrow I'll go on into town and ask the sheriff to come see you."

A fear came into her eyes. "The sheriff! Why?"

"I want him to open this letter and read the other paper too. That way the opening of it can't be challenged by Hutchinson, or anyone.

"Sophie, it's important to bring the law in on your problems. It'll be all right. I'll make sure of that. Will you trust me?"

The house was so very quiet. I could hear the children across the room breathing in their blissful sleep.

"Sophie? Your stock? Where are they?" I asked gently touching her arm.

Looking at me, she whispered, "Hutchinson took 'em as payments for the last five months. Kate? He's been a-lying ta me hain't he? All this time him pretending to be a helping. He weren't doing a thing, but a cheatin' me, and them babies! Weren't he?"

Choosing my words with care, and using as gentle a voice as I could muster up from behind a hot anger that had built in me when I read the papers; I replied to her pain. "I believe he lied, and stole from you, and the children. But Sophie, tomorrow will be his day of reckoning. You have my word on that, and the word of an O'Reilly is born in honor. I promise this to you."

With those words we parted for the night, but I doubted if the woman would sleep much.

Hutchinson was the same caliber of man that young Morris was back in Tennessee; only worse. Morris had been accountable to his father, but apparently Hutchinson wasn't accountable to anyone...yet. I shook with disgust at the guile of this man! I hoped he'd sleep well tonight, for tomorrow he'd meet me, and if all this about Sophie was true, I aimed to break the conniving, thieving, low life to his knees!

This wasn't my duty or job. I wanted to do this for Sophie; a good person who didn't have any way to fight for what was right. But mostly I needed to help Mary

Rose and John Jacob; two innocent children; pure in life, or my conscious wouldn't let me sleep.

In the barn I unrolled my two blankets; tossed my last set of clean clothes across Striker's saddle; stripped off my weapons; my dirty trail clothes, and bunched the dirty clothes in a pile under the saddle rack. I pulled my long coat over my naked body, and wearing my boots, carrying my rifle, towel, and bar soap; the empty water bucket, and went to the creek in the pasture to bathe.

The water was ice cold, and I was shivering before I'd washed half of me. Goose bumps covered my body, and my breasts were drawn tight and hard. Icy shivers raced across my scalp as I washed, and rinsed my long hair.

I surely missed my hot bathing tub back home! But I wouldn't impose on Sophie by asking to use her tub except; I would heat tub water in the morning, and wash my two sets of soiled garments.

Back in the barn I dried off; put my last clean clothes on; towel-dried my hair best as I could, and worked it into a large braid for the night.

Striker watched me with a mixture of what seemed like mild interest or boredom. The cow didn't seem interested at all in what the human in her barn was doing.

Using the sturdy, wooden, three-prong hayfork, I piled a good, high bed of loose fodder in the corner of Striker's stall; spread one blanket on it, and wearing my clothes, and coat; I laid my weary body down. I pulled the other blanket, and Striker's saddle pad across me, and didn't know when I fell asleep.

It rained, but I didn't hear it.

Chapter 14

Striker nuzzled me awake. He was standing over me as if asking, "You sleeping all day?"

He was pushy at times.

I pried my eyes open; batted them a few times to get the sleep out, and get them to focus, but still didn't see much.

The barn was dark, for dawn hadn't brightened the sky much at all, but I knew I had slept the night through, and I hadn't moved a hand; since I still clutched the blanket under my chin.

I guess my conscious was clear.

Cat stretching my body fully; I rolled to set up. There was a damp chill in the air; even in the tight barn. I unfolded; stood up, hefted the rifle, and went to have a quick chat with nature.

Coming back inside, I led the cow, with Striker following, to the creek. When they had their fill, I staked her out near the garden in a new patch of rain-wet grass that needed her attention, and Striker stayed to keep her company.

My boots were thoroughly wet.

Back in the barn, I gathered up my washing; a handful of hay, and went to the wash tub. I struck the fire with the hay, dry twigs, and sticks off the porch, and stood aside to watch the dripping world wake up.

"Dawning is the magical time." Mother used to say that. She said a lot of things that I keep remembering, and don't intend to forget.

Sometimes I feel my mind pull away, and I find myself hovering high overhead; watching me, and seeing things for miles around. It's a weird feeling when that happens; which comes unbidden to me sometimes; like right now. Other times I can make it happen.

I'm up here; looking down at the 'me' standing near the tub; seeing the garden, and the two grazing animals. Off a ways I see the lake; the streams entering, and leaving it, and the wide grasslands that fills Sophie's range. I can see more of the sunrise too, and watch its approaching line of sun light on the ground that was coming towards the 'me' down there. I wondered if I could get back down before the sun light got to me, and then I was there, standing right where I had been.

The high accents used to scare me something awful when I was little. Mother tried to explain it to me the best as she could. She said it was the Graces, a pulling me up so I could see there was more to life than just me. That I was part of it all; connected to everything that ever was, and ever will be.

They graced only those of us, she said, who were found worthy of their magic. If that were true, and I believed it could, and should be; I felt honored. I knew none of my sisters were chosen to walk in the magic...only me. Mother, and Grandmother Kate, told me that, so I knew it was true.

The morning magic vanished, and I was beside the heating tub in my wet boots. The dream of my sleep came back to me as I watched the quiet dawn.

The dream was a scene of a black, moonless night. The moon was in its dark phase; the sky was clear, and the night cold. Stars filled every spot in the sky. I sat atop Striker; we were alone, but I didn't know where.

Something tragic had happened, for a horse lay dead nearby, and I was looking at those stars asking for help.

*Help with what? From who?* I asked of my dream as the eastern sky turned a dull, gun blue gray, and I waited for the half tub of water to heat.

I smelled the wood smoke of my fire and watched the smoke rising from the house chimney fight to climb a few feet; then spread out over the yard and garden in a flat, white blanket.

The air was heavy with last night's rain, and I could taste its wetness as I breathed in.

Sophie was up. She disturbed my thoughts as she came from the house, and handed me a cup of hot, creamed coffee. Bless her!

"Morning Sophie. Thank you," I acknowledged her, and the coffee.

She saw the staked-out cow; Striker at breakfast, the tub on the fire; my pile of clothes, and knew for sure that I didn't wait for someone to see to things for me.

"I see ole Lilly be hungry this morning." Sophie's voice was pleasantly friendly, and her statement was her way of thanking me for putting the cow to graze.

"You's horse seems content."

"He's content anywhere he can put his head down and fill his belly," I answered her lightly with a smile, and small shake of my head as I lifted the hot coffee to my lips.

Striker raised his head, and looked square on at us. He seemed to know we were speaking of him. He chewed and watched us. I think he took pleasure at having the attention.

I said, "I'll have time to milk her before breakfast, and the water's hot enough to wash. Would you want to save any milk this morning?"

"You's knows how ta milk?"

"I do Ma'am. I'm proud to say I have learned how to do a lot of things. My folks wouldn't have had it any other way."

"No reason to be a-saving her milk this mornin'," Sophie replied sadly to my question.

I nodded, took up the rifle, and went to lighten Lillie's load while Sophie tended to breakfast.

Kneeling on one knee in the wet grass, I was glad to see the old cow was at ease with me, and let her milk down. I pulled her dry, letting the milk puddle underneath her.

Striker didn't pay much mind at all to my chore, probably because it didn't involve him.

Sun up was still a good half an hour away, but I could easily see for quite a distance. Again I breathed deeply of the wet air, and felt it rush through my head. Father used to tell me I was like Mother that way; head over heels in my feelings for nature. He jokingly said it was probably the way of the Pagan in the both of us.

Yes it is.

I washed my hands in the warming tub water, and entered the house to find two sleepy-eyed children, a smiling Sophie, and a hearty breakfast waiting for me.

Mrs. Alexander was a wonder for sure! Her table held fried corn pones, fried eggs, ham slices, with butter for the pones. Days of eating trail fare made me appreciate her meal even more.

Sophie said grace, and we ate while I told her what I intended to do in town.

"I'll wash my clothes, and then head for town. I'll find the sheriff first; follow his lead if need be, and then find the judge. I'll think about telegraphing my sister to get her thoughts on your problem, but I believe I already know what needs to be done, and how to go about it.

Before I ride out, if you make a list of supplies you need, I'll pick them up. I need to buy for my trail crew anyway, but I'll do that on order. Sounds like I'm going to have a full day; maybe you too." I shot her a smile as I talked.

Sophie listened intently, and offered the papers to me: "You's gonna be a-needing these I reckon."

"No Sophie, those are yours, but you will need them later."

We washed our dishes; threw out the water, and I went to carry rinse water from the creek for my clothes.

"John Jacob? Will you carry my rifle while I tote water?" I asked the boy, who appeared more comfortable with me this morning. I wanted to give the boy a man's stance in the world.

I didn't need help, or protecting, but he didn't know that.

He didn't make a move until Sophie laid a hand to his shoulder, and told him gently, "You's go on now with Miz Kate. She'll be a-needing you's help."

I gave him full credit, for he moved to my side, but didn't say a word.

"I'd be obliged if you carry this while I do the buckets." I handed him my rifle, and walked away towards the creek. I didn't look to see if he followed. That was up to him, but I didn't have any doubt he could carry the weight of the gun. It only weighed a tad over seven pounds, eight, fully loaded as it was.

He managed just fine.

Four buckets of water, and two trips to get them; the tubs held all I needed. My laundry was sparse compared to what hung on the line, and didn't take, but half an hour to scrub, rinse and hang.

## Chapter 15

The morning sun was already building a heat when I rode out. Striker was pitty pattin' his front feet. He wanted to run. Just his nature. I let him. Sophie's land was five miles from town, and Striker loped most of it as I gave him a slack rein.

The first building we came to was a church, and it had all the requirements; white paint, bell steeple, double front door, a few stained glass windows, and a cross over the doors.

A school hunkered down across the road. The same carpenter must have built both for they were identical. Except the school had a bunch of swings, and teeter totters. I recalled how many times my rear end got bruised when my balancing partner bailed off, leaving me high in the air on one end of the board, only to plummet to the ground.

The plummet stopped when I hit.

Sheridan proper was large, and wide awake as Striker worked his way forward. Rows of houses spread out behind the businesses that occupied the main street. There were a large number of stores, and I made note of the ones I wanted to visit. After seeing to Sophie's problem, I'd fill those lists the girls sent with me.

I knew the cost of another wagon would be cheaper than paying the cost of freight for all their items. Besides that, I'd still have the wagon. I'd see to its purchase, but I already had the horse power trailing towards me to pull it. I had a bank draft in my pocket for $3,000, but I didn't intend to spend it all.

The jail was easy to find. It and the bank were the only buildings with grating on the windows and doors.

The bank was inviting; the jail was not.

Sheridan was a town moving forward, but in a time when outlaws still plied their trade, the town seemed prepared for the worst.

I wrapped tied Striker's reins at a hitching rack in front of the board sidewalk, and waited for two women to pass before entering the jail.

The women gave me a look that did nothing to hide their disgust at my appearance, but I helped all I could by smiling sweetly at them; which they didn't return.

Guess they weren't raised up proper like I was.

The door was heavy; three times as thick as need be, but maybe for a jail in this town; basically an Army town, it WAS needed. Maybe Sheridan was a rougher town than I'd seen riding in.

The sheriff, and another man, who also wore a badge, looked up, then stood up as I closed the door behind me.

"Can I help you, Ma'am?" The sheriff was an older gent, but had the eyes of a man who didn't take to foul play or being lied to.

Father had taught me how to 'read' a person real quick, and I surmised instantly the sheriff was a good man. He was my height. The deputy was not.

Walking across to his desk, I reached a hand to the sheriff. He took it, and was firm, but not rough. "I'm Kate O'Reilly from Highwater, and I'm here on behalf of Mrs. Alexander," I stated quietly.

"Who's she?" The deputy asked with way to much authority in his voice to suit me. Maybe he was trying to make up for being short.

"You been around here long?" I returned his question with a question.

"Few years. Why?" He was standing just a tad on the belligerent side of me right away. Damn it!

"I know Mrs. Alexander. I've known her since she, and her family came here five years ago. She stays pretty much out of sight. Don't come to town hardly at all. She got trouble?" The sheriff offered up in a much gentler tone than his man used. He was making up for the deputy, and putting the man down; all at the same time.

"Would it be all right if I could have a talk with you? Alone? This is personal." I asked softly, and I didn't care if the deputy objected or not. I wasn't here to be his friend, or educate him.

"Billy? Will you go out for a walk?" The sheriff asked, but really ordered the man out of the room.

Billy was miffed but, as I said, I didn't care. He'd started it by not knowing who lived in his area. I know everyone who lives in my valley, and had been there not quite a full year.

Billy left, and I sat in a chair not offered. Just my way of claiming title to the command of the situation.

"I stayed the night with Mrs. Alexander, and the grandchildren. Someone's forcing her off her land with false papers. I'll be wanting your help setting it right for her." My words were softly given with a hint of the brogue, and clearly spoken.

"You have only known her since last night, and you've taken up this cause for her?" he asked. I could tell he was intrigued.

"Just last night, but like you, I have a way of sizing a body or a situation up fairly quick. You wouldn't be any good at your job if you couldn't do that, and neither would I."

"And what exactly is your job, Miss? O'Reilly?" His questioning look after the "Miss" established my status.

"Building a ranch, and seeing to my family."

"Would you care for coffee? It's decent." He was thinking; killing time; sorting me out.

"Coffee would go nicely right now. Thank you."

He made more work than necessary in getting the coffee, and I let the silence grow between us.

"It's fairly fresh. I made it. Can't drink Billy's brew," he offered a distracting note to our meeting. He sat at his desk again; took a sip from his cup, and instructed: "Tell me."

"I've seen the documents that show a $100 loan Tom Elders took out with a J.B. Hutchinson, and was paid off in full. He tells her she still owes on that loan, and that paper has Tom's name on it."

"Lots of folk still can't read, and write. What's your point?"

"Tom Elders could read, and write. So could his wife; Mrs. Alexander, and the grandchildren. Most folks I know rush to show off their schooling, not hide it." I tried to imitate my lawyer sister in words, and manner, giving a slow measured presentation of the facts.

"One other thing, sheriff, Sophie has her copies of the papers. She's never seen the one at the bank Hutchinson talks about, and there is a Trust envelope; unopened. I don't believe Mrs. Alexander knows it should have been opened, and processed."

The man sat silently sipping his coffee; his eyes were staring at nothing. He was thinking. He needed to know more, and I waited for him to ask his questions.

"What else?"

"This Hutchinson had taken her eleven cows, and calves as partial payment, and left her with an old milker. He also took her horses...effectively stranding her, and the children on the place with no way to get to town to sell the milk, and butter. She's been dumping the milk on the ground; what she doesn't use."

The man watched his coffee as if expecting it to move.

"I milked the cow onto the ground this morning. There isn't more than twenty pounds of food in the place. They eat mostly garden things. There's a rifle but no bullets. Meat isn't on their table."

He sat watching me as I drank my coffee. Holding the cup in both hands, I continued, "Stealing a person's stock is not a practice that I believe should be overlooked; unless there are different rules on such things for a woman?"

My statement was meant to be a gentle tap on his conscious, but you'd have thought I'd pistol whipped him the way his eyes flashed to mine.

"You think I'd let something like horse and cattle stealing slide because it's a woman standing the loss?"

I pushed him harder. It's just my way.

"Maybe I'm about to find out," I replied softly. "What sort of man is this Hutchinson?"

Hesitating a moment, he spoke again, his tone milder. "He's been here close to five years or so. He's from St. Louis. Hired in as replacement for Barrows, who took a bullet in a hold up. J.B. scouted around for land, but..." He stopped mid-sentence.

"But what?" I prodded.

"He just missed getting the Alexander, I mean Elders place by about a month."

"Did he buy?"

"Yep. A spread between the Elders' place and town. It stretches east to west, and is more long than wide; 2,000 acres."

"Is it good land?" I asked nonchalantly as possible.

"Yep. Level. Good grass, and water."

"The water come off Mrs. Alexander's place?"

He thought on my question before nodding, and finally said, "Yep."

I didn't say anything else for a while, but let him run with the ideas I hoped I'd planted in his head, and drank my coffee. He made a decent cup.

"You be willing to ride back with me to look at her papers?" I sat my empty cup on his desk and stood. "There's enough day left."

He rose to his feet. "I'll let Billy know."

"What's your name, sheriff?"

"Jack Copeland." *Same as the name on the paid in full receipt* I realized.

"I hope I can say later; that I'm pleased to meet you Sheriff Copeland."

He didn't respond, but put on his hat and coat; opened the door for me, and reached for his rifle with the other hand.

Deputy Billy was leaning against the hitching rack admiring Striker. "Nice horse," he said a little too hard.

"He is," I replied flatly.

"I'll be back this afternoon Billy," Copeland told his deputy, who was still leaning against the rack, and unknowingly, out of Strikers reach.

"Where ya goin'?"

The sheriff was wishing he had a different sort of man working for him. I didn't doubt that in the least. The deputy never got his answer, for it was in my introduction. He apparently didn't recall that. He seemed to miss a lot. Sheriff Copeland did not.

"Sheriff, I'll need to buy a couple of horses for Mrs. Alexander. Where would you suggest?"

"Livery. The end of town," the man used his words sparingly; like I had interrupted his thoughts, and he wanted to get back to them.

"She had a pair of Pintos, red and white," I added. "It would be good to take them back to her, but that might be asking a lot."

Chapter 16

The livery was out near the east end of town, and on the backside of some of the houses I had passed coming in. We ambled past at least fifty houses, and that was just in this part of the town. I suspected the sheriff had his hands full most of the time. Looking into a bank loan for a woman might be seen as using up his time by some folks, but there was more to this, and I wasn't using up his time…Hutchinson was.

It had been a while since I was in a town this big. I still wasn't impressed. The homes were close up on one another; which was a requirement of a town I guess. The streets were as narrow as my ranch lanes, and crowded a body close. I could stand in a spot, throw stones, and hit at least six houses.

Many had gardens not big enough to mess with, and grew mostly flowers. A wasteful use of land if a body wanted vegetables on their tables. Like Sophie.

The livery was a prosperous sight. The pastures, four of them, were long, narrow, and held maybe a dozen horses in two of them. The other two were empty and growing green. Rotation of grass. That was good thinking on someone's part.

Beyond the pastures were cut-over hay fields with winter fodder stacks piled high. The barn corrals held half a dozen animals close up, and ready at hand for rent.

What interested me the most was what caught my eye right off. As we rode up and reined in; I shot Copeland a look, and thrust my chin at the second pasture of horses.

A couple hundred yards out, two red pintos grazed contentedly.

"I'll do the talking," Copeland said. I took a second look around. Nary one head of cattle to be seen anywhere.

Copeland climbed down. I didn't.

The liveryman straightened from the horseshoe he was beating into round. He was muscled up; sweaty; about half a head taller than Copeland; colored, and I could tell from the tight, gray-tinged hair he kept trimmed short; that he was an older man.

I can't say why, but I knew I needed to get off Striker at this point. All I did know was I didn't need to be looking down on this man. Guess that might have had something to do with the Civil War that pertained, in part, to folks of his race.

"Good morning, Abraham."

"Morning sheriff," Copeland offered his hand, and the man took it easily.

"Decker around?"

"No Sir. He's out to the Tasselman place returning a spring wagon. He'll be back near midday. Can I help with anything?"

The man spoke very well. He'd spent time in a classroom somewhere; somehow, for I still didn't know any school that allowed colored; except the one on our home ground in Tennessee where everyone HAD to attend. White, red or black, Mother made sure they all learned to read, and write. She let any teacher go that didn't feel comfortable with a 'mixed' classroom.

When I went to take a year at the town school; a school for girls, I didn't like it. Only whites were allowed. That fact had brought the taste of bile to the back of my throat, but I stayed, and learned what they offered. Including their 'we're better than others' attitude, and how to be 'proper' ladies.

That attitude stayed at the school when I left. When Mother learned about this; the younger girls didn't have to endure The Higher Learning Girls Institute that I did.

Con men and women, cheated those who were uneducated, and I came out of that school with an inside track on conning. It seemed to be the underlying theme of the staff and their students, who claimed to be of the highest society.

My 'society may not have been the highest, but it was damned well the oldest.

So I slid down off Striker out of respect for what this man had obtained in his life, and for what he had had to endure to get him to where he was.

"Believe so, Abe. This is Miss O'Reilly. Miss O'Reilly, Abraham Geerman."

I shook hands with Abe, and again, he didn't hesitate. He stood tall and confident, and like me; he knew who he was.

"What can you tell me about those Pinto's in the pasture, Abe?" Copeland's request was easy.

"Mr. Decker bought them off Hutchinson. At least his foreman brought them in about three weeks back. No one wants them because of their color I reckon."

"They for sale sir?" I put myself in the conversation.

"Yes, Ma'am. Mr. Decker wants them gone. They eat more than most the other horses." He smiled wide; showing a mouthful of white teeth. "They have already cost him his profit on them."

"What would be the bottom line for both?" I asked, returning his smile.

"Decker wants $300 for the pair. But he'll take $200. That's what he paid for them." He kept smiling, and Copeland, and I joined him, but we knew Hutchinson didn't pay a penny for them.

"All right, two hundred dollars it is then. Need a hand bringing them in?" I said.

"No, Ma'am. They come to grain readily. I'll be right back." He removed his leather apron; took two leads off the wall, and went out a back door of the livery barn to fetch up Sophie's horses.

One more point for me; minus another for Hutchinson, and I knew I had Copeland solidly on Sophie's side.

The closer Abe came with the horses the better they looked. They were fat on grass, and lazy on work. Then I saw the real reason they hadn't sold. They were both 'watch-eyed'. Pale blue with lots of white showing. A bad luck sign too many horse owners, such animals were often shucked off to the first buyer dumb enough to buy them. But, they were Sophie's, and they were going home.

We stopped by a store so I could fill her list; added a few extras, and made sure the store keep could fill my order for later. He could. I think he was giddy to have such a large order, or should I say, the large amount of money the order would lay in his hand.

We left town, and we each held a lead rope of a watch-eyed Pinto.

"How'd you happen onto the Elders' place?" Copeland asked politely, making small talk, and gleaning information. That was his way of passing time for the five-mile ride.

I didn't ask him why he became a sheriff, or how many outlaws he'd had to shoot. "It was fixing to rain. Her barn was dry. We both benefited," I replied with a shrug. I didn't offer more. He didn't need to know more about me. At least not yet, but he knew I carried a powerful rifle; rode an attention getting stallion, and had a whip coiled over my saddle horn, and he knew, that I knew, he was a thinking man.

Chapter 17

Sophie was hoeing in her garden when the hound gave voice to our arrival. She cried with joy; patted the fat horses while Mary Rose jumped up, and down, and John Jacob wrapped his arms around a front leg of one horse.

Their happiness filled me with pleasure.

"Thank yous, Kate! Oh thank yous!" Sophie was short on words, but long on gratitude.

I was standing by Copeland, and taking his horse's reins, I spoke to the children, "Kids. Will you help me put your horses in the barn, and get them used to being home? The sheriff needs to talk with your Gram Ma."

They hurried to take the leads from Sophie; each child leading a horse, jabbering all the way, and excited as...kids.

Striker walked along behind me half a step as I led Copeland's gelding as we trailed the foursome. Sophie showed the sheriff inside, and he carried the heavy sack of food for her.

I kept the children occupied, and let the happening in the house...happen. Copeland may be a friend to Hutchinson, but his head was a lawman's, and full of lawman's thoughts, and possibilities.

We messed with the Pintos. John Jacob chattered so fast he said half-finished words and questions. He was a happy child. We finished Sophie's garden job; washed up at the water pump, and went to the house for a late noon meal.

Sophie was fixing some of the food I had bought, and the sheriff sat at the table reading documents.

I sat my weapons beside the door, and went to help her finish.

The children put the dishes on the table. Sophie handed them the new eating spoons and forks I had bought as a gift for them. They carefully sat the new items on the table, handling the bright metal items in wonder, and Sophie and I smiled at their innocence.

The two new boxes of bullets sat on their small shelf above the door next to the rife on its pegs. Another special purchase I made. An empty rifle isn't any good to anyone.

As the children set the table, Copeland folded the documents; laid them with his hat; washed up at the inside basin, and returned to the table as Sophie refilled his coffee cup.

We sat down; Sophie said Grace, and Copeland held our hands.

He was a good man.

"Mrs. Alexander, I'd like you to come to town with us, and put things right with Hutchinson. If these documents are true, then the man's wronged you, and I apologize for not picking up on your misery," he spoke humbly, looking directly at her, and she graciously accepted his words, and his help.

"We'll be ready directly, sheriff. Thank you."

I noticed her grammar was improving.

The meal was eaten with a friendliness that I believed Sophie had not had in her home for a long time. The children were relaxed, and chatted about the horses nonstop until they were gently hushed by Sophie.

John Jacob kept staring at the metal spoon and fork in his hands. He ate from one, and then the other in turn, which made the three of us smile.

The meal over; I washed, and Sophie put away the dishes; the kids scrambled to put on their 'town' clothes, and Copeland went to tack the horses.

I went to help him while Sophie changed clothes.

We backed the animals to either side of the wagon tongue; hitched them up; checked the wheels, and led the horses out to a beaming Sophie.

"Sophie? They've been on pasture a while. Might be a handful. I'll be glad to drive them for you," Copeland offered.

"I's...I can handle 'em sheriff. But maybes...maybe the children should ride with the two of you until the horses and I come to an agreement on who the boss is."

Copeland grinned wide, touched his hand to his hat, and helped her to the seat. He climbed into his saddle; reached a hand to Mary Rose, who hesitated a moment then grasped his hand, and got hauled up behind his saddle.

"Come on, John Jacob, you're holding things up," I said as I leaned down from Striker, and reached for his arm pits as he held his little arms high. He was light as a feather. I settled him on the saddle in front of me, and held a hand to his little belly. He held to the saddle horn above my coiled whip, and Striker fell in beside Copeland; who had positioned himself in front of the wagon.

The Pintos balked at first; fought the bits and wagons weight, but with our horses in front of them, the pair calmed down shortly, and the rest of the way was an easy ride. Sophie asked the kids to ride in the wagon, but they wanted to stay with us, which was just fine.

Midafternoon found a lot of folks walking all over town as we came in. Copeland took us straight to the bank, and waved Deputy Billy to join us from in front of the jail as we passed it.

Copeland gave Mary Rose an arm down, dismounted, and lifted Sophie off her perch.

People stared.

He hoisted John Jacob from my saddle, and stood him beside his sister as Deputy Billy walked up.

Sophie was escorted into the bank by Copeland with his hand on her elbow; opening the door with his free hand. She took the manners of the man graciously, but I could tell she was flustered. Deputy Billy allowed me and the children to go in next.

He didn't have a choice as I had already stepped in front of him.

One customer was at the teller windows. He finished his business, and I locked the door, and turned the 'closed' sign outward as he left, which made Billy raise an eyebrow. He and I stood with the children in front of the locked door, and I rested a hand on each child's shoulder.

"Cora? I need to see J.B.," Copeland addressed the woman teller. She was nice looking; dressed for the job, and had light brown hair, and blue eyes.

"May I tell him what this is about?"

"No, Cora, just let him know we're here please."

Copeland played his hand close.

Cora disappeared into an inner room marked "private" and I finally laid eyes on J.B. Hutchinson. I didn't like the look or smell of him. He looked like a sugar-coated rodent, and smelled of a bottled scent of some kind that was used overly much.

I looked for an open window, and didn't find one.

I knew the banker was the sort of person who had made his way in the world pretending to be a helpful friend to those in need. But he wasn't a friend. He was a gambler betting on their loss, and he wasn't above making a loss happen.

"Jack! What a surprise! Nice to see you! Cora said you needed to see me?" Hutchinson seemed to be at the top of his business, but he was only a manipulating thief. I knew it, and I was pretty sure Copeland was thinking along those lines too.

Father had run into a few of this kind of scoundrel, and I remember how he had shortened them up. I was very interested to see if Copeland would do the same as Father did.

"J.B.," Copeland shook the offered hand. "I'm here on business. I need to see the paperwork on the Elder's loan." He was all business. Another point in his favor, I thought.

"Sure thing, let's go into my office and..."

Copeland spoke up before I could, "Here's fine. Cora, would you get the Elder's file for me?"

She hesitated; holding her hands together, "I can't. The files are locked."

"Open it, J.B.," Copeland was stern.

"Jack, those are personal."

"You telling Mrs. Alexander she can't see her file, J.B.?"

"No...no, of course not...but she's not asking to..."

"Yes sir, I am asking," Sophie spoke up clearly, and I detected a bit of impatience in her tone.

"Well you realize its Tom Elder's file, not really yours ma'am...and I can't..."

"You are making me pay on it, and it hain't...ain't even mine? Iz...is that what you just said?" Sophie was getting riled. "You took my cattle, and horses for a loan that ain't mine?"

"J.B., give Cora your keys."

The man was sick to his white gills, but he handed over the keys from his pocket, and Deputy Billy went with Cora. She didn't take long; came back, and handed the file to Sophie's outstretched hand. Sophie handed it to Copeland. Deputy Billy stood behind Hutchinson, and in front of the open office door, and the only way out of the building for him.

Sheriff Copeland laid the file down, and spread the papers across the desk. Then he laid Sophie's papers alongside the first ones.

"J.B.? You mind telling me why there are two sets of figures for the same day? And why Cora's signature is on a receipt to Elder for a loan paid in full a year later? And...why you've not given the Trust money to Tom's children?"

Cora Copeland inhaled sharply, and stared, wide-eyed at J.B.

Hutchinson was choked silent as even more color drained from his face.

"Where are Mrs. Alexander's cattle?" Copeland asked, tight jawed, and pointedly emphasizing each word.

Hutchinson whispered brokenly, "At...at...my place...in a high meadow...south...of the ranch."

"So far I count a few charges against you, J.B. One. Horse stealing. That's a hanging offense. Two. Cattle rustling. That's a hanging offense. Three. Falsifying bank records. That's prison time. Four. Embezzling money with those false records. Prison time. Five. Using your position for illegal, and personal gain. Prison time. I don't think the bank authorities are going to take this lightly. Six. Withholding, and using for your benefit, legitimate funds of a Trust in your care. I aim to prove that, and that will be more jail time.

Cuff him Billy." Copeland was all through talking, and was having a difficult time keeping control on his anger.

"JACK! You don't understand!" Hutchinson began to say when Copeland quietly said, "No. No I don't J.B. Billy? Get him ta hell away from me."

I unlocked the door; opened it, and made Hutchinson step around the children as Billy guided the man out the door.

Copeland inhaled a shaky breath, and slowly let it out. "Cora? Can you run the bank alone...legally?" He softly asked the woman. Cora was whiter faced than she had been a few minutes ago, but nodded in answer, "I can run the teller station, but not the legal paper work that J.B. usually does."

"You would do a more honest job than he has Cora. I'll send Billy back over to watch out for you. I have to see Judge Baily, or I'd be here myself."

"I'd appreciate that; you sending Billy over."

"Then I'll see you at home," Copeland voiced softly; put his hat on; gathered up the papers, and left the room leaving me and Sophie staring blankly at Cora in surprise. I mean Mrs. Copeland. I had connected the fact that they could be related, but not married.

I watched as the sheriff gathered up the papers, and then I escorted Sophie, and the children out the door behind him. I turned the sign to 'open' as I left.

I lagged behind Copeland a ways, for I didn't have any doubt the man needed time to get straight in his head what had just happened. It's a hard thing on a heart, and mind, to be deceived by a friend.

I wondered how many times Hutchinson had done the same thing to others, and ruined their lives, or worse. The investigation would uncover a lot of wrong. I didn't have a doubt about that either, and I knew the investigation would extend back to St. Louis.

Copeland was seated at his desk when we walked in. Billy was closing the door that led to the cells. Copeland stood for us.

"Mrs. Alexander, I need to show your papers to the judge. He may want to speak with you, but it's pretty dam clear what Hutchinson has done. Will you speak up if need be?"

"Yes sir. I surely will," Sophie uttered gently. I think she knew the depth of the man's hurt. "Sheriff, sir? Will I get my money back? And my cattle? And the children; will they get what their daddy left 'em?"

"Yes you will, Ma'am, and so will the children. Hutchinson was wrong on many things, but withholding the children's Trust..."

Copeland was at a loss for words and stopped speaking. He was an angry man.

"Sophie, did you read the Trust letter after the sheriff opened it?" I asked.

"No." She replied slowly shaking her head, her eyes wide, and looked from me to the lawman.

"Tom left $5,000, and the land to his children. Hutchinson was holding the money, and was supposed to invest it for Tom." Copeland was saying the right words for Sophie, but I could tell his mind was still on Hutchinson.

I recall Copeland saying he knew the man for near five years. That's a long time to be lied to.

Sophie's tears were misting her eyes as she abruptly sat down, and shook her head. "I...I didn't know," She uttered brokenly.

"No one knew, Mrs. Alexander. Looks like he kept it all to himself under lock and key; making use of the money for himself. But he's been found out, and things will come square for you, and them," he nodded at the children huddled by her side.

"There will be an investigation, and we're likely to find other thefts. I think yours should be settled soon. Maybe even today. It'll depend on what the judge thinks."

"Can the judge be trusted?" I asked straight out.

"GOD I hope so!" Copeland words were pure anguish as he ran a hand through his hair.

"Sophie, how about you, and the children come help me get my supplies bought, and loaded in your wagon? That will give the sheriff time to talk to this Judge Baily. All right with you, sheriff?" I asked.

"Supplies for what?" He asked me right back with interest. Maybe he thought I was going to stay a long time.

"For Sophie's ranch, and my hired hands. Her house is echoing empty of food as you saw for yourself, and when my herd gets to her place; those drovers will be aching for home cooking," I answered his question.

"Your herd?"

"Horses and cattle. You know...livestock." I said, joshing him some. "You're welcome to stop by at Sophie's and see them. We'll pasture there for three or four days before heading out.

Come on, Sophie, we've things to get done. We'll be at that mercantile beyond the bank sheriff," and we left him to his business and sadness.

An hour later he found us just as the last of our supplies were being loaded by a very helpful store owner. Guess the man appreciated the business more than I thought.

Sophie bought carefully, and got everything she needed, including four new, ready-to-wear dresses in beautiful colors that I chose for her, and clothes for the children. Rose Mary was squeezing a new doll, and John Jacob had a new hat, and a toy horse, and Sophie had money left over from the eighty dollars I'd paid her.

The store keep was thanking Sophie again, "Mrs. Alexander, you come back when you need anything more," he said as he laid the last of the purchases in her wagon.

The watch-eyed horses stomped indignantly, and I had to agree with them. But maybe we were thinking on different things. Sophie was overwhelmed by the man's kind words, but responded well, "I will sir. Thank you."

She honed her grammar skills on the merchant as I was watching the Sheriff approach. Catching his eye; I lifted my head, and asked silently. *What?*

"Mrs. Alexander, the judge will meet us at the bank. You ready?" He was in a better mood than when we had left him. I could tell by his tone.

Within another hour, we were headed towards the children's ranch. New papers made Sophie their guardian, and controller of their inheritance. Sophie received a check for $500; the two percent interest that the money should have earned; which she cashed right away. Money sorely needed for the care of the children.

Best of all, the judge declared that J.B. had purchased his ranch for $2,000 just a day after Tom Elders had laid $5000 in his hand to invest for the children. And...finding no other records for another investment for that same amount of Trust money, other than the purchase of cattle, horses, household furnishings, and clothes that came to near $3,000 in the next few weeks of the ranch purchase;

the judge ruled J.B. had bought everything with the Elders' money.

May the Graces forever bless the Judge! For he ruled J.B.'s ranch belonged to the children as a legal investment of their Trust money!

Sophie was stunned to silence as was I!

The children owned 2,000 acres of good land, and a decent sized herd of mixed stock besides their parents 1600 acres!

Our little troupe of one wagon, loaded to near squatting with supplies, three horses, and four people, made it out of town before Sophie began to cry.

"Come ride with me, Mary Rose," I spoke gently, and hauled her from the wagon seat up behind me. "You too, John Jacob. Gram Ma needs to have time alone." I spoke softly to the confused children as I placed the little boy in front of me again.

I kicked Striker up, pulled ahead of the wagon, and let the stallion give the kids a wild ride, and wondered who else the judge was going to make this happy? Who else had Hutchinson stolen from to build up his social status, and bank account?

I didn't have nary a doubt that the judge, and Copeland would be digging deep; along with the bank officials, to find that out.

That evening at supper Sophie ask me to move into the spare bedroom. "Ain't proper for a guest to sleep in the barn," she said smiling broadly.

I smiled with her, and traded the hay bed for hers.


I had arrived at least three days ahead of my herd and having promised each sister I'd get the items they need from a bigger town than ours, I went back to town the next day, and went about the business of getting their buying done. Sheridan sported a better leather goods place than our town did, and I bought a large stock of the quality items; had them all packed, and loaded into Sophie's wagon, along with many items from the seven 'I need' lists of my sisters. I bought another wagon from the livery; filled it with the last of the purchases; tied Striker on to the side near me, and went back to Sophie's ranch.

I hired Abe to drive Sophie's wagon home later. The girls would think it was Christmas when I came hauling all this back home.

Back home...it had a nice ring to it.

Chapter 18

Matt Perkins' crew pushed the herd in about midday the next day, and I met them a mile out on the east side of town. Copeland had sent Billy out with word from the stage driver that my herd was close to town.

Matt had worked for Father, and he agreed to ramrod the drive for Hendrik. Matt brought his pretty young wife, Cassie, and little son, Cotton, clear from Tennessee to start over out here with us. Cotton was one of those white-haired, tow heads that seem to fall out of every tree back in those hills. Everything they owned in the world was in two wagons hitched to eight of my powerful draft horses.

The horses were a breed called Shire, and stood upwards of nineteen hands at the withers. With a short body length, a massively long head; deep set, powerful thick necks, and broad chests; the horses didn't strain much when they were hitched to a pull. They would lean forward on their thick, sturdy legs, and simply walk off.

The breed was out of Scotland.

The bridles, and harnesses were of a huge size, and each was special made for each horse. Father had been overly proud of his drafts; to the point where he'd had brass name tags attached to their jet black harnesses.

Their feet were huge; four times the size of Striker's. I had told Abraham I wanted him to check all my horses when they arrive. We had a fair ways to travel, and I wanted the animals to stay in good shape.

Meeting with Matt, I was pleased to know the small herd of young drafts, riding stock, and Herefords left at Hendrik's, were doing just fine.

You cannot operate a business and farm without stock.

I would trade stock with him in due time. It was a long way to go for breeding stock, but this way the bloodlines would not interbreed, and diminish their quality. The only outside animal we would need to buy were studs and bulls. Hendricks would have them shipped or trailed to me on order from breeders back in Virginia, and I would do the same for him.

Matt reported that Hendrik; his family, and our many friends, were doing well.

I was also pleased to see a bank draft for near $82,000 that completed our land, and timber sales by Tillison, and Hendrik. Some money had trickled into us last fall and winter, but I knew the men handling my money, and didn't worry about payment; it was in good hands.

That included the man who sat his horse opposite me, Matt Perkins, and I had an idea on how to square things with him, for what he had just done for me.

Matt had hired five Tennessee men to help bring the herd to me, along with some household furniture, and items. All five men were familiar faces, and one was an old beau of Say'ards!

Things were going to be quite interesting when HE showed up back home! Jake McFellan had been the most serious of Say'ard's beaus, and apparently she didn't know how serious he was! I always felt she had been a little too high-handed with Jake's attention, and didn't really treat him as she should have. Fact is, I thought she intimidated him, and he let her get away with it! I couldn't believe love is really that blind, but I did have a few weeks to 'educate' Jake. Things could get very interesting!

Our ride through town to the livery with six wagons: twenty-four traced teams of stout horses, along with twelve more mature drafts, and yearlings, caused many folks to stop dead in their tracks to watch us pass.

Why not? We were leading a breed of stock through their town that they had never seen the likes of before. When we stopped at the livery, a crowd had trailed us, and gathered around.

Matt handed the crowd, and their questions over to Jake, while Abraham and Matt saw to the stock.

He was in awe, Abraham was, at the size of my drafts, and he fairly glowed with the pleasure of tending them. Running his hands over their heads, necks, withers, then down their legs, Abraham smiled constantly.

He found only eight horses needed shoes refitted, and Matt hauled the heavy shoes from the gear wagon for him. In two hours Abe was finished, and Matt had hired Abe on as our own blacksmith, which made a lot of sense to me; even if I didn't think of it.

There were still the riding horses to be seen too. That herd of thirty-five was being held with the cattle just outside of town, and would be driven through town, and on to Sophie's place shortly.

Abe would need a wagon to haul his belongings, and smith tools. Matt purchased the last wagon the livery had. When we left Sophie's place for Highwater; Abe would go with us.

We were building ourselves into quite a large group, for with the last wagon purchased we had a total of nine plus the stock.

Matt sent Jake back to get the herd, and we waited for them at the livery. Folks lined the street to watch the Herefords, and riding stock amble slowly through town.

Abe; rooted to the ground; watched the drive move past him, and had a grin on his face that must have hurt. It was that big.

Abe apparently couldn't wait to tend the mounts, for he showed up early the next morning at Sophie's just in time for breakfast.

"You partial to trailing by moonlight?" Matt inquired easily when the man pulled in, and climbed down to tend the tired horses just as dawn was throwing enough light for a body to not run into the side of a building.

"It was rather a peaceful ride, and I smelled Sophie's food cooking clear from town, and couldn't resist!" Abe replied sagely with a smile as big as he was.

"Well then, you'll not be disappointed. The table is fairly groanin' under the load of food spread on it! There's even enough to fill as big a man as you!"

Did I mention Matt was from a line of Irish?

Abe was greeted by everyone again, and hands were warmly shaken. Sophie was as transparent as a piece of quality float glass, as she hovered over her cooking, and kept Abe's coffee cup level full without him asking.

Abe had apparently made a conquest the other evening when he delivered my goods to me.

Mrs. Alexander may have been an older woman, but not that old apparently! As for Abe? He was fitting right in with the crew, but his eyes strayed to Sophie more than was necessary.

I elbowed her as I helped her cook, and wiggled my eyebrows, and she flushed red. As I said before, bringing people together, and watching what may happen, even if this time it was Matt's doings, can be very interesting!

Giving the herd a rest for a few days, the children had the opportunity to run around as children should. Cotton

Perkins was taken under the hand of Mary Rose as a mother hen did her chicks, and John Jacob dragged Cotton to all the places that were sacred, and special to any boy's heart.

Abe tended his blacksmithing chores with a makeshift forge, and more dried apple pie, and coffee than any man had a right to.

None of us were surprised the next day when Abe hitched up the watch-eyed pintos to Sophie's wagon, and gently handed Sophie; dressed in a beautiful green dress and hat, up onto the seat, and headed for town.

If they thought for one minute they were going to get married by themselves; they didn't know the ways of the Irish at all! And there were eight of those folks watching the couple drive away.

Matt and Cassie smiled at me. I smile back, and raised my eyebrows. Matt nodded, and our whole crew raced each other to saddle up. No wagons needed! Matt held Cotton, I held John Jacob and Mary Rose was up behind Cassie as we raced after the soon-to-be newlyweds.

I spoke with Sheriff Copeland, and Judge Bailey in front of the eatery, and asked Copeland to arrange a wedding luncheon at that place, and to join in the wedding. They accepted warmly.

The wedding was a riotous affair as Jeb Morely, our trail cook, insisted on walking Sophie around the preacher's living room twice, on her 'bride walk,' as he referred to it, then straight up to a bursting with happiness, Abraham Geerman.

I was asked to be the maid of honor, and I was honored to take my place beside the typical blushing bride. Sheriff Copeland as asked to be best man by Abe, and dutifully took his place.

The preacher was efficient, and brief. Too brief by my thoughts, and I added my wishes when we were at lunch.

"Sophie? Abraham?" I begin gently, raising my cup of coffee, and brought all to their feet with me except those two. "In my family we extend a special blessing to those who begin a life together. I would give you that blessing:

"I ask that your lives forever be one. May the Graces lovingly protect you, and may you always feel the warmth of each sunrise, and may good fortune always be at your door.

Keep the Magic of each other in your hearts, and hold the Essence of your God in your souls. Extend your hand to those in need, for the sowing of that seed will be returned to you thrice fold.

And this is the most important part my Mother would say," I said with a wink. "Be sure to be a-leavin' a flask, and loaf on your hearth for the Wee Folk of Old so you will earn their trust, and they will bestow their luck on you! Congratulations!"

That word was heartily echoed around the table that was laid heavy with gravy, meats, vegetables, biscuits and a wedding cake. The fare was made short work of by us, and the table talk varied from horses to cattle, to the journey we would begin shortly.

Finally I broached the subject of the children's land to Sophie, "Sophie? Abe? Are you two still going to be leaving with us?" My question brought a few moments of silence as everyone, it seemed, digested the question.

Sophie looked to Abe, took his big hand, and firmly said, "We'll be going with you."

"And the children's ranch? Will you be selling that?" The judge joined in.

"Can I do that?" She questioned carefully.

"Yes Ma'am. It's theirs, and you have legal say for them."

Silence hung heavy on her as she sorted out what was best for her grandchildren, herself, and Abe. "I'll sell," she offered firmly. "What would be a fair price, judge?"

"Well, Mrs. Alex...Geerman, you've already made a small profit on the investment; so I think the return of the principle plus a profit for increase in land, and stock value would be a level even price. But you need something for your place also...say another two thousand for a total of $8,000.

Now you think on that while I tell you that the other folks Hutchinson swindled will be getting re-reimbursed from the many investments he owned. There are a few folks we have to track down, but we'll do it. Hutchinson had enough squirreled away to repay everything and more of what he took."

"Sophie? I know a buyer," I spoke up brightly.

"You's...you do?" she corrected herself, and asked wide eyed.

"That I do. Matt and Cassie here." I nodded to a stunned Matt. "Well, Matt? You came west to have a ranch didn't you? Thirty six hundred acres isn't all that big by western standards, but it's the best in the valley with good grass, and water year round."

"We...we don't have near...the money," Matt whispered as he looked to his wife.

"You would if we threw in together, and raised my herd on both places. Mother always said, "Never gather your eggs all from one nest." Remember? And we can work the details out later today," I continued while he thought on my offer, and held his breath.

"What details?" He finally questioned.

"How much stock I leave with you; what the pay back will be. Percentage split. Things like that. We have a deal?"

He studied his wife, who nodded her head slightly, and reminded him; with a catch in her voice, "Matt. This is an O'Reilly making the offer."

Matt reached across the table, grasped my hand, and the deal was signed. "Judge, will you see to the paperwork for us?" Matt's voice was a little shaky as he was dealing with the good fortune that had fallen in his lap, and the fact that he still wasn't using air properly, probably weakened his words somewhat.

"I would be glad to do that Mr. Perkins, and welcome to the valley," Bailey spoke warmly as he shook hands with Matt and Cassie.

"Tomorrow about four be all right?" Matt asked.

"That's good with me. We'll meet at the court house. Sophie, you come too of course."

Sheriff Copeland entered into the pause of conversation, and deal making with, "You'll like your home. It's a fine place to raise a family and build a life."

I noticed Sophie was quiet, and no longer eating. The thoughts in her head must have been whirling like a strong wind! This woman had gone from near poverty to having several thousand dollars cash money, a new husband, people who would stand with her, and a new life waiting for her...all at once! That much good fortune would stun anyone.

I'd provide the money to Matt and Cassie to buy the two places, and leave them enough to live on for two years as back-up. Adding the cost of a ranch and crew, I thought thirty thousand would be enough.

There would be a sale of all the Hutchinson's stock along with the children's this fall, leaving only young steers for meat on the ranches. I'd leave starter herds of cattle and horses for him to increase, and he'd repay me upon their sale. He had to put the work of training and care into them, and pay me 60% of the profit.

We'd be partners for years, and the time would come when he'd buy me out.

The sale of one well-trained draft horse would fetch hundreds of times more than the two percent interest that was the going rate on a loan now-a-days, and the money would be in our hands the whole time.

We left the Geermans to head for the smaller ranch, mounted up, and went towards Matt and Cassie's new home. Sheriff Copeland rode with us to handle any questions, or problems we might run into with Hutchinson's crew.

We had the children with us, and therefore we weren't looking for trouble.

Sheriff Copeland took the lead at the Perkins Ranch, and explained to Mrs. Hutchinson, the hired hands, right down to the cook and house staff, that Hutchinson had been found out, arrested, and waiting trail.

Mrs. Hutchinson was hard eyed as she glared at the sheriff, but gathered her personal things; climbed into the wagon that was brought from the shed, and let Sheriff Copeland escort her into town.

I had the distinct knowing that she was aware of where the money came from that she had lived so well on, and her life would not be so easy from now on. She'd probably separate herself from J.B. as soon as she could.

These folks hadn't been to town, and no one had brought them word on Hutchinson's new living quarters, as the man usually spent a few days of the week in town and I detected a note of sadness in the sheriff's voice as he made the announcement.

The men had a choice of staying or going, and four decided to quit when they learned the new owners were southerners, but four of our men, all unmarried, took their place. These men, along with two who had worked for Hutchinson, would deliver my herd, then all six would return here to work for Matt.

We spent a half hour going through the place. It was way more impressive than mine, but J.B. had had a good supply of money.

Matt and I talked after the tour, and settled on an agreement. My herd would be split 70/30, with me taking the 70. We would split the draft horses evenly, but I would again take 70 percent of the riding horses, but half of the ones left in his care were pregnant mares. The race horses would not be split; they were all mine.

Any money from dealings; timber mainly, not connected to the horses and cattle would be his, but we would do a 60/40 split on any profit on my stock sales. Matt would deduct the expenses of my stock, but not his labor. He would also hold 50 percent of breeding fees. Usually such arrangement ran closer to a 20/80 percent, but I wanted a partner I could trust, and one that was set up to prosper.

Early the next morning, we divvied up the stock, drove a herd of one hundred and four head of cattle, and horses into a large pasture at Matt's, and spent an hour or two trouping in and out of their home, unloading their goods from their wagons while Cassie gave directions.

I don't know why they needed more furniture because the large home was grandly furnished to overflowing already.

Cassie solved part of the problem by loading up the wagons again with some of JB's furniture, and gave it to me! I was speechless and Cassie hugged me tightly, and whispered through her tears. "Thank you so very, very much Kate!" She was moving more furniture into Sophie's ranch also.

Mr. and Mrs. Geerman finally showed up, and got the grand tour from the Perkins. The main house was large, with two levels, wrap around porches, and a grand staircase. It reminded me of our home back in Tennessee.

The out buildings of two large barns, machinery shed, bunkhouse, and attached cook shack, with the smelly pig/chicken pens located well behind the barns; were very efficiently arranged. All were painted red with short, grazed, grass around everything. It was picture perfect.

As I said, it was a far better place than my own, but I wasn't envious. My ranch would take shape at its own pace, and would look very different.

After the noon meal, served on the long, formal dining table to everybody; including the men who stayed on from Hutchinson, and who couldn't believe they were sitting where they were; those of us who needed to, went to town to finalize the selling of the children's property. The rest of our combined crews took a break.

I put Jake McFallen in as trail boss in Matt's place.

I was happy at how things were working out, but my night dream wasn't so far back in my mind that I'd forgotten it. I was still trying to make sense of it, as I worked over in my mind the contract Matt, and I had made.

By partnering with him, I would have plenty of room on my land to raise stock. He would raise more stock for me, and we wouldn't overgraze either ranch. It was a good contract.

Chapter 19

Cool gray dawn of the fourth day brought us into cold saddles, hard wagon seats, and my stock to their feet.

Jeb Morely, the cook, took point, and set our pace. The other wagons strung out along both sides of, and slightly ahead of the herd, but behind Jeb, and on the up wind side whenever possible. Nine outriders rode where needed. Abe was one.

Jake was a good trail boss, Abe could push stock and Sophie didn't have any problems driving their heavy wagon, with the children, when they weren't riding with me or Abe.

Abe's blacksmithing tools were in one of my wagons along with some items for the girls.

From Tennessee to Sheridan, only six young stock had been lost. They had been born shortly before the trip started. Coyotes took two down, and one got head butted by one of the bulls. That one, and the one that broke a leg, became supper for the crew, and the last two calves were swept off downstream in a river crossing. I didn't wish to lose any more in the twenty days or so it would take to see me home.

"Do you love Say'ard?" Jake and I were riding drag, and enjoying not eating dust, for a light rain had fallen last night wetting everything down proper. A week had come and gone, and we were leaving more miles behind every day. We were making good time, and were a full day ahead of my schedule.

"Yes. With all's that's in me," he replied sincerely.

"Yet you let her push you around," I said flatly. My tone carried just a hint of reprimand.

"Yeah, I know. I don't know how to win her except let her rule, but I'm full set on trying."

"Well, you should push back; ignore her, or tell her where you stand. What YOU want."

"I'd lose her for sure that way." He sounded hopeless, half afraid, and hopeful, all at the same time.

"Then I suggest you just claim her; quietly, and gently walk right up to her, and tell her how you feel. Open your heart. Let her think the decision has to be hers. Then walk away. If she loves you, she'll make the move."

"That would be…"

"Manipulatin', connivin', and the only way to handle my headstrong sister," I interrupted with a broad smile.

"Jake, I'm not above begging you to take her off my hands." I sounded as mournful as I could. "She's just more troublesome than the rest of my sisters all added up together. But if you've not the nerve to handle your woma…"

"I can handle her! It's just…I don't think a husband should have to 'handle' his wife."

"Say'ard NEEDS handling, but just a little," I responded quickly. Maybe getting him into a riled up state of mind would be all he needed to get him out of this passiveness he'd allowed Say'ard to put him in. Jake, it seemed, was a gentle giant.

"You know, Jake, if you pick her up, and get her off the ground…"

"Stop, Kate! I won't force her!"

"Nope. I'm just saying kiss her 'til she stops pushin' on you, and sees things your way. That's all I'm saying." I had my palm out to him, making him listen as I piled on more advice. "She does like a strong, take charge man.

"You go ahead and think on things awhile. We still have near two weeks of travel, but remember, it only took Abe a day to win Sophie."

I'd given Jake another way of pursuing the taming of my sister the shrew. That way being Abe. For now I'd let Jake settle things out in his mind because I'd made up my mind to haul Say'ards behind out of that saloon when I got back! And Jake was my way of going about it. Better still...he could do it for me!

As for Jake, I watched him riding more with Abe in the following week, and needn't have been a mind reader to know what they talked about.


Little John Jacob took to riding with me almost every day right from the start. He was also getting talkative. His questions were kid questions like: "What's that?" "Do cows think?" "Why don't birds fall down from up there?"

His little brain put mine to the test!

Bless his little wondering mind! I was glad to hand him back to Sophie most of the time. The one time I didn't want to hand him back, was the day he asked me in a very, very hushed voice, "Is that man, the dark one who's with my Gram, is he my Gramps now? And why is he dark?"

I searched around in my brain for a 'kid' answer to his question until I realized he wasn't asking a kid question. "Let's go find a place to sit a spell," I said gently. "I want to talk with you about your question."

"All right," he whispered back.

I looked Jake up, told him we were going for a ride, and be back soon, and turned Striker off towards a hill to our left which happened to be upwind of the herd. It was a fairly tall mound without trees, and it was covered with a splattering of large gray rocks.

I chose a patch of grass for Striker, and John Jacob chose a rock for us to sit on. It had a big angled notch almost at the top for us to sit in. We could see the herd, and everyone below us.

I began to talk easy, but seriously.

"Yes John Jacob, that man is now your Grampa. He's here to take care of, and love your Gramma, you, and Mary Rose. Do you know what I mean by 'love,' John Jacob?" I asked softly as I put him on my lap, and wrapped my arms around him.

"I's reckon so," he quietly answered.

"Well, I know you love that old dog of yours, and I saw how happy you were when your horses came home. That's love. That's when you care for something, or someone very much, and you want to be with them, and take care of them; watch out for them, and see to their needs. Do you understand what I'm saying?"

"Yes'em, I does," he spoke after a pause of deep thinking.

"Your Gramma is very happy, and that's why they married each other. So, are you happy with him making Gramma happy, and being your Grampa?" This time his answer was given with a firm head nod.

"Yes'em, I's happy. But. Why's he so dark?"

I thought swiftly, searching my mind for a comparison that would explain to this child in my arms the difference of color, and color not meaning a blessed thing!

"Look down there John Jacob," I pointed towards the stock below us. "See the pinto horses pulling your wagon? They're red and white. Right?"

"Yes'em."

"See the other horses? How many colors are they?"

"Three," he said holding up five fingers, which made me smile.

"What about the big wagon horses?"

"They be whitish."

"And my horse over there eating grass?"

"He be black," the child squinted over to look at the stallion noisily chomping grass. "But whats about Grampa? He ain't no horse."

*One problem solved. Abe was now Grampa in the child's mind.* "Well, as you can see, the horses are different colors, and sizes, but they're ALL horses. Right?"

John Jacob looked at Striker a while, and then out over the moving line of stock before he softly said, "Right."

*Good! All right, here goes!* I thought, and took a breath. "People are like those horses. We come in different sizes, and colors. Didn't know that, did you?" I squeezed, and shook him gently.

"Yes I does! I's seen some brown people, but they spoke funny, and I's didn't know what theys said."

"That's something else about people. We speak lots of different ways, not just English. English is how you, and I talk.

When we get to my place, one of my sisters has lots of books, and she'll show you pictures of people in all different colors. Red, white, brown, yellow, and black; like your Grampa.

That difference is what makes the world very interesting, because we not only are different colors, and talk different; we live different, and eat different foods, and some people don't even ride horses."

"Theys don't?"

"Nope. Sometimes they ride a really funny looking animal called a camel."

"What's a camel?" He asked with a scowl.

"There is a picture in one of the school books. I'll show it to you when we get home. Is that all right?"

"Yes 'em," he said slowly, but I could tell he didn't quite believe me.

"But John Jacob, we are all people. Just like all horses are horses. And it really doesn't matter the color of a person; that's just on the outside, like horses are, and we can't change that. But what really matters most of all; is what we are on the inside. Here, in our hearts." I whispered softly to him, and watched his face as I touched my palm to his chest.

"If you're a good, loving person who cares for others, people or animals, that's all that truly matters. Do you understand what I'm saying?"

His beautiful brown eyes held mine for a long, quiet moment. "Like Grampa Abe is good?"

"Yes. Like Grampa Abe is good,"

"Is I's good?" he questioned suddenly.

"You're more than good! You're great!" I choked out as I hugged him close.

"Does yous like me?" This question startled me, and was filled with the hope of me wanting him, and he was more than damned serious!

"Yes, I LIKE you, but more than that, I surely do love you!" I whispered from my very soul.

His little arms went around my neck, and I let time march right past us as I rocked him in my arms.

*This is the innocence of children,* I realized, and something the Graces had just re-enforce in my soul.

Later, and after supper when I saw John Jacob climb up into Abe's lap, I knew the child had accepted what I'd said, and took his new Grampa into his little heart. Watching from a distance, I felt the swelling fullness of happiness for them; what they had, and surely was proud to be part of what I watched.

The next day I found that I'd lost my little riding partner to Abe, and that was all right.

The days were bright, clear, and the air cool. Gold sunrises gave way to sapphire blue skies, crowned by white wavy clouds that deepened into purple clouds lined by pink reflections of the setting sun.

While we pushed the stock, I slowly led Jake into believing that Say'ard needed a strong, take-charge man. Firm yet gentle and IN control. To win Say'ard, he just needed a little inside help. Who better on the inside than me? Maybe if I worked this right, Say'ard would be someone else's worry. Now THAT had a nice ring to it, but I really thought Abe had more of a hand in helping Jake than I did.

Men had a way of understanding one another.

As the days followed each other, Abe and I coached Jake. He was getting the message, but I made it clear that everything depended on him; not what we said.

Now maybe you recall one of the Rules? The one about lying? I wasn't about to break that Rule; it's just I

KNEW Say'ard. I really did know her. Her wants, needs, dreams, faults, and the kind of man it would take to ride herd on her. Jake had the love in his heart to be that man; I just hoped he had the nerve!

Jake was a good-looking man with a charming wit, and square chin. He had reddish brown hair, and most of all, he was Irish. I let him know just how important to us O'Reilly's a man of the blood was. Now don't get me wrong, Jake knew his faults, his strengths, and what he wanted. He'd made up his mind to marry, and Say'ard was the woman he set out to have. She would have to be impressed by a man who traveled the most part of two thousand miles to claim her! I surely was!

Throughout my ride to Sheridan, and now trailing the herd back home enjoying the beauty of the land, I still had a dark feeling riding around in my mind. I couldn't see it. I couldn't shake it off; identify it, and it was starting to worry me more than I cared. The dream came often; maybe because I dwelled on it during the day. I don't know.

The herd was apparently getting tired of the long walk from Tennessee, and wandered farther out of line than we wanted. We were constantly ranging from the main line of travel to recapture the wayward stock. Jeb and Abe solved the problem at just about the same time by tying two cows to the last wagon. The sight of the cows in front of them plodding along placidly, pulled the rest of the herd along without any more problems.

We moved into the homestretch as I saw the town of Highwater on the horizon the morning of the sixteenth day.

When we picked the road up far outside of town, the travel became smoother, and faster for the wagons, and a few local people passed us on their way into town. I hadn't any doubts my sister would receive word of our arrival.

We were ahead of my schedule by four days, and I was home.

But there was still that 'something' bothering me. It was much stronger today, for last night the same dark dream of Striker and I had come again.

Chapter 20

The first week of September lay upon the shoulders, and peaks of these mountains when we drove the herd into town.

Jake was nervous, and kept wiping his hands on his thighs. He was somewhat amusing, for I knew this man had ridden a pretty hard trail getting here, but the thought of Say'ard had him sweating like an anxious race horse! Love was a four letter word that had just about taken the wind clean out of this grown man!

The town folk came out of doorways to watch us push the mixed herd through town, and the dark feeling I had been carting around, was now so heavy, I could hardly breathe!

I glanced around, and saw nothing unusual. Nothing seemed out of sorts. Nothing to help lift that dark feeling from me.

Up ahead at the bookstore Mary stood waiting. I saw Say'ard, Ellen, Hal, and Matilda join her from across the street. Say'ard and Til were dressed for riding. I grew tense, my back came up straighter, and there was a cold quiver in my belly. Whatever the dark feeling of dread I had been dreaming about was here; now; waiting for me, and the Graces were ominously silent.

I was scared, and not like it was with the bear. This was a helpless kind of scared. Something bad had descended on my family, and I hadn't been here to try to stop it!

Jane brought Shannon from the store, and to stand in front of the others. Say'ard had stopped next to a pack horse. He was one of ours, and geared for a long haul. Hank and Chuck stood next to the same horse, and had their hats in their hands.

Jake sided me as I reined in in front of my family.

Shannon was crying.

The sheriff, an older man; wise in years, but not up to the hardness this job seemed to demand from him; came up alongside Striker. Art Curtland looked up at me with the sad eyes of a grandfather, and whatever it was he had to tell me was hurting him deeply. I glanced at my sisters, found them pale, and sad.

"Where's Meagan?" The voice that came from my mouth echoed in my head, and came from a hollow space deep inside me.

"Kate. Kate she's not with us anymore," Art said softly. "Yesterday three men robbed the bank, and one shot Meagan. She was dead before she hit the floor. We killed two of them. I should say Matilda did, but the third man; the one that shot Meagan, got away."

Art stopped speaking for a moment while I tried to take it all in; except I couldn't. I surely couldn't believe my little sister was dead!

Shannon! I pulled my eyes to her. Her sister! Her TWIN sister was dead! The pain she must be feeling made mine feel small!

I leapt down, and gathered her to me just as she started to wilt to the ground. She clung to me like a lost waif, and I hugged her tight! Bending down; I scooped her small body into my arms, and with our sisters following; I went into the bookstore, and someone closed the door. We needed privacy. We needed to talk. We needed family.

Muffled sounds from outside told part of my mind that the crew was pushing the herd on through town. Hank and Chuck would show them the way to our ranch.

I sat in a big chair near the stove for long time, rocking, and holding Shannon. I listened to her sobs, as I listened to Matilda tell the short time it had taken for someone to kill our Meagan.

"It was just past noon Sis. There were five or six people in the bank lobby area. These three men came in, and I knew what they were going to do. Like you get a feeling sometimes? You just know?

I dropped my hand to my gun lying in my cash drawer. They pulled guns, gave their orders, and everyone did as they were told; including me. One went to Earl's window, and one took things from the customers. The men were disarmed, and everyone was told to line up on the wall. Earl emptied his drawer, and they forced him to the wall. Then the man came to my window.

The door opened, the third man wheeled, and shot. It was Meagan; Shannon was right behind her. Meagan fell backward. Shannon caught her, and they both fell down.

I grabbed my pistol, and shot the man in front of me. I tried for the man who shot Meg, but I missed, and he went out the door over the girls. I put a bullet in the other man. The whole thing was over in an instant, and I ran to the girls.

Meg had taken the shot high in the throat. She died quick Sis. She never knew any pain.

Shannon was covered with blood, and I gathered her up, and started for Jane's. The girls met me, and we took her the rest of the way; cleaned her up; changed her clothes, and tried to soothe her. That's all there is to tell you Sis. Except; I tried. I really tried to kill him! I'm sorry Kate! I'm so very sorry!"

'Til was crying deeply, and losing control. I gave Shannon off to Jane; went to 'Til; pulled her to me, and held her tightly.

"It's all right 'Til. You did just fine. Don't be sorry. Don't ever be sorry. You did the best any one of us could have done."

My tears were falling as freely as hers and my other sisters. I cried for 'Til, for Meg, for our parents, for the long days, of hard work, and for the injustice done. And I cried for me. When my tears finally stopped, I found out they hadn't helped, or changed a damned thing! Meagan was still dead, and her laughter was only an echo to us now.

"Why didn't anyone go after him?" I spoke with a bitterness that I tasted on my tongue. "Art and most of the town men were still here."

"I told them not to Kate," Say'ard said. "Art is the only law and an old man. The rest are businessmen, rancher, and farmers. They have families to stay here for. Meagan was ours. This is our chase. I told Art to deputize you, me, and 'Til. We'll go after him. Everything's packed, and ready to go. We can leave right after the burial...today."

I looked at Say'ard as she spoke. She'd aged somewhat since I'd left. They all had. I wondered if we'd ever be the singing, happy family we were a month or so ago?

I nodded to Say'ard, "You're right Say'ard. It's our chase," but I knew this was my job.

I had forgotten about Jake, and I think Say'ard had too, but he was standing by the door beside Hal; hat in hand.

"Say'ard, Jake rode from Tennessee to marry you. You'd better go speak to him," I told her with no ridicule in my words. The feeling of gaiety or cut-downs wouldn't be in us for some time to come.

She nodded, and went to Jake. "Jake, I'm going with 'Til, and Kate. When we get back, I'll marry you. You'll just have to wait a while longer for me. I've loved you a good long while, and it hurt to leave you behind, but you couldn't come with me then, but you're here now, and when this is done; we can be together."

She turned away, not giving him time to speak, opened the door, and asked Art to come in. "Art," Say'ard spoke clear, and firm. She had made up her mind. "We're going after him. You can deputize us now?"

"You can't be serious! You're women!" He spoke in disbelief.

"We're women to reckon with Art," I said quietly. "We're going with, or without your blessing. Make up your mind."

He looked me up and down. I was wearing my trail clothes. Pants, chaps, vest, shirt, hat, boots, and a gun belt. He looked at all of us, then back to me, raised his hand, and we took his oath, and he went to his office for the warrant, and our badges.

Jake had started to object to everything he heard, but Say'ard stopped him flat. "When we're man and wife Jake, you can have it your way, but not now. This time it has to be my way." With that said, Say'ard kissed Jake passionately in front of everyone, and amid all the sorrow; his smile and shining eyes; filled with pure love, were a sight to behold.

Jane handed me a piece of paper. I didn't need to ask what it was, for I knew it was a drawing of the man who killed our Meg, and I handed her the two bank drafts I carried and kept some cash money for travelling.

"I described him to Shannon, and with what she could recall, she drew him out for us. It's an exact likeness," Til said.

I turned to Shannon; her eyes were wider than ever, and full of grief. The fear was still in them too. "We'll be back before you know it Imp, and with your picture; we'll get him for sure. Don't be afraid for us little Sis. There's three of us going, and we'll take care of each other. You let Jake, Hank, Hal, and Chuck, take care of all of you while we're gone," I whispered gently. "Right now Imp, let's go tell Meg goodbye," I said as I pulled her to me again.

Tears welled up in her eyes as I spoke as I had heard our Mother speak: "Save the tears for happiness Imp like Mother used to say. Remember? 'Tears don't do a thing for those gone, but they surely put meaning to the living. Let's all save our tears for happier times. All right?"

"Oh, Katie." Imp's childish voice, filled with pain yet grown old in the past two days, twisted at my heart!

Our parents had taught us that we should not harbor hatred for anyone, but a hate started deep in my soul as I stood by Meagan's grave. I felt it swell until I nearly burst. Slowly it drained down, and settled itself in my hurting heart. In that intense emotion of hate, I heard the faint whisper of Mother's voice. *We have her. Give justice to her Kate.*

A hard, cold, vengeful feeling rose inside me, and I gave it voice. Silently I told Mother and Meg, *One way or another; I will give you Justice Sis. I promise."*

I carried a great hate for a man I'd never laid eyes on, for he had taken from us, someone who would never be replaced. Someone who would never quite leave us, but never again share our lives. The man was mine. My sisters would ride with me, but this was my job, and this bastard was mine!

The Reverend was saying, for my benefit I do believe: "Vengeance is mine, sayeth the Lord."

The man was right, but as for the Lord, I'd send this man to Him to do with as He wished, for the Graces didn't have a use for such scum!

This was the shadow that had haunted me for so long. That shadow took the form of a heartless killer, and he had hurt my family beyond measure. If I were to be the instrument of his justice, so be it. I couldn't stop this from happening, but I sure as hell would hand him O'Reilly justice!

## Chapter 21

The temperature had dropped during the mid-afternoon services, and as I pulled my body up on Striker, he stood steady beneath me, as if he could feel the way I felt, and knew the job ahead was deadly serious.

The chill that slid over the high valley as we rode out didn't take any heat from my soul.

Hal was going to off saddle Striker and tack a fresh mount for me, but I said softly, "I need Striker for this."

Jake rode beside Say'ard for a little way, and 'Til and I gave them privacy by riding on ahead. She caught up with us, and we settled into an easy lope that would cover a lot of ground by nightfall.

The peacefulness of yesterday seemed eons ago. It was hard to shake the feeling that Meg wouldn't be waiting for us, and it didn't seem real that we were hunting a murderer.

But we were.

His trail was easy to follow, for he was riding hard; the horse making deep tracks, for the man had been in too much of a hurry to hide his trail. His sign was an open book to us. We could all read trail sign. Broken Wing, an old Creek family friend from our childhood, had taught us. Father had hired him on, and he taught us well by demanding, it seemed at the time, impossible things from us, but now those teachings were going to pay off.

'Til had said the horse the man was riding was a flea-bitten gray. Gray flecked with brown. Not too uncommon a color. The left hind shoe had a nail bent down at the outside of the hoof; instead of up along the hoof leaving a little hole in the ground beside the shoe print.

He was a big man, for the hoof prints were deep; indicating a heavy load. He had stopped at a small water seep, and his rundown boots with uneven heels showed an oblong chunk was missing from the edge of the left heel; like he had stepped on a hot coal at a campfire, burning or melting the indentation. Whatever made it, it marked him well for us, and he probably didn't know it was there.

He smoked. Not unusual again. Most men did. He rolled his own, for a paper lay on the ground where he had stopped for water. Again, not too outstanding a single item, but added to the hoof nail, burnt boot heel, and the gray horse; it was helpful. Leaving the paper was a bit careless on his part, but by now, as far behind him as we were, he probably didn't think anyone was after him.

The temperature kept dropping as night slid over us, and knowing we wanted to remain silent, and out of sight; we made a cold camp. Neither of my sisters complained as we ate cold food, and huddled together for warmth in a bed made of our heavy deer hide coats, and blankets.

The next morning we found his night camp hidden in a swale full of dry brush.

Matilda stood guard as Say'ard and I worked out the camp sign. It would have been hard to creep up on anyone with all the dry branches, and leaves on the ground. He had chosen well. Maybe he was smarter than we thought, for the camp ashes had been picked up, scattered, and the area had been feathered out with a branch; including his tracks for a quite a ways. But we worked out his trail anyway.

Luck was with us for the heavy moist air had intensified the arid smoke smell of the ashes, and led us to the camp. With the two of us working at it; we put the camp sign together in short order, and trailed him to where he had bedded down, and tied the horse.

A piece of broken rein lay half hidden under a bush near where the horse had been tied. I picked it up, and put it in my saddle bag; another link to tie him to us. The broken rein told me the man was border line poor, for a man with money always tended to have good tack.

The size of his body print showed a man over six feet tall, and wide of shoulder.

"A man that size should be working for a living," Say'ard noted.

"He is," 'Til answered her, "He's working at staying free, and alive."

"Not for long Sis. Not for long," I breathed out softly.

We took the time to water the horses again, and graining them a couple of handfuls each; we mounted up. Say'ard led out.

The murderer was still moving fast; covering his tracks where he could, and riding hard where he couldn't. Matilda voiced the fact that this could turn into a long chase. Say'ard and I accepted that statement as a possible fact.

He knew things we didn't. He knew where he could find friends, where to go for help, water, and shelter. He knew the towns, lay of the land, and he knew he could ambush us at anyone of a hundred places.

On the other hand, I knew one thing that he couldn't know, or maybe even understand if he did know. The one thing that outweighed all his knowledge.

I didn't intend to turn back. Ever.

## Chapter 22

We were two weeks on his trail when we followed him to a town in Idaho territory. It was a small, robust, town that had a muddy quagmire that passed as a street. Boards were laid across in places for the folks to tread across on. It didn't boast a sign board, or anything with a name on it. It was just a town.

The weather had warmed some in the past few days, and the occasional snow had changed to frequent rain showers. The mountain slopes were a rich golden landscape; heavy with the last of fall's colors that clung to the Aspens. A clear, blue sky kept watch over us, but I could feel the coming winter in the north wind.

"'Til? See if you can find a post office or stage depot, and send word back to the girls". Say'ard voiced.

"All right. No use letting them fret any more than necessary," 'Til replied, "Where are you two going to be?"

I'd been looking around as we rode in. "Probably be a good idea to get some supplies. Say'ard? Will you do that? I need some personal things. It's close to my time. I'll find the local law, and I'll meet you both there." I spoke quietly, not wanting too many folks to overhear us. We split up and rode off.

The jail was laid-up brick work with a heavy double-planked door. The place looked about as unpleasant a place as I'd ever seen. On the other hand, I reckoned jails weren't supposed to be hospitable. This one wasn't.

The town sheriff was a lean, well built, dark and handsome man, with hard green eyes. I showed him the drawing without saying a word as I made a scan of his wanted posters on the wall.

As I said, he was handsome, but he didn't do a thing for my heart.

"Sheriff, my name is Kate O'Reilly. Have you seen this man within the last day or so," I said indicating the paper he held.

He had stood up when I came in, and he towered over me. I'm an even six foot, very tall for a woman, and tall as many men yet he was a couple of inches over my height.

Sheriff or not, he was a gentleman raised. "Ma'am. Please sit down. You look like you've come a long way."

His questions were easy and probing. All right, let him probe. I'd answer what I wanted in my own fashion.

"Thank you," I said taking the chair he held for me. "Yes, I've come a long way. Judith Basin in Montana Territory."

"Judith Basin? That's a two, two and half week ride from here." He glanced down at the drawing like he was studying it.

"You're after this man?" His question was redundant. Why would I hunt up the law if I wasn't after this man?

"Yes."

"Why?"

"He robbed a bank back there, and killed a bystander."

"Why didn't the law come for him?"

"I am the law. Deputized by Sheriff Curtland. I have a warrant for this man's arrest."

"You have a name on him?"

"No." I studied the man. What was I missing here?

"You're sure this is the man?"

Something about the way he asked that last question caught my attention. Then it hit me! He KNEW the man!

"You know him don't you?" I pared.

"Let me see your warrant and badge."

I handed him both. One at a time. He leaned back, tilted his chair on the two back legs, and looked at me steadily. I had the uneasy feeling of being sized up for a coffin.

"You sure you want to find him?"

"I'm sure. Who is he?"

Taking a deep breath, he let it out slowly. "The name's Alan Stillwell. He's got a bad reputation. He's wanted in most of the territories for robbery, and murder."

"Do you know where around here he might be found?" I spoke easy; trying to hide my anxiety! I had a name to go with the drawing!

"I hear tell he visits Ruby's place. I've never seen him though. He slips in, and out before I know it."

"Where's Ruby's place located?" I asked, starting to rise from the chair.

"You don't want to go there."

"That's not your concern. I'll go where I need to. Where is it?" I was done with his questions, and was irritated at being held off.

"Over on the west side, outside of the town limits. You can't miss it. It's painted bright red."

"Thank you. Is there anything else you have to give me, anything at all, no matter how small it may seem?" I asked.

"No, not really. Why are you so hell-bent on finding him? Excuse the remark, but you're a woman, and most men wouldn't want to meet Stillwell; much less go looking for him!"

I might as well tell him as it surely wasn't a secret. Besides, all he had to do was contact Art, and ask.

"He killed a fifteen-year-old girl in that holdup, for no reason. He shot her in the throat. She was my sister."

The sheriff was a good man, and knew the hardness that men could fall to, but I could see his jaw set a little more when I told him about Meg.

"I'll go with you to Ruby's," he said as he reached for his hat.

We went outside to find Say'ard, and 'Til, sitting in front of the jail on their horses on either side of Striker.

"Sheriff these are my sisters; Say'ard and 'Til. The sheriff's going with us across town to a place called Ruby's. We might luck out," I said.

"By the way sheriff, what's your name?" I asked.

"Harrigan. Ray Harrigan."

The sheriff touched his hand to his hat to my sisters. He looked a little bit longer at 'Til I noticed, and she looked right back.

I walked to Striker as the sheriff went to his horse. We mounted up, turned, and rode four abreast down the muddy street.

More than a few folks took notice of us, and one or two hurried out of our way. There was a look about us that could not be mistaken.

I held the reins left-handed as my right thumb slipped the hammer string off my hip gun, and I held the grip. I didn't need to glance at Say'ard to know she, and 'Til, had done the same, and the sheriff didn't miss any of our actions. My whip was around my shoulder.

Ruby's place was bright red, and looked like what it was; a whore house. A block back, 'Til swung out to the left, and Say'ard went right. I went straight with the sheriff.

Tying our horses to a hitching rail off to the side of the building, we went to the door, and the sheriff knocked as I eased to the handle side of the door jam.

After some time passed, a woman opened the door. She wore a gaudy orange dress that clashed with her dyed red hair, and red lip color. More of her hung out of that dress then was in it.

"Ruby," the sheriff said as he touched his hat. *Still the gentleman, even here.* I thought. *Impressive.*

"Ruby, is Stillwell here?" He asked her quietly, touching a finger to his lips.

"What do you want him for? "

"He killed a fifteen year old girl over in Judith Basin. Is he here?" Ray Harrigan asked again.

"He's here, but you don't want to tangle with him Ray. Besides, my place is outside the town limits, and your jurisdiction."

"But it's NOT outside mine!" I gritted out harshly as I pushed her aside, and moved inside. "I've a warrant for his arrest. Which room is he in?"

I was angry or mad, and I didn't take the time to figure out which.

"And just WHO the HELL do you think YOU are?" Ruby sneered at me.

"She's a deputy acting for the sheriff of Judith Basin," Ray said. "What room is he in, Ruby? I won't ask again."

"This floor, last room on the left," she said with her hands on her hips, and a jerk of her fake red hair.

Ray finished moving through the doorway, around Ruby. She reeked of cheap perfume, stale smoke, and sweat.

She hadn't bathed in a while either.

Easing down the hall, we each had our guns in hand, but we hadn't reached the halfway point in the hall when a shot rang out behind us, and we wheeled; our weapons pointing; to see Ruby with a pistol in her hand pointed at the floor, and I almost squeezed off a shot.

"Alan! It's the law!" She screamed.

Ray and I spun back around, and raced down the hallway. Ray put a good, solid kick to the door, and took a bullet along his left ribs in return for his actions.

He went down, and I fired over him; splintering the window frame where Stillwell's head had just been.

I should NOT have missed that shot!

I leapt for the window; took a headlong roll out of it, and heard shots fired around the back of the house as I landed.

Gaining my feet, I ran to the corner, and around the back of the building. A horse's hind quarters were going out of sight behind the outhouse, and Say'ard was firing at the horse and rider from her side of the alley.

She didn't hit him, but he had hit 'Til! She was down near the back door with a bloody thigh. She was white with pain, holding her leg, and rocking her upper body in agony, but mad as hell with anger!

"I didn't get him Kate! He's got my bullet in him, but I failed again! I can't shoot for beans!" She said through her clinched teeth. Her pain was intense and she was just short of tears.

"It's all right 'Til. We caught up with him once, and we'll do it again. Besides, your bullet will slow him down some." Say'ard talked quietly to her as I knelt, and tied off the leg wound with 'Til's neck scarf.

Standing up, I spoke to Say'ard, "The sheriff's been hit. I'm going back inside to see about him."

"The sheriff!" 'Til spoke quickly. Too quickly I thought with half a smile, and as I turned to leave, I could hear 'Til saying, "Say'ard? Get me up!"

I went in through the back door of Ruby's. Ray, with blood all over the front and side of his shirt, was leaning against a connecting hall wall, confronting Ruby, but I couldn't see her.

"Drop it Ruby. You're under arrest for helping Stillwell escape," he was saying. Her gun was leveled on him, and his on her.

"Hell Ray, I've lived a good life, enjoyed men, and a hell-of-a-lot of money. Been places, and seen things most women wouldn't have the guts to do. But there's one place I ain't been, and that's jail, and I ain't about to take up residence in one now!" She was arrogant in her words, and stance.

Ray knew I was there, and kept talking as I slipped back around the building, and through the window I rolled out of just minutes before. Ruby's back was just visible to the side of the room's open door, but she couldn't see me without leaning back and turning her head, and she wasn't about to take her eyes from Ray.

I uncoiled my whip, and laid a streak across her back; drawing a welt of blood from the bare flesh. She shrieked; jerked backwards, and Sheriff Harrigan knocked her gun to the floor with his.

I figured Ruby didn't fit the description of a lady, and the names she called me right then proved my theory. That poor excuse for a woman used words I have not EVER heard!

"Shut up Ruby." Ray threatened, with nothing to back up his words.

"Go to HELL!" she screamed at him.

When she turned to yell at me, I laid my whip handle hard alongside her head, and things got real quiet as the lady in orange crumpled to the floor.

Ray looked at me, Say'ard, and 'Til, as they had come up behind Ray by now, and he glanced at them. They both shrugged, Say'ard smiled, but 'Til's smile was a grimace as she clung to Say'ard.

"It's been a rather interesting morning I'd say," Say'ard said lazily.

"I wouldn't put it quite like that," Ray said in acknowledgement through clinched teeth, and asked 'Til, "Are you hurt bad?"

"Bad enough I'm afraid," Sis replied tensely.

Ruby was coming around, and Ray handed me the cuffs. I put them on her none too gently. Ray told Say'ard where the doc's place was, and we took 'Til out; put her on her horse, Patches, and Say'ard started walking off with her.

"I'll take Ruby to your office for you. You go on to the doc's with the girls." I told Ray, and I could feel the tension still in me as I pushed him into the saddle.

"'Preciate that Miss O'Reilly. "

Ruby had come to life enough to discover her mouth still worked. "Keep your...hands off 'n me!"

Now THAT sort of talk made me see red! Not like the fake red that this woman had attached to her head either! Angry red and the kind of anger that makes you cold, and dead calm inside. The kind of calm that destruction is born from.

Backed up by what Stillwell had done to my family, and the fact that this woman had helped him get away; I'd had all I was going to take from her! Reaching out, I grabbed her hair high on her head, and pulled it backwards; bending her head with it.

"If you don't want your neck broken, I'd think you'd be a very smart woman to keep your mouth closed!" I whispered tensely in her ear. "I don't care if you die here or in prison. You understand me?"

I was WAY past being angry.

Tears stood in her eyes, then ran down the sides of her face. Her face paint ran with them. I'm not ashamed to say her pain made me feel good. Much later on, I would come to realize that I needed the release from the day's actions, and to take some of my hate for Stillwell out on someone, and she asked for the burden. She surely did.

She walked meekly to the jail as Striker and Blarney, Say'ards horse, brought up the rear.

The deputy locked her in a cell after I did a body search on her, for I did not know where the gun she used came from, and I wasn't about to trust her not to have another one handy.

I came out of the cell, and waited for the deputy to lock the door. He made the statement that they'd never had a lady in the jail before, and I expressed my opinion to him that he still didn't, and with that I went out, climbed on Striker, and went to see about my sister.

'Til was propped up on a table with her pants leg cut open; exposing a wicked looking, black hole with blue flesh around it. There were traces of tears alongside her temples and into her hair just above the ears, but she was silent. She saw me look at the ugly bullet wound, and smiled faintly.

"It's got a twin on the other side," she said, and then caught her lower lip with her teeth. "Damn. I'm sorry, Sis. I wasn't thinking."

"Nothing to be sorry about 'Til. A pair of anything born at the same time are twins, and those two holes surely were born at the same time," I answered her gently, smoothing back her hair from her forehead. "Besides, we can't go through life choosing our words all the time can we?'

The double meaning of 'twins on the other side' wasn't lost on Say'ard either. I reached to hold her hand, and smiled tightly at my sisters. We sure were packing a lot of life into our short years! The kind of life women weren't supposed to live.

The doc was in the room, and was busy getting his gear out to work on 'Til and the sheriff, who was laying on a bed next to 'Til.

Say'ard spoke to Matilda, "'Til when you can travel; take the coach back home. Tie Patches on behind. We'll be along when we're finished with Stillwell," she was speaking to 'Til, but was looking at me.

That Say'ard! She'd dropped all the trapping of a saloon singer. I knew that she had finally seen life for what it truly was, and was meeting it head-on, and doing a right fine job of it.

"You take it easy, and get back home as soon as you can Sis," I added. "We'll keep in touch as best as we can, and we'll come back this way in case you're still here."

Say'ard was all business as she took the lead in what to do next: "Kate? I'll go get another letter ready to send back to the girls."

"All right. I'll see about lodging for 'Til. Then we best head out. The weather won't hold for long. There are some pretty heavy clouds coming in."

## Chapter 23

Say'ard and I were gone within the hour. We didn't even know the name of the town we had ridden into, but now with 'Til laid up there, we had gotten a mailing address on her. The town's name was Slate, Idaho Territory. It was one of those places that sprang up overnight at a wide spot in the road; exploded into being, and then died just as quickly within a year or so. Most of the town was made up of tents, and it was a small scale mining town. The few buildings were squared off, with room enough for the essentials, and faced with false fronts.

Ruby's was one of the few totally constructed buildings along with the jail, bank, and doc's house.

Sheriff Ray Harrigan was Irish, and offered to see to Matilda's comforts. Say'ard and I had kept straight faces; thanked Ray for his help; his offer with 'Til and left.

Say'ard voiced her opinion that she thought we might be seeing Mr. Harrigan again. I thought the same thing. That fella that was trying to court 'Til back home had competition. Serious competition!

We left our injured; rode around back of Ruby's place, and picked up Stillwell's trail. You might wonder why one of us didn't go after him right away. We didn't have too. He'd keep. I, for one, had a lifetime to find him, and family came first.

The tracks were easy to follow, as easy as when he ran after killing Meg. He was going to put distance behind him again.

We had wiggled our poncho blankets over our coats, and I set Striker into a mile eating canter as I led out this time.

Stillwell's trail was steadily paced in the wet ground, and that he was heading somewhere in particular seemed possible. If he was, I sure wish I knew. I didn't like the idea of being led along on a nose rope! On the other hand; I really didn't have much of a choice.

We put many miles behind us before making camp for the night in a spruce thicket in a narrow gulch. Stillwell didn't make camp at all we found out later. He had ridden through the night, and had miles on us by daybreak, or so we thought.

The night had turned colder. Snow swirled in the air, and come the morning breaking dim, a skiff of it covered the ground. His trail would be hard to follow as the ground was freezing up, and the little bit of snow would do the rest to hide his trail.

We had to work at keeping his track.

We didn't say much that morning, for we both knew the snow was a bad omen. We also had known this would happen any time; we just thought the chase would have been over long before now.

I wasn't real sure as to exactly where we were, and I really didn't think on it too much. Stillwell was ahead of me; out there somewhere, and that's all that concerned me at the moment. We had supplies, good cold-weather gear, and there were still two of us to his one.

Say'ard led out heading in the direction we knew Stillwell was going last night on a single horse trail, and well used by riders, and it headed south towards the Salt Lake area.

Say'ard led most of the morning. I thought her tracking, and other outdoor talents were standing her in good faith. She was as skilled as I in these matters, but if we didn't find him soon, winter could force us to a standstill. I didn't want that, and neither did Say'ard.

Near mid-afternoon we climbed a low ridge, and pulled up just below the crest to keep from sky-lining ourselves. It was a good thing we had the caution, for below us lay a mud sod house. The barn, as rough looking as the house, had half a dozen horses in the corral.

It seemed quiet, and looked like a normal, run down homestead.

The trail led down towards the place, and since Stillwell had ridden this same trail, we became even more cautious. One of ours lay behind us with his bullet hole through her leg, and he wouldn't be easy to surprise again. We backed off the ridge, separated, and each taking a side, went around the hill, coming up to the buildings from each side.

I had the barn.

Ground-tying Striker at the back corral, I eased into the sod barn's side opening, and, waiting for my eyes to adjust to the dim interior, I listened.

A horse snorted. Somewhere in the dimness another stomped a hoof. A bit rattled. A small animal scurried. Cat? Rat? I passed it by in my mind. I heard each sound, identified it, and tossed each non-threatening one aside.

Moving carefully, I went silently through the barn, and in the last stall I searched near the main door, I found what I had hoped to find. The flea-bitten gray!

From the slightly open doorway, I spied Say'ard as she was working two other structures. I waved her to stop, and I crossed behind some stacks of dried fodder hay to her.

"The grays in the barn; still saddled," I whispered. "You work that side of the house. I'll meet you back here."

Three minutes or so later we were squatted down talking things over as to what we found. Which was nothing because there wasn't any side or back windows. I decided on a nonchalant frontal approach as travelers looking for warmth, and a hot meal. That particular request of hospitality was common out here.

"All right. Let's get the horses." Say'ard voiced her approval.

We split up again, and went to our mounts. I had the lead rope to the pack horse still looped over my saddle horn. Say'ard joined me, and we rode straight down the trail, and up to the sod's door.

"Hello!" Say'ard called out in a pleasant voice. "Anybody to home?"

A long pause followed her greeting before the door opened slightly.

"Who are ya and whadda ya want?" The man's voice was hard, and brisk.

"My name's Miss O'Reilly. My sister, and I, would like to warm up some if you'd be kind enough to allow us to," Say'ard answered him. She had let her hat fall back on her neck so he could see her clearly. My hat followed suit.

"What are ya women folk doin' out here in this weather? Are ya alone?" he asked the questions quickly.

"Yes sir, we are alone. May we come in for a spell, and warm up?"

He wasn't at all sure of us, and his actions were none too polite, but he said, "Sure, step on down, and come in.

Martha? We've got company," he called out over his shoulder.

He opened the door wide, moved out onto the small board porch, and his did a quick scan of the trail behind us.

A bandage, with a blood spot seeping through it, was wrapped around his head. A fresh blood spot.

The family was poor by anyone's take, and two small children were huddled on a bed in the far corner. It didn't take but a moment to see this family was stiff with fear!

"It's surely not a fit day to be riding," Say'ard exclaimed, her voice light, and pleasant. Her Irish charm was coming through loud, and clear.

"Where ya ladies be aheadin'?" the man asked.

"Down to the Salt Lake area," I replied easily, watching the children. They kept glancing up at the sleeping loft. Say'ard caught their glances too.

"Ain't you askin' for trouble; being women, and alone, and all. That's a fer piece to ride. 'Specially this time of year," the woman finally spoke. Her voice was strained, and her hands shook as she poured us some kind of tea.

"My hands sure are cold. Might I warm them at the fire Ma'am?" I asked, smiling up at her from the crude table I now sat at.

"'Course ya can, Miss. What's yer name again. From the looks of ya both, I'd be thinking you're of the Irish blood. Am I right?" the woman spoke gently.

I smiled at her again, more to comfort her fears than anything else.

"I guess we can't be denying the Irish in us. Not that I'd want to. My name is Kathleen O'Reilly, and this is my sister Say'ard," I replied indicating Sis.

I went to the fireplace next to the woman as she hung the pot on the hook, and slid her hands down the front of her dress. She was very nervous!

I was hidden from the loft where I now stood. I reached out, and touched the woman's shoulder with my right hand; drawing my coat back with my left hand. I put a finger to my lips, and pulled my coat back enough for her to see the badge, and if I ever live to see hope spring from someone's eyes, it was hers.

"Say'ard? Why in the world I let you talk me into this trip, this time of year, I'll never know," I went on talking.

"The only good thing I've found so far on this whole ride is this fire."

I motioned Say'ard to me. She picked right up on the conversation as if we had rehearsed it for a stage play.

"Oh, Sis, you always were a complainer, but I do think I could stand a little of that fire's warmth too." She kept up our pretense.

"I didn't realize how cold I was," she continued. "I may never be warm again!"

While Say'ard talked, I leaned in close to the woman, and whispered, "Big man, leg shot, long brown hair?"

Her eyes were wide as she wrung her hands, glanced at her man, nodded, and then looked up to the loft.

"You're crib's empty. Where is your babe?" I didn't really have to ask, for I knew Stillwell had the child.

Tears sprang to her eyes, she caught the sob behind her finger tips, and glanced up again.

Say'ard was still jabbering on about our trip.

"Anyway out for him?" I whispered.

Shaking her head, she whispered back. "You really the law?"

"Yes." I nodded back.

What changed my idea of climbing that ladder, and finishing his hunt was the babe he had hidden behind!

I looked to Say'ard, pointed up, rocked my arms; as if holding a baby, and motioned for us to leave. We made more small conversation, took our leave, pulled up into our cold saddles, and rode off on the trail south making sure we stayed in plain sight. The land dipped into a wash in a half mile or so, and we pulled the horses into it.

"Kate! He hid behind a baby! The yellow, murdering coward!" Say'ard exclaimed. Sis's emotions were running high.

"He's a survivor Say'ard. He'll use what he has to, to live. He'll use anything or anybody," I gave her my answer that rang with the truth of what this man was capable of doing.

I had slid from my saddle and ground hitched Striker by droppings his reins. Sis tied Blarney to my saddle horn. From our pack horse we each took our deer hide robes, re-checked our weapons, and started back to the sod barn on foot. We knew Stillwell would move out at night, and once he was outside, and away from the family; we'd try for him again. We didn't know if he'd leave the family alive or dead, and that weighed heavy on us.

It wasn't too awfully bad cold, but our breath hung on the air in white plumes, and frost formed on our long hair that was loose around our faces. Under our robes we were fairly comfortable as we snuggled down in the pile of hay next to the gray's stall.

"How long you think Kate, before he comes out?"

"I don't know, but I'd say when it's full dark. It's the dark of the moon now, and he'll feel safer then. Go ahead and sleep Sis. I'll wake you in a spell."

Say'ard snuggled even deeper into the hay pile under our coats and poncho blankets, and in a few minutes her easy breathing told me she was asleep.

I thought about Say'ard. She was twenty-two years old now, a woman grown. All we O'Reilly's were, even Imp. These last twelve months had thrown life at Say'ard in such a way that she had had to grow up. Every one of us was a year older, and wiser too, but I believed Say'ard had changed the most. She no longer rushed headlong into things. Instead, she waited, looked things over, set her mind, and then simply did it. Just like me.

I grinned. Just like me, like Mother, like all the Grandma Kates. Like an O'Reilly. She'd come a long way indeed.

We lay there together, bundled under our robes, one on guard, and one asleep. Two women, hunting a killer. Are we crazy? Or are we just plain stupid? I didn't have a notion which it was. All I knew was, I HAD to be here, for this was my job, and I wondered if this was the moment I had been born for.

Grandmother Kate said that everyone was born for a moment in time that was theirs alone. Maybe she was right. I don't know if this was the exact moment I was born for, but...born for? What day is this?

I had reached town with the herd midway through the first week of September; we'd been on Stillwell's trail right at three weeks, so that would make it around the end of September.

Well I'll be; happy birthday Sarah Kathleen O'Reilly the 10th, you're an old maid for sure, and working on spinsterhood at the ripe, old age of twenty six.

I hummed to myself old Irish songs. I let many a tune rattle around in my head, tapping my fingers to the melodies, and remembering.

You know how one thought leads to another, and another, and another? In a span of six hours or so, I'd relived my girlhood days, some school events, a passel of dances, Grandma Kate's last days; her glittering green eyes shining with deviltry as she whispered she was looking forward to the experience of dying, meeting all the other matriarchs, Wee Folk, and Graces, but mostly to put her feet on the soil of her kinswomen; Skara Brae. That knowledge was a secret that belonged to us alone.

It's truly amazing how much can be contained inside a person's head. No wonder we get headaches from time to time!

It had to be near eight o'clock when I touched Say'ard awake, and it took me about two sprinkles of fairy dust to fall asleep. I dreamed of Cuchulain, catching spiders, chasing the Blarney Stone that wanted to move around a lot, and the brave Wallace and his devoted men.

None of my dreams were making much sense lately.

Robert the Bruce, at least one of them, for there were at least nine we know about from the old records, watched spiders; not caught them, and the Blarney Stone didn't move at all. Cuchulain was a knight of the Red Branch, and didn't have a lot to do with spiders. When Say'ard nudged me awake I was totally confused.

"Someone's coming," she whispered.

The night was moonless, as I had predicted; pitch black with only a billion stars to shed a faint light. We eased to each side of the door just as it creaked open.

It sounded like two people came in. Someone scratched a match; it flared briefly, was cupped to a lantern wick; the chimney set back over it, and the wick turned up. In the flare of the match, I saw the man from the house. Stillwell was right behind him in the darkness, for I could see his faint outline.

"Get over there, and get my horse!" Stillwell growled at the man; giving him a shove that sent the smaller man sprawling.

Before I wanted to make our move, Say'ard came out of the darkness on Stillwell's right, and hit his gun hand with a pitchfork. He groaned, swore, and brought his left hand around in a fist; hit Say'ard, and knocked her into the blackness behind her.

She didn't get up.

He followed through with his swing on Say'ard, and lunged back out the door.

The house man wisely stayed on the floor.

I fired, but my shot was slightly high, and I heard Stillwell grunt, then he was gone into the night, and I wasn't a ten steps behind him. All I could hear was him running around towards the back of the barn.

I took off after him, and for a big man; carrying two bullet wounds, he sure could move! Fear could inspire a person I guess, for I wasn't gaining on him, and I wasn't that slow! I ran light on my toes, the way Broken Wing had taught me so I could hear things, and I could hear Stillwell's heels crunching hard on the cold earth, and leading me on into the darkness.

I ran hard to catch him. I could hear him gasping for breath, and stomping the ground, and now I was gaining on him.

The direction we were heading gave me an anxious feeling in the back of my mind, for Stillwell was headed for our horses! He somehow found them in the darkness, and was hiding in between the three horses.

No place was clear for me to take a shot, and I wasn't about to fire on Blarney and Striker! That is where I found out more about the worthless breed of human Stillwell was.

Controlling my breathing, I stooped under the pack horse's neck; intending to shove the muzzle of my rifle into Stillwell's back. He was breathing hard and I was totally quiet, but somehow he heard, sensed me or picked up a movement from the horses, for he pointed his gun backward over his shoulder, pointed it down, and fired.

I caught a flicker of his movement, dropped to one side as he fired, and I felt the tug of the bullet on the shoulder of my coat.

Then all hell broke loose!

Striker leapt sideways. The pack horse, shot high in the whither, and down through its chest; screamed in agony, and went down kicking! I rolled to the left under Striker, and the sound of fading hoof beats told me Stillwell was gone.

I shakily rose to my feet, and listened to Blarney run. He was running hard!

The pack horse was still alive; groaning, and thrashing in its suffering, but not for long as my one shot split the cold night air.

Stillwell was making a fool out of me, but things were about to change! He was on Blarney now. Blarney and Striker had spent a lot of time together. A horse has a fine sense of smell. I wouldn't have to hunt Stillwell's trail, for Striker would follow Blarney's scent, and we could move almost as fast as Stillwell.

I gathered up Striker's reins, calmed him some, and started for the barn. I'd get the pack off the dead horse later. Right now I needed to see to Say'ard.

The barn was empty, for the farmer had taken Say'ard to the house.

I wrapped the crude door with my gloved knuckles, and the man cautiously let me in. The woman cuddled a small infant close and sat on the bed with a child on each side of her.

Say'ard wasn't too bad off, but enough so that I'd go on alone from here. A big purplish bruise was making itself known on the side of her face, and where she had landed on a blacksmith's anvil; she had broken ribs.

"I messed up didn't I Kate?" Say'ard mused, her eyes full of regret, and pain. More regret instead of pain I think.

"You tried Say'ard. The timing wasn't right that's all. I messed up too. The pack horse is dead. Stillwell shot it aiming for me. He's on Blarney now.

Her eyes were full of despair for her faithful horse. She knew how hard the gray had been treated, and now the bastard was on her Blarney! Blarney had never had a hand raised to him, and wouldn't know how to take a hard rein or whip.

"I'll take the pack off the horse, and go after him. If you can, ride the gray back to town, and stay with 'Til. When you're both well enough, go home. I'll come back through here just in case you two might still not be able to travel.

Tell Sheriff Harrington what happened out here, and send provisions to these good folks for their help."

I turned away from my sister's sad eyes, and went to the door. Stopping, I looked back to Say'ard. "You take care of the girls Say'ard. Always take care of them." I said softly, and the lump in my throat was as big as when I stood at Meg's grave.

Say'ard stood up painfully, leaned on the plank board table, holding her side, and spoke in a tight, strong voice,

"YOU come home Kate. YOU hear me? YOU come home!"

I couldn't speak, and when I finally did, I croaked out, "I will Sis. I will."

I knew what she had been thinking because my thoughts were the same. We may never see each other again, but neither of us could say it.

A calmness was in me now as I walked Striker back to the pack horse; more so than the anger I had had at Meagan's grave.

I wondered how long it would be before I saw my sisters again. Soon? A month? Never? I would not contemplate those thoughts.

There was a feeling of things finally being right in my mind. Was I supposed to have gone after this man alone after all? Is this how it should have been from the start? All I knew was, I wasn't afraid anymore, and I wondered what that meant. I didn't have any more doubts or worries. I just knew this was the way it was to be. This is what the Graces were asking of me. I will give all I have, for this is my job.

Striker, and I stood quietly in the darkness near the dead pack horse. The things I needed from the pack were tied on behind my saddle, and Striker was under me. I had what I needed. Almost.

Sitting on that great horse and friend, I looked up to the stars. The wind was still, and the stars were formed into that band of shining, twinkling dots called the Milky Way.

This was my dream.

I looked at the celestial roadway and said aloud, "Blessed Graces? Help me do this." This was the help I had needed to ask in the dream.

Striker warmed to the idea real quick that I wanted him to follow Blarney. Giving him his head after a few yards, he set a fast pace; I rode easy and loose, and the miles started to fall behind us.

As I said earlier, Blarney was a fine horse, but Striker was his father, and the better horse.

Chapter 24

Stillwell headed southwest. He traveled well-used roads, and went through a whole passel of hog-wild little towns, but he kept to his southwest direction.

At each town I contacted the local law, and yes, they knew about Stillwell, and furthermore, they knew about me. Word was spreading through this sparse territory that the manhunt was still in progress, and I hadn't any doubts that when I left a town, the word went out that I had been there. I hoped it traversed the distance to Slate, and Highwater, and to my family.

Say'ard's statement of people knowing the O'Reilly's when they see us, and remembering us when we're gone; briefly passed through my head.

Sis was right; for all the wrong reasons.

Stillwell was making a habit of stealing what he needed where ever he could, further proving that he was flat broke of money.

Three more weeks passed, and it was getting on toward the last part of October as near as I could keep track. We were in a warmer climate, but snow was still messing with me in the high places. At home the winter would be taking hard jabs at the ranch, and I hoped the girls would be planning an All's Hallows Eve; with or without me.

Four times during past weeks, I'd missed Stillwell by a few hours. He wasn't making any mistakes that I could tell, but he wasn't taking time to get medical help either, and he was still stealing supplies. He knew someone was behind him, and he continued pushing Blarney hard.

By my guesswork of how the mountains lay in this part of the country, and information I gleaned from each town, we'd crossed the Sierra Mountains, and were working our way down the west slope, headed towards the Pacific coastline.

At least it was warmer.

Then for some confounding reason, he swung inland, and crossed the Sierra Mountains again.

We were now into a dry, arid desert country. The Nevada or Arizona territories would be my guess. I had thought at one time that he might be heading for somewhere in particular, but now I knew he was just moving; staying ahead of his tail, and hoping he'd lose me eventually.

There was a dam slim chance of THAT!

The worthless hunk of skunk meat hadn't bled to death, and was probably mostly healed by now.

I grinned. *No mistakes this time Stillwell.* I had a really deep feeling that it was going to end today. For one or both of us. I didn't know which. What I did know was: I surely was tired of chasing the child killing coward!

When such deep, sure feelings, erupt into my thinking; I know the Graces are with me, and my instincts are being guided by them.

My Paganism again.

It had been a grueling hunt. Striker and I had leaned down considerably. My pants were bunched in at the waist, and I'd had to tighten another notch or two on my gun belt.

I tried to buy only the barest supplies I needed when we passed through towns, but the sheriffs gave them to me; in gratitude for going after Stillwell I guess, or shame on their part because they didn't stop him.

Anyway, I surely hadn't been eating too much. On the other hand, I grinned again, neither had Stillwell.

It seemed I grinned a lot lately. I wondered if I was going mad. Better people than me had been pushed to their limits for too long, and lost their tenacious hold on their sanity. *Tenacious. Now why in the hell, am I using words like that out here?* Funny, I didn't feel insane, but insane folks, I hear tell, are always the last to know. Sort of like the woman whose man is cheating on her; always the last to know.

Between being bone tired, saddle sore, dirty, underfed, and smiling too much, no wonder folks I met gave me a dumbfounded look, and side-stepped me. I must be quite a sight!

Let them look! I just kept my mind tuned to Stillwell, and one eye on the skyline. "No mistakes this time Kate. No mistakes."

I shook myself! *Did I say that out loud? Did someone say it to me? That voice wasn't mine? Was it? Dear Graces! I am tired!*

Striker was working us up a dry stream bed between some magnificent red colored boulders. There were a few hardy cottonwood trees growing here that indicated deep ground water. Blarney's fresh prints led straight down the dry bed toward an opening in the rocks. There was probably a good chance of water up ahead.

We were easing along and Striker was cat-footing it quietly when he suddenly stopped, and stood fence post still. I reached out a hand for his nose as I slid down, and stood a while to get my land legs, so to speak, under me, and stroked his left leg lightly.

I'd been up on Striker all day, and my backside was numb. Regardless of what folks tell you about horse riders; our rear end still goes numb.

Taking one of the two canteens down, I opened it, poured water into my hat, and gave the black a good long drink as I lifted the canteen to my cracked lips. I took a small drink, held it in my mouth before swallowing, and felt the water go all the way to my belly button. I took another longer draw off the canteen, held the water again while I put the cap back on, and swallowed again.

I had moved us into the shade of a big tree as we took our water. Now that I could move easier, I light-footed up a mound of rocks, and into a dense brushy area of some kind of stunted bush that was all twisted into odd shapes.

I didn't worry too much about snakes, for the weather was too cool for them to be out and about. I wormed, and turned my way through the stiff brush for a ways when I came upon a pool of water that lay at the base of a big overhanging boulder.

The source of the water was a decent trickle that came out of a crack in the side of that boulder, and flowed about twelve feet down the face of it. The water trickled through a mass of green that clung to the rock face, and ended up in the pool below.

If it wasn't for the three men that occupied the little glen it would have been an inviting place. Especially the water. It looked cool and sweet.

The three men were on the shade side of the boulder and pool. Two were off their horses. The third man sat on his horse, or I should say Say'ard's horse, for the third man was Stillwell. I finally laid eyes on the bastard!

Blarney was lathered, head down, fighting the bit, and wanting to go to the water, but Stillwell held the reins short. That action made Blarney open his mouth wide, and I could see the white lather around his mouth.

I couldn't hear them from where I crouched, and maybe these men were Stillwell's friends, but I didn't get that impression from my mind.

The men had apparently walked to the pool for water. They finished filling the coffee pot, and canteens, and moved slowly away with Stillwell following; kicking Blarney hard to make him move away from the water he so badly needed.

I eased from the brush, and followed them on foot. In a hundred yards they came to their camp. Their horses were off saddled, and their bedrolls were still laid out. I knew they had been there a while, and didn't intend to move out today.

One of the men, the younger one, sat the coffee pot near the fire, and dropped a handful of coffee into it. Stillwell dismounted at the camp, and half hitched Blarney to a gnarly tree.

"Hold on Blarney. Hold on." I whispered dryly.

I hustled back to Striker, and took him into the water hole. He drank deeply once, and quit. I knew he was still thirsty; so was I, but we both had enough sense to back off from bloating ourselves. Filling the canteens with the freshest water from near the trickle, I led Striker away.

We eased back the way we'd come in, and started to cut a circle around the men.

The distance was perhaps a quarter mile, but it took a half hour to get where I wanted to be; downwind. I rode low on Striker; keeping myself out of sight as much as possible. I silently let him take me up a stretch of sand to within fifty yards of the camp.

I eased down, and took my whip from my shoulder. A whirling rope would sound the air, and give me away. On the other hand, the snap of a whip wouldn't be heard at all until it was way too late.

I'd been practicing all my life with that whip, and had shaken the kinks out of it even more as I followed Stillwell. It had become a part of me a long time ago. Did my hate have a way of making me practice?

Using the whip on Stillwell wasn't going to satisfy my hate, but it would help. I didn't want to actually kill him; not yet, and with a gun, I'd be sorely tempted to do just that. This way, I'd just soften him up for the ride back, because I promised myself I'd take him back for justice if I could, and I always tried to keep my promises. Either way, I would give Megan justice; now at my hand, or later before a judge.

If Stillwell was alive to make the ride was up to Stillwell.

The men were making supper, and the coffee was starting to smell really good. So were the beans, and fried bread pones the younger man had in a skillet by the side of the fire.

Stillwell sat with his back to me, facing the trail he's just rode up. The wind was blowing toward me, and along with the food, I could actually smell him, and he stank

I was on his right somewhat, and walking into the campsite, I called to him softly. "Stillwell?"

He hesitated for a brief moment; lunged to his feet; his right hand going down for the gun he carried. My whip was ready, and snapped at that hand, and the gun was pulled from his already bleeding hand.

The other two men were instantly on their feet.

"You with him?" I asked, with my left hand holding my hand gun on them.

The older of the two eyed me carefully, and finally said, "No Ma'am. He rode up on us a short while ago."

I didn't know what to make of them, but I had the knowing the man spoke truthfully, and only glanced at them, for my eyes were mostly on Stillwell.

"Then back off. He's the one I want," I spoke again softly, but maybe that was because my throat was still parched, and they both moved back.

"WHO the HELL are you?" Stillwell swore at me as he grasped his bleeding hand.

"I've been trailing you all the way from Montana Territory. You do remember Montana don't you? Judith Basin? A small little bank in a small little town? You had to have known someone would come after you."

His eyes showed clearly that he remembered, and he shifted his look to my auburn red hair. Then slowly a smile...a queer, dirty smile broke over his face.

"That little filly back there, she had red hair like yourn. Didn't she?" He was moving toward me a step. "And that other gal, at Ruby's, she had red hair too." He went on talking, and slowly moving another step or two, and sideways this time.

I heard words, I saw him move, and if he thought either one of his actions had fooled me, he really should have thought again. He couldn't make me give him an opening. Stillwell was stalling for time as he edged closer to his fallen gun. He was now within two steps of the gun where it lay half buried in the sand.

"Stillwell, you see this whip? It belonged to my Father, and he taught me well the use of it, and I'm going to use it on your murdering, yellow hide.

You rode in here on one of our horses, and that's called horse stealing, and you treated Blarney badly."

I waved a hand at Blarney, and he jerked back hard, having taken the hand command just like he'd been trained to do. Pulling the reins loose he ran for the water pool.

"This hair? All the O'Reilly women have auburn hair. That girl back at the bank in Judith Basin? She was my sister. My little sister, and she was fifteen years old. The one back at Ruby's. Another sister. Then of course there's the sister whose face you almost broke at that sod-buster's house outside of Sandpit. They're both alive, and probably back home by now; waiting for me to bring you to them."

I didn't smile as I dropped my handgun back into its home: "But first Stillwell, you're going to hurt. You're going to hurt like my family has hurt. Almost.

For starters, the first lash will be for my sister's horse you've been pounding into the ground. There isn't any call to treat a horse like that. The rest of the beating I'm going to give you is for the sister you killed."

He had quit smiling, for he knew trouble when he stopped running long enough to turn around and face it, and he knew then that I was trouble, and he knew I was very ready to kill him.

I was WAY beyond calm.

He made a scramble for his gun, and the whip wrapped itself around his head, and eyes; drawing a goodly flow of blood from the eye lids. He screamed, covered his face, and stumbled away. I stepped forward, picked up his gun, and tossed it into the brush.

Leaping up, he swiped the blood from his eyes, and started for me.

I laid a bloody strip down his belly.

He stopped, bent over, clutched his grimy shirt, and welted belly as I quickly laid another lash across his back, and jerked it off just as fast! Methodically I went to work on him; taking out my hate, and hurt on Stillwell with each lash I laid on his body.

I'd been told a body in good shape could take a goodly number of lashes from one of these whips.

He didn't even take fifteen; Meg's age.

Although he'd tried for me time, and again, I held him off with the whip. When he finally turned to run, I coiled the slender tip around his neck and pulled hard!

Where I got the strength from I don't know, for I felt myself trembling with fatigue, or was it hate?

He flipped over backwards, and lay there trying to unwind the coils. He was bloody, gasping for breath, and crying! This big, stinking man, who had killed my sister, hidden behind a baby, and killed horses, was crying! Not just tears of pain running down his face either, for this crying was from fear, and the sobs came from deep inside him.

Just like Shannon's had as I held her in my arms so long ago.

I was exhausted! More than that; I was sick! I thought somewhere in this punishment I had handed out to Stillwell, I'd find satisfaction. But I didn't.

Revenge, nor retribution, was there. Nothing was. Just an emptiness without any words of explanation, for what I had accomplished over the past two months, and had just done to another human. Except in my mind, he was a long way from being human.

The job was all but over, and I found not a bit of pleasure or satisfaction anywhere in me.

Walking, in what felt like slow motion with heavy legs, and breathing hard, I went to one of the saddles, took a rope from it, walked back to Stillwell, and tied him up. I left him face down on the hot sand.

"You lay there Stillwell, and you think about a little girl lying in the frozen, winter ground of Montana. Then you think about hanging because you will. Either I or the law will do it. And right now; I am the law, but you will hang."

I didn't have any emotion in my voice. I just said it.

I called Striker in, and knowing Blarney would come with him, I turned with the thought in mind to get another drink of water. Somewhere at that point I faintly remember hitting the ground.

Chapter 25

I woke up to the smell of coffee, and Striker was lipping his velvet muzzle along my cheek. Reaching up to him, I heard him nicker to me deep in his throat.

"You finally going to wake up?" A man's voice broke the quiet of the camp glen.

Sitting up slowly, I gazed at the man kneeling beside me, holding a warm hunk of fried bread, and a cup of coffee.

My eyes went quickly to Stillwell. He'd been moved, and was sitting up, but still tied. He was bloody, and wide awake.

"You've made a bad enemy Ma'am," the man at my side said softly when he saw me look to Stillwell.

"No I haven't," I answered hoarsely, taking the food from his large hands. "He made the enemy."

Tasting the coffee, I couldn't help but smile, for it tasted so good, and refreshingly wet! "Thank you for this," I said raising the cup.

"You're welcome, Miss?"

"Sarah Kathleen O'Reilly."

"A beautiful name, for a beautiful woman."

I raised my eyes from the cup, and looked straight into his. He wasn't making light of me as far as I could tell. He was totally serious.

"Thank you." I replied. I had to change this line of conversation for I felt like a whole jar full of butterflies had just taken wing in my stomach!

"How long have I been asleep? You should have awaken me earlier. The day's almost gone!" I said.

"The second days almost gone," he answered my statement.

I looked to Stillwell again, and back to this man who knelt beside me.

"You looked like you needed the rest, and as for him," he nodded toward Stillwell. "He wasn't going anywhere, not the way you tied him up."

"You could have let him go while I slept."

"No I couldn't."

"Why not?"

"Two reasons come to mind. One. That horse of yours hardly lets me near the man, or you. It took a while to earn his confidence."

"You said two reasons, Mr.?" I prompted.

"Callahan. Clete Callahan. The other reason is, there isn't any way I'd want you, that horse, and that whip, on my trail. No way."

He was smiling a wide bright smile that was reflected in his pewter gray eyes, and down to the small cleft in his beard stubbled chin. His nose had been knocked a little sideways at some point, and it was slightly hooked, and there was a scar in his left eyebrow, but it was a good bold face he had.

"I think you'd not ever be having that worry Mr. Callahan," I said impishly, slipping into the auld brogue.

"Where would you be heading?" I asked quickly, dropping my eyes to the coffee cup, and away from his enchanting gray ones.

He stood up quickly, and went to the fire. "We're just drifting around. No place has taken our eye yet to settle into," he said.

"Our eye?" I questioned.

"My brother Jess, and I," he indicated the younger man with a chin thrust; talking, but not looking at me as I gingerly knelt beside him.

I was sore all over.

"There's work back in Judith Basin, and I could use the help getting Stillwell back there. I'm willing to pay good wages. Think about it while I go for a walk," I told him.

Rising stiffly to my feet, I went to my saddle bags that lay on the ground next to where someone had placed my bedroll, and me on it; took some personal items in hand, and headed for the thick brush.

I couldn't help thinking that he had cradled me in those hard, muscled arms, and laid me on that blanket to sleep.

It was quite a while later when I returned. I had taken the time to wash up, brush my hair, change into a clean shirt, wash out the dirty one, and fling it over a small bush to dry.

Taking the time, when I returned I studied his face more. I flicked my eyes over his face, and hands. He was sunburned! I was a dark tan. That meant one of two things. Either he was new to the heat of this land, or he had been inside for a long time. His actions, and manners told me he had been around here long enough to know his way around this lifestyle. I knew he wasn't a stranger to the outdoors. So he had to have been in prison.

I never did like beating the bushes for an answer, and it was a bad habit of mine.

"Why were you locked up?" I asked gently, looking at him full on, and steady.

He flicked his eyes to mine. We looked at each other for a long silent minute, and he glanced at the badge pinned to my shirt.

"I killed a man."

"I don't know you at all, but something tells me you had a good reason for it."

"I think I did. So did the law to a certain degree."

"But the law locked you up anyway? Why? I'm sorry," I said with a wave of one hand, and a shake of my head, "I don't have any right to pry."

Clete let some time pass before he answered: "He forced himself on my sister, and I beat him until he died. The judge gave me a year. He said only the law can sentence a man, and take his life. That man had taken two lives; my sister's, and the baby. They died in the birthing."

A cold shiver sliced through me! How close had I come to doing the same thing, and at the moment, I was the law!

"The law's not always right. The judge was wrong. Some of us have to take that right," I spoke gently. "I almost did."

"Yet you didn't. You stopped," he said. "Why?" His voice was gentle, and probing.

"Why?" I paused the space of a few heart beats. "I didn't want to stop," I replied softly, "other than the fact I promised myself I'd bring him back for the justice he's earned for killing Meg"

"Who's Meg?"

"My sister. The one he killed. Her name was Meagan."

Clete was deep in thought for a while as I sipped coffee, and ate another wedge of fried bread. He sat staring at Stillwell, and at a point somewhere off behind the man.

"I'll help you take Stillwell back, but you don't have to pay me. I want to go with you. If that's a good enough reason?" He lifted his chin as he said those words. I knew why he wanted to go with me, and it gave me a rush of warmth.

I stood, so did he, and I didn't know if it was manners, or that he wanted to keep eye contact with me. He was tall. I liked that. In fact there were a few other things I liked about this man.

"It'll do," I told him with a small smile, as I raised an eyebrow, "for now."

As I went to tend Striker and Blarney, I swear I heard Grandma Kate's light laughter in my ear. *He's a keeper, Lass! He's a keeper!*

I smiled to myself, and replied silently, *He surely is Grandma. He surely is!*

Chapter 26

The long ride that would take me home to my sisters, and Stillwell to a gallows, lay before us. With part of the day left we decided to head out, cover as much ground as we could, and make a late camp.

I went to clean up again, and have the first real bath I'd had in weeks, and it surely felt good, as did having clean hair. The homemade, flower-scented soap we had carried all the way west with us, made me feel a whole lot more like a woman than the horse-smelling, saddle tramp I had become over the last weeks.

As I cleaned up, I guess I started to calm down from the anxiety of the long pursuit, because for no good reason that I could think of, I began to weep. Just tears streaming my face at first that gave way into silent, broken sobs. I couldn't stop them from racking my body and soul. Finally they quit on their own, and I washed my face in the cool water again, finished cleaning up, and spent some time soothing Blarney, or me. I wasn't sure.

Someone, I think Clete, had off saddled him, and Striker earlier. I wiped him down, fed him the grain and corn mix I carried for Striker. When my sniffles were gone, I walked slowly back to the camp.

Clete's long look of approval, taking me in from head to toe, didn't hurt my feelings one bit, and I hoped he didn't notice my puffy eyes.

Deep down in my soul, I knew I had met the man I wanted to spend the rest of my days with, and I didn't feel a bit giddy like the girls. I felt settled and sure.

I'd get around to letting him know, when the time was right, and it was alright that he didn't have brown eyes.


The trip started easy enough. Clete led out leading Stillwell, and then me with Jess riding tail. Clete evidently knew this country well, for he set us on a straight line for Idaho, which was more than I think I could have done. Though I had always paid attention to where I'd been led, I still don't believe I could have taken us out of here as straight as he did. I hoped he could lead us back to Slate in half the time it had taken me to get here.

Before we left, the brothers cleaned and dressed the whip marks on Stillwell again, but I didn't go near the bastard. He could get infection, and suffer all the more as far as I was concerned! Stillwell looked like a half wrapped mummy.

Clete more or less took charge, and I let him. It was kinda nice to be looked after somewhat; even under these conditions.

Late that evening we made our first camp some twenty miles up country, and if we could keep this pace, I would see my sisters back in Slate in about two weeks, barring bad weather, and if they were still there.

The camp was sheltered from sight and nature's tantrums under an overhanging stone ledge. The fire reflecting off the sides and ceiling made the place seem almost homey.

Jess had taken a small javelina, a kind of wild pig that inhabited parts of this country, and hung it over the hot coals of the wood fire. It was delicious, and we ate every bit of it.

Stillwell got his share, but the brothers made Stillwell clean up before eating; which amused me. Clete took Stillwell to the bushes, and then tied him for the night to a large boulder. Jess spread his bedroll near the horses. When Clete, just as calm as you please, walked over, and put his bedroll next to mine; I smiled into the night.

I didn't mind smiling now.

The next morning brought another skiff of snow to this high country, and Clete cut a hole in a blanket for Stillwell to wear.

I had told Clete earlier, that Say'ard and 'Til might be in the town of Slate, why, and that I wanted to swing by, and get them if they were still there. Otherwise we would keep moving, and I'd see them at home.


This country sure was different than just about anything I'd ever laid eyes on. Everything was sand, and rocks. The whole place was dull brown, and dry. The scrawniest trees I'd ever seen in my life were trying to stay alive on bare rock, but when you least expected it, a hidden, green glen would appear with sparkling, clear, cool water running amok through boulders.

I was very glad Clete knew his way around this land. He found these water places, where I would have sworn there shouldn't have been any, and feed for the horses too.

I moved up beside Clete at the start of the day, and asked, "Does this country always look like this?"

"Yes Ma'am, for the most part of each year it does," he replied.

"Please, call me Kate; we're going be together for quite a while." *A life time if I have my way!* I thought. "And I'd be pleased if you use my given name."

"Yes ma'...Kate. I take it you've never been in this area before?

"No I haven't, and from what I see, I surely haven't missed much!"

"I can differ with you there ma'...Kate. In the spring time, all these mesas, as far as you can see, are covered with millions of flowers in colors of every hue. It's a beautiful thing to see, and smell."

"I can't imagine it lasting too long." I commented, trying to envision the brown, dead looking sand, alive with such color.

"That it don't, but while it's showing its colors, it is a delight to behold!"

"You sound almost poetic."

"Not me," Callahan replied with a wispy smile, and a shake of his head. "Jess is the one what has that trait. He's even written some down, but he won't let me read any of them."

"Really," I said. "Why is that? That he won't let you read them? Do you think he'd let me read them?"

"I don't know why he won't let me read them. Maybe he thinks I wouldn't understand them or give them their due." He paused a long time before adding. "You really want to read his words?"

"Yeah. You see, I have another little sister who has a flair for such things, and I've read her 'words,' as you put it."

"He'd probably let you read them. He's always been a sucker for a pretty girl."

"Well then, he probably won't let me read them," I said coyly.

"Why not, I just said he's a...."

"...sucker for a pretty girl. Which I'm not. I'm twenty six years old, and that makes me a woman not a girl," I interrupted him.

Clete studied on me a long time, and then with a devilish grin breaking all over his handsome face, he said, "That you are, Kate. That you are."

A feeling of total happiness ran through me, and I wondered who was chasing who? Not that it mattered, for I had made up my mind to let him chase me, until I caught him. Mother, and Grandma Kate, used to tell us that was how it worked.

I dropped back in line by letting Stillwell pass. He threw me a dirty look, and spit. The man had the manners of an ass, which was an insult to the animal!

"You won't get me back to Montana Red," he taunted me.

"One way or the other. It doesn't matter to me, but you're going back," I told him in a soft voice. "The way you get there is up to you; in that saddle or across it. The choice is yours to make." I smiled slightly as I said it.

Jess and Clete had come up from the Texas hill country. It was some of the prettiest country that Texas had to offer a body Jess said. Their parents, and two brothers, were dead in a land war. The man that Clete had beaten, and killed, was a rider for the large spread that was dominating the valley. I knew about this kind of range war. A large, powerful, and rich concern, would ride in, and take over a county, or valley. Then legally or otherwise, push the smaller spreads out. Not unlike what was going on back home. It usually turned into a very bloody affair.

While Clete was in prison, Jess had lost their spread for lack of payment because the larger concern had rustled off all the stock, or killed it. There wasn't any way for Jess to raise the money for the bank loan, and the bank was controlled by the same concern.

I'd lost my family home, but not to another concern. Unless you wanted to call the ramblings of nature a 'concern.'

I was still at odds with Nature over that incident.

Their sister and the baby died, and when Jess met Clete at the territorial prison they just struck out for new places.

A little better than a year had passed since it all began. Only two weeks had passed since he was released. The words came slow for Clete, but they came. With each word the hate slowly ebbed its way out of his heart, and that helped Jess to heal also.

I was doing a little healing on my own.

Each night we talked about their lives or mine; what we thought we wanted, and what I wanted to accomplish with the stock. They both thought it was a solid plan, but only time would prove the good of it.

During the evening talks, Stillwell got mouthy a few times until Clete put a gag in his mouth. Stillwell got the idea that keeping quiet would help his comfort, and breathing. I knew that the two men exchanged words from to time, and Clete seemed to have the last say, as Stillwell usually went real quiet.

Clete was more open to talking with me as each day passed, and each night he spread his blanket beside me, and we talked of other things; more of a personal nature. I mentioned my Pagan beliefs in passing, and he was curious, for his grandfather had said something along those lines a long time ago. His great grandfather, on his mothers' side, was a McTavish.

Was that just a coincidence, or were my Graces giving me a head nod that I had chosen wisely? Or did they arrange our meeting? They could be sly. I didn't expand on that information to him, but I knew our meeting wasn't by chance. The Graces arranged it.

His warmth next to me felt good, and just his presence aroused feelings in my body that I had to find a way to deal with. Those feelings were different than any I had ever known, and they grew more intense with each passing day. I can't say for sure when I started to look forward to lying alongside his long body, but I did. That was about the second night.

Four days into the trip, I dropped back to ride with Jess. He was just eighteen, and almost as big as his brother, but a tad shy. I had the feeling that when he finally 'came into his own', whatever he took ahold of would move. He would help build this land into something good, yet with the care, and respect it deserved.

"Clete tells me you're a poet," I struck up the conversation carefully.

"Oh," he replied with a little red blush creeping up his neck.

"Don't let it set too hard on you. Some very great men have been, and still are, fine poets, and highly honored for it." I went on speaking casually, surveying the lay of the land around us, but mostly watching Clete's broad back.

"Not just any old body can say or write words that express joy, and beauty. It's a rare gift you have Jess Callahan. Recognize it, and enjoy it."

We were riding down a stream bank, and had worked apart; as we each found a crossing, and the horses were breaking the covering of thin ice on a shallow sandbar to ease across to the other side.

Right about that time Stillwell thought it was a good time to try to make his way alone in the world again, as Clete had dropped Blarney's lead rope over Stillwell's saddle horn for the crossing.

Stillwell really should have given it more thought.

Blarney made the crossing, and was a horse length behind Clete. Jess and I were about three lengths away, and off to each side of Stillwell. This wasn't the best of places to make a getaway, but the fool tried anyway.

Wheeling Blarney around, Stillwell lunged back across the creek we'd just forded.

Jess yelled for Clete, and I slipped my whip off my shoulder, and grasped its handle.

Striker had already made his spin at my command, and was racing for Blarney to head him off.

The weapon in my hand made a hiss; bit hard, and laid Stillwell in the ice shards of the stream.

I rode up to him, looked down, and with words full of sarcastic disgust said, "If that's the best you got Stillwell; it's not near good enough."

While Stillwell struggled to his feet I told Jess, "Put a rope on him, and let him walk. That should warm him up. Blarney needs the rest."

Jess took the order like the hired hand he was. He pulled Stillwell up the other bank while I kept Blarney close to Striker, and patted him reassuringly. We rode half a day before making camp. The bastard was slowing us down, but he didn't get back on Blarney that day. Jess relented a little, and let Stillwell sleep close to the fire that night to finish drying off.


The weather was growing colder with each passing day, and the nights were down right frigid so we built brush shelters for ourselves. They were simple things that we left for other travelers when we rode out. We piled brush on a lean-to of tree limbs, or one low hanging limb, and covered it with the tarps from the Callahan's pack. We had to put up with Stillwell in the shelter, but he was content to behave, for the alternative was outside with the horses, and his one blanket.

I didn't object to the closeness the shelter put me with Clete. The first morning I woke up to his arms around me, and our blankets over us both, was very, very good, and from that time on we shared our blankets for warmth, but that was not all I wanted to share with this man.

It was plain to see that we were of one mind on many subjects.


Late the next day Jess asked me if I'd like to read some of his work. He'd been studying me for some time that day, and I think he finally came to the fact that I wasn't jesting him about his poetry.

"I'd be honored to Jess. Thank you."

Jess's work was a little rough, and uneducated I found out as I read what he'd written. The next night I read a few more poems, and I could see that he had a natural flair for putting the right tone to the words to make a body feel what he himself felt. He just needed someone to help smooth out the rough spots. I thought how hard a row he'd have when Imp got a hold of him! Somehow I had the feeling he'd enjoy every grueling minute of it!

At each camp, I told the Callahan's more about the O'Reilly's. Where our immigrant grandmother came from in Ireland, and why she made the trip over. I spoke of her mothers' Rules that she laid down for us to follow; why my seven sisters, and I came west, and what I hoped to see them accomplish in their lives.

"You mean you, and your sisters came clear from Tennessee to ranch by yourselves?" Jess exclaimed in disbelief.

"Yes we did, and that has bothered some folks. They have a problem with independent women I guess."

"I reckon some folks would think it was a bit...uh... different...you know what I'm saying?" He replied meekly, and poked at the fire with a small branch.

With a light laugh I told him I knew what he meant. He was embarrassing himself, and getting his words all tangled up.

"BUT. You haven't met the rest of the O'Reilly women. When you do you'll see why we most generally finish what we start." I finished the last words looking at Stillwell, who didn't, or couldn't, hold my eyes.

"Are the others as good with whips, and horses as you are?" Clete asked intently.

Those bottomless gray eyes had a deepness to them that pulled me to him, and I wasn't fighting the pull much at all. He shook my very soul more than I'd ever thought any man could, and hadn't…up till now.

"Not quite, but I'm the oldest, and I have to admit, I'm not the most ladylike at times, but I can be fairly lady like. I do own a few dresses and know how to dance." I said with a smile for him.

"The others can do anything I can except Imp. We're overly protective of her, but you'll like them," I said looking to each man.

"Are they as…uh…pretty as you?" Jess asked without looking up from what appeared to be a very interesting cup of coffee.

The boy had a natural curiosity in a man's body, and he was still feeling his way around through the complex world of life.

Hell! So was I!

"Prettier." I replied to the crown of his hat. "Say'ard, is spoken for. I think Matilda, we call her 'Til, is interested in someone. Jane is seventeen, and was keeping company with a nice ranch hand when I left, but I don't think it's serious. Ellen married last July."

Jess's face took on a forlorn look of disappointment.

"But there are three of us left. Shannon is past fifteen, and Mary is twenty three."

Jess brightened up immediately, and so fast it was obvious. Clete and I shared a warm smile at the expense of his brother.

"This Shannon, you call her 'Imp', is only fifteen? That's a might too young for most men," Jess went on seriously.

I turned my head to scan the ridge crest to my right, but mostly to hide my smile as I answered easily enough. "Sure she's young, but she's an O'Reilly, and THAT balances things out just fine. Imp's a business woman already. She's part owner of a book and clothing store. She draws pictures of anything and everything." I went on trying to be casual, "She's worth waiting for by any man worth his pay."

"A bookstore! Well, I'll be! Do you think she has any real good books? Not those dime novels, but real books?" He asked excitedly.

"Between what she's bought, and what we brought west with us; you would have to spend a few years just reading to get through them all," I told him honestly. "In the store are books that a body can read, and learn ideas, and things from. We have some very fine old books. She has a number of them by the best poets in the world. She also has lots of school, college books, and career manuals too."

With that I called it a night saying, "I better get some sleep. We should meet up with Say'ard, and 'Til tomorrow, if they're still in Slate."

Clete went to see to Stillwell's needs as usual, and I was glad to let him have the chore. I tended to Striker, Blarney and myself, and anxiously waited for Clete to lie down next to me on his side of our blanket bed. I surely didn't know how much longer I could lie beside this man and behave myself! He seemed to have a whole lot more control than I did!

He brought Stillwell into the shelter; tied him up, threw a couple of blankets over him; then went back into the darkness. Much later he came back, and after putting a few larger limbs on the fire coals, he lay down next to me as was our routine.

He was overly quiet, and didn't smile at me or say 'Goodnight.' Something was eating at him, for I saw a distance in his eyes when I had spoken of the girls finding husbands. Never one to let a body stew on a problem that might be my doing, I jumped in, and asked.

"Did I say something tonight that bothered you?" I whispered.

His answer was a long time in coming, and I knew he had to think his answer through; choosing the right words. His answer seemed very important to him; as it was to me.

Finally he turned on his side to face me, and I could see by the dim firelight the serious set of his jaw line. "I wondered if you had a man waiting," he whispered back, trying to keep our conversation quiet even though the other two were already snoring

This was the time I'd been waiting for! The time I would hear him say he wanted me! "No. I don't have anyone waiting for me."

He watched me quietly as his eyes wandered over my face, and stopped at my mouth. *Please let him kiss me!*

"You...I...love you Kate...but I don't have a thing to offer you."

I touched his lips, and to my surprise, I found them trembling just a bit. Maybe he wasn't in all that much control either! I couldn't help but smile a tiny bit at this big man, and his loss for words of love.

"Clete Callahan; I love you so very much, and if you were to offer yourself to be my husband; YOU'D be more than enough," I whispered, as I leaned toward him for the kiss I needed to give him.

Then. Right then. His eyes brightened with moisture; or surprise, and he pulled me tightly into his arms, and kissed me like a woman should always be kissed by the man she loves.

Coming up for air, which I surely didn't need yet, he laid his big hand alongside my face, and with his forehead touching mine, he whispered in a broken, emotionally filled voice, "Sarah Kathleen O'Reilly. Will you marry me?"

"Clete Callahan. I've waited all my life for you, and I'd be honored to be your wife."

The night was warmer than I thought a cold winter night could be, but the glow of love can produce miracles I've been told. He asked me when I'd like to have the wedding, and I told him tomorrow in Slate with my sisters, and Jess to stand up for us. He held me tighter, and kissed me again saying he'd have a hard time waiting a whole week, for that was how long it would seem to him.

Chapter 27

The morning couldn't come quick enough, and yet it was too soon, for that meant I had to leave his arms, but this was my wedding day! I smiled way too much, and so did Clete. Jess gave a bear hug to his brother, and a kiss on the cheek to me, when Clete told him we were to be wed in Slate today. My lips were his anytime he wanted them, and he found many times to want them!

Jess led out today with Blarney on the lead rope. Clete rode beside me, and gave me kisses every chance he could!

"What will you do for a wedding dress Kate? My bride should have one."

"I'll find one that will do just fine. You won't be ashamed of what I'll look like."

With that said, he pulled to a stop, swung his horse alongside, and faced me. He laid his hand alongside my cheek; pulled me close to him, and said sternly, "I WILL NEVER BE ASHAMED OF YOU...NEVER."

The tenseness in his voice made me take deeper notice of the depth this man's love, and I looked him straight in the eye, and said evenly, "And I will never, as long as we live, question your love for me, nor be ashamed of you."

Those words were more of a commitment between us than any wedding vow could ever be. These words went beyond wedding vows, for they came from our souls, and we were not repeating words someone had written down. From that moment on I was truly a married woman, and the happiness that brought to my heart was beyond words.

The early afternoon was cold and clear, with a pale blue sky covering the world when we rode into the half deserted town of Slate. It was rapidly becoming a played-out mining town, and we passed a wagon, loaded down heavy with a family heading out, as we were headed in.

I half expected the girls to be gone, but they weren't. They came through the door, and onto the porch of the doc's house where I'd last seen 'Til. Say'ard was first, and 'Til was right behind her. Ray Harrigan was with 'Til;

holding her arm. Matilda looked fit, as did Say'ard and Ray.

We pulled up, and I jumped down, and met my sisters' welcoming arms!

Weeks ago I'd left alone; to finish what we had begun, and I'd come back with two good men, and Stillwell.

"Kate," Say'ard said. That was all. "Kate" But it surely did make a lump in my throat as I hugged them both.

"You look like hell Sis," Matilda finally whispered, trying to make it sound gruff, but it didn't come out that way at all, and I didn't say anything deriding.

"Yeah. It's been a long ride. Clear down into Arizona country," I replied softy. "You two look good enough to travel. How are you both? Fairly healed up? You too Ray? How are you feeling?" I asked.

"Better than better," he said brightly as he eyed Stillwell's scabbed face.

"We're ready to go home. We were just waiting for you to show up. This morning we packed our gear, and the horses are ready," 'Til said.

I looked at her with the question on my face. "How did you know I'd be here today? Someone see us coming?"

"No. I had thoughts about you last night, that you'd be here…with Stillwell."

"You should have more thoughts like that 'Til, they're good ones," I said honestly.

"The three of us are all set to travel," Say'ard added.

That 'three' was something I'd half expected. "Three? Who's going with us?" I questioned Say'ard with a faint smile on my face knowing full well the answer.

"I am," Ray said still standing next to 'Til, only now he had an arm around her waist, as she looked up into his smiling face.

"Looks like there should be a wedding before we go," I said.

"We talked it over, and I'd like to be married with all the family attending, and Ray has agreed," Matilda said in a gush of words.

I smiled; nodded my head slightly to him, and said "Welcome to the O'Reilly family Ray.

Say'ard, Matilda, Ray, this is Clete and Jess Callahan. They helped bring Stillwell this far, and I've hired them to work at the ranch."

Clete and Jess had dismounted when I had, and now touched their hands to their hats to the girls, and shook Ray's hand.

With a devilish grin, Say'ard whispered to me quickly as the men exchanged greetings, "Hired on hell!"

It was good to be with family again, I think, but right now I still had a surprise for the two of them.

"I still think there should be a wedding before we go. If not yours 'Til, then mine and Clete's." The statement took them both by surprise, and rendered them speechless.

Which doesn't happen too often.

It took some time for them to understand that I could find a husband all by myself, and I felt rather smug as I watched their faces, as it dawned on them what I had just said. Clete dropped an arm around my waist, and expressed the rest, "We'd be pleased to have both of you, Jess and Ray, to stand up for us as soon as we can get things arranged today."

The girls shrieked with delight, and started talking about all the plans to get in order when I held up a hand, and stopped them.

"All we need are some clean clothes, a preacher, and put Stillwell in the jail. I'm tired of babysitting him," I explained to my sisters.

"I'll put him in the jail for you Kate," Ray said, and reached out to take the lead rope.

"Get another horse for him to ride, and get him to hell off Blarney!" 'Til said coldly.

That was Sis! Warm and loving one minute, and madder than hell the next, but I couldn't blame her, Blarney WAS her horse.

Pulling Stillwell of Blarney, Clete said quietly, "He can walk that far Ray. He's walked before."

"Clete? Jess? If you tag along with me I can show you the hotel. You can get a bath, and there's a store where we can get you trucked up for the wedding," Ray said, ignoring my prisoner.

"We girls will make do here, and Ray, will you hunt up the judge or preacher?" I added to the sparse wedding plans. "But first I'd like to see if that store has a wedding dress."

We were all about to part ways when Ray stopped, and turned to 'Til. Moving close up to her he took her hands, and said gently, "Matilda? Will you marry me today?"

Love, it's been said, looks well on a happy woman, and my sister was a happy woman as she said, "Yes."

We waited patiently in the cool afternoon wind, as they shared a very long, passionate kiss.

"We'll take the horses to the livery on the way to the mercantile," I said as Ray reluctantly lifted his lips from 'Til's.

Say'ard and 'Til took the reins of the other horses, and we started for the livery, and do some shopping. There were three of the family here, and that was enough to witness our weddings.

"The girls are really going to be surprised when we get home!" Matilda bubbled.

"I sure wish Jake were here. We all three could get hitched together," Say'ard said sadly, and I gave her a one armed hug.

"When we get back; Jake will want to marry you on the spot, and we'll let him," Matilda said.

"What makes you think he'll want to marry me right away?"

"Cause I wrote him a letter, and said you couldn't wait, and for him to be ready when we got there," Matilda answered. "Besides. YOU did tell him you'd marry him when you got back. Didn't you?"

"Well, yes, but I thought it would be a day or two...after we showed up."

"Nope. I told him THE day we showed up you'd be ready, and for him to have everything arranged. YOU can't back out now. It's a done deal. Now let's get these horses stabled and go shopping!" Matilda squealed.

I draped an arm around Say'ard's shoulders again; gave her a pull to me, and asked her if I could give her any womanly advice before her wedding to just let me know, for I'd be an old married woman by then.

She threw an elbow into my ribs!


The livery was at the east end of town, and we had ridden in from the south end. Our men, those words sent a shiver of pleasure down my frame, our men were on the walk in front of the sheriff's office when I glanced back and Clete caught my eye, and touched his hat to me. I just about let the girls take the horses to the livery, and went to him. I wanted to be by his side. Right now! Forever!

Where ever! It was a feeling I just couldn't put words to, but he turned and went into the sheriff's office.

Matilda pulled me onward, for I had stopped when I looked back at Clete, and she smiled wickedly at me. "You wouldn't be having any indecent thoughts about that man would you?" she asked in a teasing voice.

"Not any more than you are about yours," I told her truthfully.

## Chapter 28

We made it to the livery in the high spirits only truly happy women can be in on their wedding day, when the sight of a horse in the barn corral stopped me in my tracks.

Say'ard and 'Til stopped with me, and looked at the horse I was staring at. It was a highly decorated, Indian's, buckskin stallion. I must have gone pretty pale for the girls were asking me questions, and I wasn't answering.

"Kate? What's the matter? You know that horse?" Say'ard words were finally getting through to me.

"Yes. I know that horse," I said in a breathless whisper.

The owner of the livery came out, and greeted us in a business manner, not knowing something was twisting my insides into knots!

"Help ya ladies?" He asked, looking me up and down, and probably thinking he shouldn't be using that term on me.

"Yes," I spoke up. "Would you have room for our horses for tonight?"

"Yep. Only have my own in here, and three that belong to these ladies. Got a fresh cutting of fodder 'livered just yesterday that ought to suit your horses' just fine. Dollar for each horse. That'll be four dollars."

"Can we leave the tacks here also?" I questioned.

"Yep. That'd be fine. No charge for that." The old livery man was just about done with his working years, for he had to be nearing eighty years if a day.

"That buckskin out there. He for sale?" I asked as I counted out the money, and put it in his hand.

"Yep. Took him in couple of airs ago. Didn't think I'd have a sale fer him so soon, being an Indian horse, and all. He's a might painted up. Too much fer white folks, but he's solid, nothing wrong with him I can tell."

"How much?" I asked again.

"Well...like I said, he's..."

"How much?" I repeated sternly.

The old man took a good long look at me, the badge on my shirt, and studied a minute on whom he was talking to, then said, "I figured he's worth 'bout $100."

"Fine," I said, and I handed him the money for the stallion. "Did he have any tack with him?'

"Shore. Indian gear back in the corner over thar," he nodded with his head.

"That part of the price?" I asked, and he nodded, "Ain't got nary a use fer stuff like that."

I was already moving to the 'stuff', and knelt to sort it out. Her blankets were there as were the girth straps for the saddle blanket, the hackamore, and their travel bag.

There was dried blood on the side of the saddle blanket.

I walked up by the old man and asked, "Who did you buy the stallion from?"

"Rancher by the name of Carl Braeburn brung it in behind his surrey this morning."

"Where might I find him?" I pressed gently.

"He and his family are over to the eatery. The Mrs. has shopping to do. Oldest boy's getting hitched come Sunday."

I wondered what day of the week today was.

I thanked him and left. I was taking long strides and hitting the ground hard. 'Til and Say'ard caught up with me quickly, and 'Til, gently taking my arm, asked, "Sis? What's the matter?"

"I need to find Carl Braeburn and ask him about that stud."

"Kate? How do you know that horse?" Say'ard asked carefully, for my manner was tight, full of anger, and controlled, but I was seething! They could tell that much from my clinched fists!

"The people who owned that horse are friends of mine. They wouldn't have given the stud up freely, and there's blood on the saddle pad," I said tensely.

We met Jess, Clete and Ray just coming out of the sheriff's office. Clete read my face, and knew something was tearing at my heart!

"What is it, Kate?" He asked softly, and I couldn't say a thing for the life of me. I didn't know where to start! How could I tell him I was afraid a young mother was dead, and the baby...what of the baby!

"There's a buckskin stud in the livery corral that Kate knows, and she said the people who own the horse are friends of hers, and they wouldn't have given him up freely," Matilda said to Ray for all to hear.

"The livery man said a Carl Braeburn brought the horse in a couple of hours ago, and the family is still in town, at the eatery," Say'ard added the rest of what they knew, but not what I knew, and dreaded to find out.

"Kate. Tell me about it," Clete said gently, wrapped his arms around my shoulders, pulled me to his chest, and rested his chin on my head.

Standing there on the sidewalk, I told them what I knew of Rebecca Braeburn/Little Walking Fire, her son, Strong Boy, and her loving husband, Talks to Horses.

When I finished I looked to Clete and said, "They're all dead, and whoever brought that stallion to town knows how they died, and I need to find that out."

Together, as the family we now were, we turned, and started to the eatery. Ray led the way with 'Til, Clete and I followed them, and Say'ard and Jess were last.

We had taken Clete and Jess's rifles from their saddles when we left the livery, and those rifles were handed over by my sisters. I still carried my own rifle, along with my whip.

Ray led the way into the establishment followed by Clete and Jess, we girls came next, and I closed the door behind us. We waited while Ray went to the table where the Braeburns sat with a couple, of what looked like, hired hands.

I eased over and stood to the side of the door.

This was Ray's play, for he was still sheriff of Slate. Jess stood with my sisters, and Clete moved to the side of the table opposite Ray.

"Mr. Braeburn? I need to have a talk with you, and your family, about that buckskin down at the livery. I think it best be done down at my office."

Ray was polite, even to the point of taking his hat off in the presence of Mrs. Braeburn and nodding to her.

Carl Braeburn started to rise, but his wife didn't, and Ray said quietly, "All...your family, and your workers too. This is important."

Silence is a virtue, and an important tool of control when need be. And control, on everyone's part right now, was important. I had a knowing deep inside me, that things might get out of control real soon, and I needed to protect my sisters if that happened.

The room, half full of customers, was eerily quiet as the Braeburn group rose. The men donned their hats as Carl took his wife's arm, and turned for the door.

They hesitated briefly at the sight of Jess and I with our rifles pointing at them, but went through the door that Matilda opened for them. Ray led the whole group to the jail.

I surveyed the men as they walked past me, and three of them had a look about them that I understood to be fearful. That they knew something was amiss showed in their eyes. One had the look of Carl Braeburn all over him; face and build. Little Walking Fire looked like her mother.

Ray walked beside Mrs. Braeburn with her husband on the other side. The son and two hands followed, and then Clete and Jess, and then we girls. The entire group was probably more people than had been on the street in a month, and the few folks we met, hurried aside and let us pass.

The office was crowded by the time all eleven of us were in there, and from somewhere, Ray found chairs for the Braeburns.

Clete and Jess stood next to Ray, one on each side. The girls were next to the door, while I stood off side of Clete so I could see all the faces of the Braeburn group.

Ray led out with careful questions concerning the horse I'd just bought.

"Carl? There's been a question as to that Indian stud you sold to old Ike? I need to know where you got him."

Taking a moment to answer, Carl looked to his son, "Brad and the boys here," nodding his head backwards to indicate the two hands, "brought him in yesterday. They found him up in the high country north of here. Don't have a use for a damned Indian horse. I knew old Ike'd be able to sell it, and take it off'n my hands. So I brung it along today; since we was making the trip anyhows."

His German brogue reminded me of Little Walking Fire as she struggled to speak the tongue she was born with, and had not used for so long. That he hated Indians for the supposed theft of his little girl was probably behind that misplaced hate, for the Indians had saved her life! Which was a thing he didn't know, but would if I were given the chance.

Ray turned his attention to Brad Braeburn and asked the same question, "Where did you get the stud from Brad?"

Brad shifted slightly in his chair and looked at me. "You the person asking?" he said, locking eyes with me.

Why he picked me out of the crowded room was unclear, but he was dead on in his question.

"I'm asking Brad," Ray said softly. "There's a problem with the ownership of that horse. It now involves the law, and I'm the law Brad. Where did you get that horse?"

The son was stubborn, or belligerent; I didn't know which, but he didn't, or wouldn't answer. Ray turned his attention to the hands, and put the same question to them, but they dropped their eyes, and didn't say anything.

"We can sit here all day if that's the way you want it, but one of you will give me the answers to the questions I ask," Ray said.

"Ray?" I spoke for the first time. "May I take Mr. and Mrs. Braeburn aside? In the back?"

He knew what I was going to say, and that I was going to show them Stillwell, but he nodded anyway, giving me leave to follow my instincts.

The couple stood; she had a worry on her face, and his was grimly set, but they followed me towards the cell area. I stopped in front of Stillwell's cell, and let them look at the man who killed my sister.

"This man killed my little sister. He was robbing a bank, and he shot her in the throat as she entered the place, and then he ran. For weeks I hunted him. I found him down in the Arizona Territory. I did that to him with this whip.

I want you to know that I won't be letting this problem go. I will find out what happened to the girl who rode that horse. I do not intend to go away until I know. Do you understand?"

The woman could hardly look at what was Stillwell's face, but her husband knew I meant what I said. As we started to leave the cell area Stillwell reminded me that I'd never get him to Montana, and I reminded him whatever way he wanted to make the trip was all right with me, and the Braeburns heard every word said.

I stood beside Clete as Carl Braeburn started to relate how the stallion came to be sold to Ike. "Day 'fore yesterday, Brad and these two come riding in with the stud on a lead and..."

"Shut up, old man!" Brad Braeburn shouted. "You don't know nothing! Keep your mouth shut! They got nothing on us! Nothing! It's just a God-damned Indian horse!"

"What Indian Brad?" Ray asked.

"I don't have to say."

"Yes you do. There is cause to believe that someone has died over that horse. Unless you can prove otherwise; I'm going to lock you men up while I back trail you, and find out what happened."

"They weren't no account! They was just vermin!" Brad ranted.

My anger flared white hot as his words were said, and that anger straightened me taller.

"They were people Brad, and had a right to life just like you," Ray said carefully.

"What about my sister? Didn't she have a right to life too?" Brad yelled.

"Son?" Carl reached out a hand to his son, who shoved it off with a swipe of his hand. "Son, that was a long time ago and…"

"And nothing! She's gone! The Indians took her, and God knows what she suffered!" He calmed down some, but spoke in a tight voice, "They all should be dead, and if they die one at a time; then so be it."

"Brad? Did you kill someone for that horse?" Ray asked quietly.

Brad just smiled, and looked at Ray confidently.

I asked Ray if I could ask some questions. His look cautioned me to go slowly, and I would, for I knew that Brad Braeburn had a twisted soul so full of hate that he would never find his way out of it, and...he was deadly.

"Did you two take part in what happened to the woman who sat that stallion?" I asked the hired hands, and before they could answer Brad leapt to his feet to face them, and Clete racked a shell into the chamber of the rifle he held and moved to the side of Brad and between him and the door. For a second, there was a deep silence.

"You keep your mouths shut! Both of you! They can't touch us if we don't say nothing!" Brad bellowed.

"You both going to go down with him?" I continued softly, and Brad whirled to glare at me, as if I hadn't been glared at before, and he had to look up to do it.

It didn't work before, and it didn't work now.

"I'm going to back trail you; find out what you did, and then there will be a hanging...his, yours, or all three. I don't care, but I bet you do?" I spoke quietly, but to their credit, or their fear, they didn't speak.

I spoke to Mr. and Mrs. Braeburn this time, and I spoke gently, because I knew the hurt my words were going to bring to them would just about kill them. The truth needed to be said to bring an end to a lot of years of suffering, and torment of not knowing what happened to their daughter.

"The woman who rode that horse was named Little Walking Fire because of the red tint in her dark hair.

I met her just over five months ago. She and her husband, his name is Talks to Horses, had made a camp for her to give birth. It was a breech birth, and I didn't know if I could help her or not, but she, and the baby lived. They named him Strong Boy."

I reached for, and held Mrs. Braeburn's hands, as I knelt in front of her, and spoke woman to woman.

"She was a white woman, about seventeen years old, and she remembered how to speak some English. We talked all the next day, and into the evening. She told me as much as she could remember about her white life, and she told me her name. It was hard for her to say, because it came strangely to her mouth. It had been a long time since she used the old language. Her name, the one her white mother used to call her, was Becca Brayburnt."

The parents of Rebecca started to cry and hold each other. Brad lunged for the door, but Clete swung his rifle stock into Brad's midsection and floored him.

The hired hands had both their hands in the air, and were stepping all over themselves trying to out talk the other. Brad was trying to get his wind, and reached for his pistol, but Ray got to it first, and Jess had his handgun locked on the hired hands.

Jess and Clete hauled Brad off to a cell, and locking the door, came back to the room to hear the rest of what I had to say, and what the hired hands were now volunteering.

"If this young woman was your daughter, I want you to know that she was adopted by a woman named Blue Cloud, and she raised your daughter with love. Rebecca was a daughter; not a prisoner, and she stayed with them because she wanted too. You were long gone, and she didn't know where to look for you.

Rebecca loved her husband, and he loved her very much. They were planning to come to find you as soon as Strong Boy was big enough to travel, for she was searching for where you lived, and she wanted you to see her son.

Talks to Horses knew the danger in bringing her to the white world, but I think he'd do anything for her.

That stallion was their horse. They rode away on him the day after your grandson was born."

I eased up; moved away, and left the Braeburns to console each other. IF that were at all possible!

Ray questioned the hired men quietly, as Clete slipped an arm around my shoulders, and leaned me in close to him. He felt so good!

"We didn't know what he intended to do when we found the three of them inj...Indians camped on the ranch land up by the spring. I swear to God we didn't know!"

"What happened up there? Are any of them alive?" Ray said tensely.

The two hands looked sick, and surely wanted to be anywhere but here, but they swallowed hard and spoke up; weakly.

"We rode up on them easy like and they were quiet. She was standing; holding the kid, and the man was on the horse. Brad just pulled out his gun and shot the man in the head, and body after he was on the ground. Brad got off his horse and started walking towards the woman. She put her hand out and said "I speak your tongue."

Brad back handed her; she fell and dropped the baby, and he booted it out of the way. Then he...hit her hard...a few times; ripped her clothes down, and...."

The two of then stopped talking; looked down, and one started to softly repeat, "Oh God, Oh God...he just went on and on with her, and we couldn't watch, and when he joined up with us later he said we sure missed a good party."

We were all silent for as long as it took for the two to gain control and talk again. "He was leading the stud, and we just went along with what he told his Pa about finding the horse."

Finally the other man spoke up, He said he'd never seen Brad so crazy, and he was afraid of him. He couldn't tell the boss what his son had done, and that this wasn't the first time Brad had killed Indians.

I was so sick to my stomach that I wanted to vomit, but I swallowed hard, and I knew Say'ard and Matilda felt the same, but I asked in a low voice, "The baby? Is there a chance it's alive?"

The look of horrible regret, and disgrace, sat hard on their faces, but each of them said the baby was crying in the grass where Brad bad booted it to. They were sure the man and woman were dead, but they didn't know about the baby.

"Take me to where this happened." I clinched my teeth together so hard that my jaws ached, and I wanted to march back to that cell and kill the bastard! From the look on the faces around me, I knew I wasn't alone in that terrible thought!

Clete was reading my mind, for he drew me tighter and whispered, "We'll go together."

Jess, Clete and I went to the livery, and saddled all the horses without talking. Til and Say'ard went to the house where we were going to be married, and changed into their riding clothes. Ray had us a food and medicine pack; two shovels, and extra blankets ready by the time the girls arrived. The two hired hands were up on their horses waiting for us.

We swung up; headed west with the two men leading, and Clete pushed them hard right off by slapping their horses with his hat.

"Ride!" He yelled. "Ride hard! Don't stop until we get there."

Later, when we returned, Ray told us that Carl Braeburn had walked back to see his son; shot him dead in the jail cell, and then turned the gun on himself. Mrs. Braeburn had collapsed; was taken to the doctor's house where, she awoke; got a kitchen knife and killed herself.

There are things that go beyond what a person's mind can understand, and this was something those two people couldn't begin to cope with.

I almost couldn't, but I had a hate; a boiling, hot hate in me that they didn't. I had held Strong Boy in my hands; saw the love his parents shared, and had been privileged to share their joy. Maybe that's what kept me from going into that dark place in my mind that the Braeburn's had given in to.

The two men took Clete at his word, and they rode hell bent for as long as it took to cover the twenty odd miles to the spring.

We found the camp without any trouble. Little Walking Fire was dead, and it had not been an easy death. She had fought her brother. He had beaten, and violated her something awful. She had been strangled. Talks to Horses was missing.

I covered her immediately with a blanket, and Say'ard found sign where someone had crawled off into the brush, and was leaving a blood trail. We knew it was Talks to Horses.

The baby wasn't anywhere to be found. I prayed that Talks to Horses had the boy, but I also saw the sign of coyote tracks around the camp as did everyone else. I don't know about the others, but inside I was pleading. *Dear Graces! Not the babe!*

We followed the marks in the dry ground, and they led us to a rock filled gulley. We split up; searched the banks of the dry gulley, and Jess whistled up that he had found something.

Hurrying over to him and Say'ard, he pointed out the faint marks of where someone had crawled through and broken off brush.

I asked the others to stay back and let me take the lead, for I was the only one that Talks to Horses would recognize...if he were alive.

His trail led around a large boulder, and that's where I found him and Strong Boy.

They were tucked up next to the rock, and under a pine tree. He had his knife in his hand, and the look in his eye was truly wild.

I knelt to his level; opened both my hands, palms up, and came forward slowly; stopping at his feet.

The side of his head was caked with his dried blood. One eye was swollen shut, and the blood on his chest was caked dry over the three bullet holes. Strong Boy was asleep, or dead on his chest, and the side of his little face was swollen and blue.

I think of myself as a strong woman, but the sight of those two; the defiant father, and the helpless child, added to what had happened to Little Walking Fire; was just about more than I could stand. Tears sprang from my eyes, and I let them fall.

Slowly I gained my mind, and held out my hands to him. He waited a long time before a look of recognition surfaced in his eye, and he lowered the knife.

I scooted to his side and reached out to touch the baby. His little chest was rising and he BREATHED! THANK THE GRACES HE BREATHED! And my tears fell for the joy of it!

I wrapped an arm around Talks to Horses' shoulders; laid my head next to his, and held him for a few moments with my hand on Strong Boy. Then I called in the others, and that was how they found us. Huddled close together.

Talks to Horses moved slightly at the sight of all the white people, but I shushed him gently; pointed to my eyes; pointed to my sisters, and hoped he understood.

I gently pried Strong Boy from his arm, and Clete and Jess lifted Talks to Horses, and tenderly carried the gravely injured man down to the small creek, but not too close to where the body of Little Walking Fire lay.

The night before had been cool, but as sheltered as they were under the low tree branches. They were chilled, but alive.

Say'ard took Strong Boy from my arms, put him down on a blanket, and gently undressed him. Jess went to our pack horse and got our medical supplies. Matilda found a baby bottle full of lukewarm milk in the supplies. Ray had wrapped it in newspapers, and thoughtfully tucked it into the supplies.

Clete helped me with Talks to Horses, and Matilda laid a fire beside Say'ard, as she tended Strong Boy.

The two hired men stood with the horses, totally ashamed at what they watched, and had let happen.

The bullet had passed completely through the side of Talks to Horses' head, leaving a huge gash that traced the side of his skull. Only his head band had prevented the bullet from angling deeper into the skull, and bleeding more than it had, or killed him outright, but it was still a deadly wound.

Brad Braeburn had carefully shot three more bullets into Talks to Horses. The shots were not meant to kill the man, but allow him to slowly bleed to death. He had lost a lot of blood. Perhaps too much, for he was extremely weak, and couldn't but move a hand, and he was wet with sweat.

I didn't know if he would live, and that was mirrored in Clete's eyes as well, but we were surely going to try to give him that chance as we busied ourselves with the job at hand.

No one spoke a word as we worked on the father and son, but I noticed Clete's eyes strayed again and again to the dead body of Little Walking Fire, and the barely alive child. I didn't need to think twice to know what was in his mind, for he and Jess lost people; one being a child.

Evening time came and we had laid Talks to Horses near the fire for warmth and light. He stirred awake, and I rose from my bed next to him, and looked into his eye as I touched his brow. Clete had made a bed next to mine, and he too rolled up and came to Talks to Horses.

To my surprise Talks to Horses spoke in broken English! "My...son...lives?" He forced the faint words out with a great effort.

"Yes. He lives," I spoke gently as his eye sought mine in a desperate plea for assurance of that fact.

"My woman...is dead." It wasn't a question. He stated a fact that he knew. Looking at Clete he asked, "Green-eyed...woman's...man?"

Clete answered gently in a proud, but breaking voice, "I am."

"Bring...her...to...me. I would die...with her near." This he asked of Clete, and with a nod of his head, Clete rose to bring Little Walking Fire to her husband.

We all watched as he lifted the small body of Rebecca Braeburn, and bringing her to her husband, he knelt to lay her next to him on his arm that I had stretched out.

Rolling her body to his, Clete and I tucked another blanket around them.

Struggling to open his eye, Talks to Horses spoke once more to Clete before closing them forever.

"My son...I give...you," and with those words he rested his cheek on that of his love, and gently slipped from life.

We buried them high above the flood line of that small water flow, and covered their bodies, still wrapped together, like my parents, with many rocks, and a ton of dirt.

We buried them as deep as we could in that high valley, and set a large red stone upright over them. We worked far into the night taking turns with the two short shovels we had brought with us, for none of us could sleep.

Clete and I took turns with Say'ard, 'Til and Jess, tending Strong Boy, and feeding him often. The two hands that allowed this to happen worked on the grave more than the rest of us.

I don't know if the burial was how their people would have done it, but it was performed with honor, and compassion, and feelings so profound that none present could speak a word.

I silently asked The Graces to accept them home.

Going to our horses, we loaded up, and with Strong Boy snug in Clete's left arm; we rode into the night.

Chapter 29

Early morning brought us to Slate and Ray Harrigan was waiting for us at the edge of town. He wasn't wearing his badge.

In the breaking dawn I saw he hadn't slept either, and sitting quietly on our tired horses in the moist morning air, he told us about the Braeburn family.

Our response to the deaths of Strong Boy's family, was silence. My thoughts were a mixture of understanding, sadness, expectedness and waste. But Strong Boy had us.

We took our son to the doc's for a better assessment, and the doc confirmed the babe had broken ribs, and a broken arm. The lump and the bruise on his head were subsiding, and the doc felt confident he would be all right; after all, he'd made it this far.

Clete carried our son tenderly in his arms, while I held to one of his elbows, as we walked into the house where our family waited.

I carried my rifle and Father's whip was coiled on my left shoulder. When we got home, I would ask Clete to put the matriarchal ring of old, on my finger.

We stood with Strong Boy in front of the preacher with Ray and Matilda, and repeated the vows of man to make us man and wife. The whole affair was like an afterthought for we had considered ourselves that for a few days now.

We were still dressed in the clothes we rode out in yesterday, and we all had our guns on. The clothes a person wears doesn't matter as much as the person wearing them, and the six people in that room, who were my family, mattered a whole lot to me.

Life's trials have a way of putting things in perspective. That's something Mother said. They, those trials, reminded me again of what is truly important.

I know my namesakes, probably every one of them, were standing with me, as I joined my life with Clete's. I could feel their presence, their strength, their love. I took comfort in this, and drew my strength from them. I felt Megan near, and I was aware of a smile coming to my lips, as I imagined the unseen guests crowded into the preacher's small parlor. I knew we were blessed by The Graces.

The words we exchanged, were not as meaningful to me as were the ones we exchanged days earlier on our way here. Clete's eyes reflected those other words also, as he whispered, just before he kissed me, "I'm proud of you...wife."

"And I of you...husband," I answered.

We were happy, and sad, all at the same time as we left the preacher's house, and headed up the warm, dusty street to the only hotel in town. We meant to have a long overdue meal and unwind. Strong Boy needed to be changed, and it was time for his feeding.

As man and wife, we would file adoption papers for him, making him our son legally, but the sweet child was already ours.

We would discuss a name for him. One that would take him into his life, serve him well, yet let him know who he was, and who his parents were. Most of all, he would know that they loved, defended him, and that Clete and I would do the same.

I much imagined that his new aunts and uncles felt that way too. His name; red and white; along with his parents; the Braeburns, and Clete's, would be written into the O'Reilly family Bible.

Sometimes things in life are linked together without rhyme or reason. Sometimes they are personal links, although unexpected, like the Braeburns and Strong Boy through a lost daughter. Then there is the very personal link of Stillwell to me, and my family, by a trail of murder, and soon-to-be, justice. But as I reflected, it seemed to me, the most profound link was that of Clete and Strong Boy; through the trust of a dying father.

Come daybreak tomorrow we would take that link back to our ranch to begin a new chapter in our lives.

I was still determined to keep the promise I had made, and deliver Stillwell to the law there, and see him hang. He was the same class of animal that young Braeburn was and I will settle for nothing less than his death.

Clete and I were walking arm in arm as he cradled Strong Boy in his left arm, and I held lovingly to his right one. Ray and Matilda followed behind us, and Say'ard and Jess brought up the rear.

We were all dead tired and pushing hard. It was getting on mid-morning and the sun was starting to show its hot, belligerent side in an un-seemingly warm winter day as we moved along the street.

The jail was just up ahead; on this side of the street. We would stop there. Ray would check on Stillwell, and leave instructions for the deputy, and we would go on to the hotel from there.

My mind and heart were filled with thoughts of Clete and our long-awaited time together tonight. Say'ard was going to keep Strong Boy for us.

Clete looked down at me with a wide smile and I was so lost in my feelings for him that I was slow to recognize the appearance of a man bursting from the door of the jail.

It was Stillwell!

A cold, black chill of pure hate ran through me! How the hell he got there wasn't as important as the fact that he was there, and the barrel of the rifle he carried was coming up fast, and centered square on me!

I didn't think, wonder, or speak.

I let go of Clete's arm, ripped my handgun from its home, and fired from my hip. I aimed my second shot, and the two bullets opened holes, not three inches apart, in Stillwell's chest. Stillwell jerked backwards, as each round hit him, and he fell in front of the jail door.

As the echo of my shots faded into the morning stillness, I was aware of Clete and Ray, with guns drawn, standing on either side of me.

For a long moment life was still and silent; the very air seemed to stop movement.

Ray sprang into action, and ran straight for the jail. Clete handed Strong Boy to 'Til; as I had already started to walk to Stillwell, and went to back up Ray. Jess stayed with my sisters. I was aware of all their actions, but didn't look to them.

I walked to Stillwell and looked down at the sorry piece of humanity. There was a calm finality in me I couldn't explain; except I knew this was the way it was to be. My job was complete. My promise fulfilled.

I knew Ray and Clete were checking the deputy, who I could see sprawled on the floor near Stillwell's open cell door. He wouldn't be getting up, but neither would Stillwell.

That fact didn't bother me a bit. I thought it would...if his death came by my hand, but it didn't bother me at all, for I knew this had been my responsibility all along.

I felt Clete come to my side and slip an arm around me. I held my gun, hanging down, in my right hand, as my sisters came to stand with us.

Looking at his lifeless body, I silently repeated my earlier words to him; *I told you Stillwell; you weren't near good enough.*

Like I said, some things are linked together. Stillwell and I were certainly linked, and I had the same feeling I'd had weeks before when Say'ard had gotten hurt. That night I'd sat beneath that black, starlit night before going after Stillwell. Just me and Striker. The way it was meant to be.

Far away in the depths of my mind, I heard my mother's soft voice whisper gently, *No regrets Sarah Kathleen. Tis the end he surely asked for and Megan has the justice due her.*

My mind answered gently, *No regrets Momma. No regrets at all.*

The End